Fashionistas

Irina

Sarra Manning

Irina

Hodder
Children's
Books

A DIVISION OF HACHETTE CHILDREN'S BOOKS

Text copyright © 2008 Sarra Manning

First published in Great Britain in 2008
by Hodder Children's Books

1

A Catalogue record for this book is available from the British Library

ISBN-13: 978 0 340 93222 3

Typeset in Bembo by Avon DataSet Ltd, Bidford on Avon, Warwickshire

Printed and bound in China by Imago

The paper and board used in this paperback by Hodder Children's Books
are natural recyclable products made from wood grown in sustainable
forests. The manufacturing processes conform to the environmental
regulations of the country of origin.

Hodder Children's Books
a division of Hachette Children's Books
338 Euston Road, London NW1 3BH
An Hachette Livre UK company

Acknowledgements

Thanks to style supremo, Iain R Webb, for his invaluable help and knowledge of the fashion industry and particularly his experience of working on *Vogue Russia*. I'd also like to thank super stylist, Jill Wanless, for all her wonderful behind-the-scenes modelling stories.

Thanks also to my wonderful agent, Kate Jones, and Laura Sampson and Karolina Sutton at ICM Books. Props as well to my editor, Emily Thomas, and all at Hachette Children's Books.

And may I finally say, thank God for Wikipedia and *The Rough Guide to Moscow*!

http://sarramanning.blogspot.com

BOOK THREE:
Irina

Previously on

After years of being the prettiest girl in town, Laura gets a rude awakening when she realises that she needs to lose her attitude and her excess weight to make it in the world of modelling. But Laura never expected that she may have to lose Tom, her devoted boyfriend back home too...

Read all about it in *Fashionistas:*

Laura

Hadley Harlow was once the world's biggest child star. Now she's strictly C-list and launching herself on the London celebrity circuit to revive her flagging career. Hadley's a tough cookie; she can handle her flatmates – even jealous co-stars – but has she met her match in notorious modeliser, Reed?

Read all about it in *Fashionistas:*

Hadley

Prologue

Irina checked the pocket of her coat *again* for the bulky but reassuring weight of the bolt cutters and cast an anxious look at Sergei, who was chattering animatedly to the two glacially unimpressed sales assistants.

She scanned the rails for the black silk dress that Sergei's client had requested. This was the bit that Irina hated the most because she could never tell the difference between silk and satin, charcoal and grey. Actually the part she hated the most was setting foot in Kitai-gorod where everyone looked at her shabby clothes and knew that she didn't belong, even wearing the voluminous fur coat that Sergei had stolen from his grandmother.

There were three black silk dresses hanging from one rail: so understated and elegant that Irina was convinced they'd disintegrate from one touch of her grubby fingers. She grabbed the collar of the first dress, checked the size and reached into her pocket for the cutters.

'You're gorgeous,' she heard Sergei say behind her. 'You ever think of being a model?'

Irina scowled. She knew that he was only flirting to distract the salesgirls. And she also knew that guys like Sergei, with his twinkling blue eyes and easy smile, weren't interested in girls like her. But still, it was pathetic the way the sales assistants were fawning over him now, even though he looked just as out of place in their stupid, ritzy boutique as she did.

Her fingers were shaking as she manoeuvred the bolt cutters carefully between the stem of the security tag and the delicate material. Not because she was scared. Irina wasn't scared of anything, but Sergei was laying it on too thick now and their cover could get blown.

'Wow! I've never seen such beautiful women.'

Irina shifted to one side so she could glare at the simpering sales staff and make sure that a well-dressed couple were between her and the security guard stationed at the door. Sergei would punch him when she ran for the exit, Irina assured herself as she tried to cut through the thick plastic tag.

But then Sergei's phone started ringing.

'Lilya, baby, I'm a little busy right now. Can I call you back?'

Lilya was tiny and blonde and punctuated everything she said with a high-pitched giggle.

Irina yanked impatiently at the dress, which gave up the fight and tore under her impatient fingers. She swore softly under her breath. Keep calm. Keep calm. One black silk dress was much like any other. Irina seized the next one on the rail, vaguely aware that the guard was walking towards Sergei who was badgering one of the girls to open a glass display case. They could get 1000 roubles for Prada sunglasses. It wasn't part of the plan, but that's what she liked about Sergei – he was so spontaneous, so exciting . . . and so very about to get busted.

'Leave the store now,' the guard ordered tersely. 'Out, or we press the panic button.'

He hadn't seen her yet. Irina fumbled with the cutters again, heard Sergei remonstrate with the staff.

She felt her body grow clammy, beads of sweat popping up on her forehead as a hand clamped down on her shoulder. 'Any second now, that security guard is going to see you,' a voice advised her. 'If I were you I'd leave the dress and come with us.'

Us? The well-dressed couple had her book-ended. Irina's eyes darted wildly around and came to rest on the man's polished black shoes. He spoke Russian with an accent. The woman was younger, blonde, elegantly dressed in a soft leather coat and staring at Irina incredulously. What a bitch!

'Go away,' she spat loud enough that the security guard slowly swung round. 'I'm not going anywhere with you.'

She could already see Sergei sidling towards the door, not even bothering to look back and check that she was OK. Then he was gone, an indistinct blur streaking past the window, and she was on her own with the guard striding towards her. They didn't carry guns, Irina was pretty sure about that. Not here, where the rich came to shop. Though you could never tell with the private security firms.

Irina tried to put the dress back on the rail; wrinkling it in her sweaty hands, messing it up like she did everything. 'I . . . I . . .' the words were stuck in her throat, but the woman was calmly shielding her from view, taking the bolt cutters out of Irina's hands and dropping them into a capacious Gucci tote.

'Do something, Henri,' she hissed in English. 'And do it quickly.'

Henri was already pushing Irina towards the sales desk. He presented the dress that she'd already torn with a flourish. 'I'm terribly sorry but my niece has had a small accident. We'll pay for it, of course.'

Irina waited until he was taking a credit card out of his wallet before she bolted, the worn soles of her trainers skidding across the highly polished marble floor, but the blonde woman was blocking her exit.

'Don't even think about it,' she rapped out. 'Just stay there and smile and remember to thank your "uncle" for getting you out of this mess.'

Her 'uncle' had a stiff cardboard bag in his hand, as he nodded his head at the staff before hurrying over to them. 'Let's get the hell out of here,' he gritted between clenched teeth as they bundled Irina out of the door.

'What do you want from me?' she demanded brusquely, trying to wrench away from them as soon as they got outside. 'You want me to pay you back for the dress, huh? How do you want me to do that?'

She knew about rich tourists. There were girls that hung around on the edges of Sergei's gang who'd come into the city and go to the fancy bars attached to the biggest hotels. They came back the next day with tearstains, bruised lips and fistfuls of dollars.

The woman was pulling Irina into the weak sunshine spilling down on Tretyakov Drive. There was nowhere to hide from two pairs of beady eyes that swept over the moth-eaten fur coat, the grubby tracksuit bottoms and trainers poking out from under the hem, and Irina's face. Her stupid, sallow face with the blotchy brown marks all over it.

Irina sized them up – the woman could easily be knocked over, but Henri was tall and she could feel the tensile strength in his hand as he kept a tight grip on her arm. 'I didn't ask you to pay for the dress,' Irina insisted again.

It was like her words were made out of air. They simply brushed them away and continued to stare at her.

'Have you ever seen cheekbones like hers?' the woman said in English because they thought she was some dumb hick. 'And she's tall.'

'Thin too,' the man added, actually daring to pull back the side of her coat, even as Irina hissed at him. 'Rangy, she's got long legs.'

Any moment now, Sergei would roar up on his bike. Except Sergei was probably halfway to St Petersburg by now and Irina was on her own. They didn't know that she could speak English and that was something at least that she could use to her advantage. Maybe even take the woman's bag while she was at it.

All Irina needed was to come up with a plan while they talked about her like she was a slab of meat on the butcher's block.

'I wonder how she photographs,' the woman was saying and Irina couldn't help the shudder that ran through her. Everyone knew a girl who'd gone off to Sweden or Germany or Switzerland with a rich foreigner who'd promised her a passport, and they were never heard of again. Sergei said that they got sold into prostitution rings. They'd sit there wide-eyed, listening to him go into lurid details. Then he'd ruffle Irina's hair. 'Not like you have to worry about that,' he'd say. 'You'd have to pay them.' And they'd all laugh. And Irina would laugh too, though actually she didn't think it was that funny.

'I'm going now,' she said decisively, because the icy panic washing over her was making it hard to think clearly. 'Get your hands off me or I'll scream.'

She'd never screamed in her life but they didn't know that.

But they weren't letting go; instead the man nodded and the woman turned to her with a smile. 'Tell me something, have you ever thought about being a model?'

Chapter One

It had been a strange two weeks. Busy, which Irina wasn't used to. She was used to boredom in the crappy jobs she'd managed to find, until she'd inevitably got sacked for her bad attitude. And she was used to interminable periods of waiting. Waiting for her mother to get paid. Waiting for Sergei to come round with that careless grin which got to her every time. Waiting for something, anything, to happen.

And finally something was happening and she wondered why it was happening to her. Like, when she'd thought about the future, it was always vague and indistinct. The sum total of her ambitions was maybe going to America to become a nanny, which was why she'd persevered with the shouting and the rapped knuckles when her mother had taught her English from the primers she used at the language school where she taught.

Mostly, she thought she'd stay in Moscow and end up pregnant and penniless. And the closest she'd ever get to the outside world would be the rap tapes that Sergei lent her.

Her mother hadn't believed Henri and Claire when they'd said that Irina could be a model. She'd sat stiff-backed and accused them of being human traffickers.

'Tell her about the money,' Henri had said to Claire in

English. 'They usually sell their children down the river for a couple of hundred dollars.'

Big mistake, Mr Hotshot, Irina had thought to herself with a grin. Big fucking mistake.

'A couple of hundred dollars isn't going to cut it,' her mother had snapped back in perfect English, as Henri had flushed and shrunk back like he wished the threadbare sofa would swallow him whole. 'I teach English for a living, French as well. If you'd like to insult me in another language, I suggest you try Spanish.'

Irina's snicker had been cut off by her mother's most vengeful glare, which was saying something. 'Did you tell them you spoke English too?'

She'd shrugged. 'Didn't come up.'

'And I still want to know what you were doing in Kitai-gorod and where you got that coat from.' Her mother's eyes had narrowed suspiciously. 'Have you been stealing again?'

'No!' Irina had looked pointedly at Claire and Henri because any time they wanted to leap to her defence would be just fine with her.

But it hadn't gone down like that. Claire had reached into her bag for the bolt cutters as Henri pulled out the torn dress. 'Your daughter doesn't need to be co-opted into a human-trafficking ring to get into trouble,' Claire had said flatly. 'She seems to be doing fine all by herself. Well, and with the help of a friend who ran off and left her.'

Her mother had started shrieking, threatened to call the police herself, then asked how long it would take to have Irina packed off to England.

Irina still had a horrible feeling she was about to be sold into prostitution, despite the promises of fame and fortune from the Russian modelling agency which had organized her visa and taken hundreds of Polaroids of her scowling face. But the only other choice was going to live with her Uncle Igor in Vyasma, who slapped her when he thought she was being cheeky, which was all the time.

But her mother was made of stone. 'All I do is worry about you and the trouble you get into. You can be someone else's problem for a few weeks.'

It wasn't much, but it was something. 'Just for a few weeks?' Irina had asked hopefully. 'Then I come home?'

'A few weeks is long enough for them to realize that you're bad news,' her mother had said matter-of-factly. 'Then they'll send you home so you can cause havoc with your friends and I have to keep feeding you and clothing you. You'll never to amount to anything, Irina, but at least you might make some money in England.'

She'd heard it a million times. *You're no good. You're just another mouth to feed. You've disappointed me from the moment you were born.* They were just words, so why did they always give her a dull ache right in the pit of her stomach?

'At the model agency, they think they I'm special,' Irina had protested.

'Then they're bigger fools than they look.'

And so Irina was on a plane to London; flying across countries she'd only ever seen on a map, all her worldly goods stuffed into two bin-liners because her mother wouldn't let her take the cheap plastic suitcase that had sat on top of their wardrobe for as long as Irina could remember.

It took hours to clear Customs, even with all her paperwork in order and a letter of accreditation faxed over from Fierce Talent Management. Eventually Irina's visa was stamped and they even held the door open for her so she could manoeuvre herself and her bags into the arrivals lounge, where a man was holding up a sign with her name on it. A girl could get used to this.

Irina pressed her nose against the car window as trees and hedges sped past; she didn't want to miss a single blade of grass. Moscow was always grey, from the dirty piles of sludgy snow, to the swollen, grimy water of the Smolenka canal that she could see from the rattling window of their kitchen and the endless blocks of identikit buildings. Even people's faces in the housing project where she lived were grey. But here there was colour everywhere, and it was even better when they got closer to London and the foliage was replaced by advertisement hoardings for food she couldn't wait to eat and clothes that she wanted to wear.

She didn't want the journey ever to finish. There was suddenly this exhilarating mix of scary and excited coursing through her veins at the thought of it all: London; getting paid stupid amounts of money to have her picture taken; sharing a flat with other girls, other models. Would she have to share a room? Or a bed, like she did at home? Would they speak Russian? Or English? Or would they be from exotic places like India or Japan or Mexico? The questions whirled around her head and it was a surprise when she realized that the car had stopped outside a neat little tow of terraced houses.

'Here you are,' the driver told her slowly, like she was retarded or something. 'It's the one with the red door.'

It was like a doll's house, with a white painted trim above the door and bright yellow flowers fluttering along the garden path. 'I'm staying here?' Irina asked doubtfully.

'Yeah, I know it's a little poky but you're near the tube.'

Irina didn't know what he was talking about. It wasn't poky, it was a palace – and what was a tube? A face appeared at the window and then disappeared, as Irina climbed out of the car and hoisted her binbags over her shoulder.

The door was already opening as she shuffled down the path and she hadn't even got her foot on the doorstep when she was suddenly confronted by three girls with long limbs and hostile faces.

'That must be the new girl,' one of them said in Russian and Irina gave the tiniest sigh of relief. 'What is she wearing and why the hell does she think she's staying here?'

Chapter Two

She hated them. All three of them: Masha, Famke and Oksana, who had ushered her into a room, pushed her down on the sofa and stood over her with their hands on their tiny hips. All three of them looked like angry swans who lived on a diet of nectar and lark's eggs.

'It's Russian girls like you that give the rest of us a bad name.'

'They already think we're peasants.'

'No one wears clothes like that here. Is it meant to be that colour or has it never been washed?'

Irina looked down at her lilac tracksuit and then back up at their spiteful faces. 'I'm not a peasant. I'm from Moscow.'

'You *look* like a peasant,' Oksana spat. 'My father is in oil and Masha can trace her family back to the sixteenth century and Famke trained with the Bolshoi. We have heritage, you have rubbish bags.'

Irina gathered the black plastic bags closer to her. 'I'm a model,' she stated emphatically. 'I've done a shoot for *Vogue Russia*.' Which wasn't even a lie. She'd met a British photographer called Gerry at the Russian modelling agency who'd shared a spliff with her and taken some pictures up on the roof, which he said he was going to show the editor.

'You have brown spots all over your face,' Masha informed her acidly. 'And a gap between your front teeth. You're ugly.'

They all had this look on their faces that Irina had seen before but just couldn't place. Then she remembered little Lilya's resentful expression whenever Sergei wanted Irina to go on a job with him. He'd put his arm around Irina and Lilya's eyes would flash and she'd pout because she was getting jealous.

They were jealous of her! Which made no sense. Still, Irina was going to savour every second of it. 'In Russia they even bought me a Prada dress,' Irina said. She shook one of her bags. 'I think I packed it, I can't remember.'

The bag was snatched out of her hand and upended so Irina's greying underwear, dingy tracksuits and the carefully-wrapped Kransky sausage that her mother had sneaked in there sometime during the night tumbled to the floor.

'I don't see a Prada dress,' Masha sneered. 'I just see a peasant. And I *smell* peasant food.'

The faint aroma of caraway and dill was gently drifting upwards as Irina grabbed the sausage before being unceremoniously hauled up. If people didn't stop yanking at her . . .

'You want to see a Prada dress? I'll show you a Prada dress, Miss Moscow!'

14

She was frogmarched down a hall into a pretty, light room with a huge bed covered in cushions in an array of sherbet colours. Irina wanted to stop and soak it all in, but Famke was already striding over to a big cupboard and flinging open the door.

'Prada, Chanel, Versace,' she chanted, brushing a careless hand over a rainbow of silk and velvet.

'I don't know why you're bothering,' Oksana said witheringly. 'She's too ignorant to know who they are and she's probably contaminating the fabric just by being in the same room.'

They were right in a way, Irina thought. She didn't belong here where everything was too light, too pretty, too delicate. But that didn't mean she was going to let these horrible girls know that. No one talked to her like this and got away with it. No one.

And she was still holding that stupid sausage, which normally she liked to fry with onions and eat on rye bread. Irina could only imagine the reaction that would cause. But her peasant food did have other uses.

She dug her thumbnail into the greaseproof paper, felt it rip and marched over to Famke, who was still caressing her over-priced clothes like they were her one true love.

Irina grabbed for a dress, any dress, a fragile confection of pink chiffon and cobwebby lace, and slowly and deliberately smeared the sausage over it, leaving greasy streaks on the fabric. 'I guess I have contaminated it now,' she announced in her most bored voice.

Famke packed quite a blow for such a skinny girl. An hour later, Irina's head was still ringing from her right hook. Then they'd pushed her out of the house. 'I'm phoning the agency so they can fire you!' had been Famke's last threat before she slammed the door. A second later her bin-liners and a stream of curses had floated out of the window.

Irina was sitting on the garden wall, looking helplessly at her London guidebook and the small amount of English money that she'd been given as an advance on her earnings before she left Moscow, when a car pulled up outside.

A girl got out and gave Irina a cursory look before she did a completely unnecessary double-take. What the hell was her problem? Did no one wear tracksuits in this country?

But Irina was staring too. The girl looked like she should be on MTV or something, with blonde hair pulled into pigtails and jeans and sneakers that didn't look like any jeans or sneakers that Irina had ever seen. The denim was too dark, too well cut and the sneakers had little red cherries printed on them. How could a girl like that afford to travel in such a fancy car?

'Irina Kerchenko?' she asked, glancing at a piece of paper.

Irina nodded tersely.

'I'm Sofia from Fierce,' she said in Russian. 'I'm

your booker. I look after all the new Eastern European girls.'

There were that many of them that they got their own boss? So why had everyone in Moscow told Irina that she was special? 'I don't like it here,' she growled.

Sofia ignored her. 'Let's get this sorted out.'

But it was un-sort-outable. The three stuck-up bitches refused to let her back in the flat, which worked out fine as Irina refused to take even one step over the threshold. And she didn't appreciate the way that Sofia kept ordering her brusquely about. 'Just come in and see your room,' she demanded. 'I don't have time to babysit you.'

'No way,' Irina said firmly, climbing into the back of the silver car, which was still waiting by the kerb. Gerry had told her that they liked grumpy Russian girls in England. Well, she was going to be the grumpiest Russian girl they'd ever seen.

In the end, Sofia had no choice but to get in the car too and tell the driver to take them back to the agency.

'This is not Russia,' she said angrily. 'Here, everyone says please and thank you. Also, they smile. You have to be friendly all the time.'

Irina glared so hard that she could hardly see. 'Those girls weren't. They were spiteful just because their families have some money. I bet they have mafia connections.'

'Don't be silly,' Sofia snorted, but she didn't sound that convincing. 'There's nowhere else for you to live, but you can spend an hour at Fierce to calm down. Have you eaten anything?'

There had been a meal on the plane, garlicky and unidentifiable, and the Kransky sausage had ended up in a flowerbed. 'I'm starving.'

Sofia smiled for the first time. 'I'll get someone to go out for McDonald's. It's so cheap here, also Burger King, KFC and pizza. Pizza everywhere!'

'I've never had pizza before,' Irina grudgingly confessed.

'You'll love it.'

She did love it. Once they got to the agency, Sofia pushed Irina into a room with a huge TV and half an hour later someone brought in a pizza the size of a car tyre and a huge bottle of Coca Cola – all for her. No one trying to grab the food off her plate when she wasn't looking, or telling her they had to keep something back so they could make soup tomorrow. Irina stuffed slices of pizza in her mouth so fast that she barely tasted them, and stared through the glass walls at the bustle of the agency.

Irina had thought that the Prelestnyjj Model Agency was fancy: there had been computers and pictures on the wall, even carpets that weren't stained or full of holes; but this place was like something out of a Hollywood movie. Yeah, it was like a film set, with blinding white walls and bright pink sofas that were far too frivolous to be sat on. And there were people rushing about in these chic little outfits that Irina hadn't even seen on the rich, fashionable kids that hung out in the cool parts of Moscow. Everyone at Fierce looked young, sleek and happy, like the models advertising perfumes in the fashion magazines that Gerry had given her.

It felt as if Irina hadn't got on an aeroplane this morning (had it really been this morning? It seemed like weeks ago), but a spaceship which had taken her to another planet.

Irina licked the last blob of melted cheese from her fingers and looked up as Sofia came in.

'I love pizza,' Irina said, and she even tried out a smile, which felt unfamiliar.

'And I love that gap in your front teeth,' Sofia said with a straight face, like she wasn't joking. 'It's so early Madonna. Get your stuff.'

Irina gathered up her bags, which were looking decidedly ragged, and followed Sofia out of the room.

'You have to go back to the flat now,' Sofia said without preamble. 'You go back to the flat or you go home. Your choice.'

The smile had been a mistake. The smile had made Sofia think that Irina was weak; that she could be walked all over. Boy, did she have a surprise waiting for her.

'I'm not going back there,' Irina said flatly, dropping her bags so she could fold her arms and exude hostility from every pore.

'Then I can have you on a flight back to Moscow this evening,' Sofia replied implacably.

Irina was staying right here, where people actually paid attention to her and there were huge pizzas. She followed her bags down to the floor and sat on the polished wood boards. 'Make me.'

Sofia tried. There were threats and a bit of arm-tugging, but Irina was unmoveable. She'd already been slapped once today and her mother used to chase her round their flat with a cast-iron saucepan, so Sofia never had a chance.

'You're an ungrateful beast!' she yelled. 'A thousand girls would die to be in your shoes. Get up and get your arse in the car.'

'No! Find me somewhere else to live or I'm staying on the floor. For ever, if I have to.'

'There is nowhere else. All the model flats are full and we want you to stay with girls who speak the same language as you.'

Irina was just about to point out that her English was good and her French was adequate when a door at the end of the corridor opened and two men walked out.

'Sofia, what's all this racket?' one of the men asked.

'Another damn Russian princess,' Sofia snapped, which wasn't true, but it was funny that she hadn't been told about the whole speaking English thing. 'She's meant to be staying with Oksana and her two minions, but there was a thing with a sausage and an Alice Temperley dress and Irina says that she won't go back there.'

That about covered it, though Sofia had missed out the

part where Irina had been assaulted. She tried to assume a blank expression like she didn't know what they were talking about as the man who'd spoken came towards them. He was tall and thin, with a big pair of black glasses and a supercilious expression as he peered down at Irina.

'These bloody Russian girls, we should pack them all off to charm school as soon as they arrive at Heathrow,' he said to Sofia. 'What's this one's story?'

'She signed up with Prelestnyjj a fortnight ago, but her mother insisted that she was sent here or she wouldn't sign a contract. They weren't going to risk another agency spotting her, so they agreed, but she hasn't done a single shoot.' Sofia lowered her voice. 'You'll never guess what she was doing when she was scouted.'

The man was still staring at Irina, who had to resist the urge to stick her tongue out at him. 'What?' he muttered vaguely.

'Shoplifting from Prada. With bolt cutters!' Sofia supplied. 'But in her Polaroids she looks like a dream, Ted. A bloody dream. Her eyes turn silver and her cheekbones just pop out at you.'

Ted, or whatever his name was, clicked his fingers at Irina. 'What's Russian for "up"?' he asked Sofia.

'*Naverkh*,' Irina told him sweetly, getting to her feet. 'Though I hear that everyone in England say please and thank you.'

Ted looked horrified for a split second before he smiled.

Then the smile became a snigger. And the snigger upgraded to full-throated howls of laughter.

When he was done shaking with mirth, though there was nothing particularly funny about any of it, Irina stuck out her hand. 'I'm Irina Kerchenko from Moscow and I only shoplift because my family was starving.' She wondered whether that was overkill, but at least she had Ted's undivided attention again. 'Those girls were horrible. They call me a peasant and one of them slap me round the face.' She pointed at her cheek, though it took a lot for her to bruise. 'Please don't make me go back there—'

'There are no spare rooms anywhere else,' Sofia interrupted. 'And we agreed that if any of the girls caused a fuss again, we'd send them home.'

Irina tried to look suitably penitent, and Ted hadn't taken his eyes off her so maybe it was working.

'Take your jacket off please, Irina,' he asked and she unzipped her tracksuit top so Ted could get the full benefit of the 50 Cent T-shirt she'd stolen from a street stall. 'Turn to the left, but keep your face to me.'

'Ted, we agreed!' Sofia barked. Irina wished she'd just shut the hell up.

'Do you like Moscow?' he asked Irina, who shook her head.

'I hate it,' she said fiercely. 'You not know what it's like there. Is miserable and grey and nothing works properly. I want to stay here.'

22

'If you stay here then you have to live with the other girls. It will be fine, you can bond over . . . I don't know . . . how much it doesn't snow over here.'

And maybe she *could* stick it out with those three other girls. Or she could hit them daily or something. But Ted was still eyeballing her and now the other man was doing it too. Like, they'd never seen a girl with two eyes and a nose and a mouth before. And Gerry had told her not to let people walk all over her and he was a famous photographer so he obviously knew what he was talking about.

'No,' Irina stated emphatically. 'I'm a hard worker and I make you lots of money. I even answer phones or clean for you, but I'm not living there.'

There was a moment's tense silence and Irina knew that she'd blown it, like she always did, by opening her big mouth and being wilful and defiant and all the other things that made her mother so angry.

There was a cough from Ted's friend, who'd been silent up until now. It was a relief when Ted and Sofia swung around to look at him instead. He shrugged. 'Before you put her on the plane back to Moscow, I'd like to book her for the autumn promotion we were talking about, Ted. Is she free Thursday?'

Chapter Three

Sofia booked her a hotel room with its own bathroom. There were even free bottles of shampoo and bubble bath and the hot water never dwindled to a cold trickle no matter how many times Irina refilled the tub on that first night. She'd never felt so clean in her life.

Ted took her out to breakfast the next morning and watched in amusement as she demolished a plate of what he called 'full English' and a basket of flaky pastries as he told her he'd decided to take a special interest in her career.

'Cool,' Irina said around a mouthful of bacon, because she had a feeling that Ted would be easier to handle than Sofia. If she never had to deal with another Russian person ever again, it wouldn't be soon enough for her.

'I think you're a very unique girl, Irina,' Ted said, pouring her another glass of milk. The milk in England was thick and creamy, not like the watery stuff they got back home. 'You have the potential to be a very successful model. Why are you smirking?'

'Because I look in the mirror every morning and I not see a model.' She waved a hand in the direction of her face. 'But if you think so, then whatever.'

'So, let me guess, the other kids would tell you that you

were ugly and that you looked like a freak because your eyes were too big, and your face was too pointy, and you were taller than all the other girls and most of the boys?'

It was like Ted had had a back seat in her classroom at the Academy. 'The boys were OK because they not want to get in my pants, but the girls were vicious.' Normally she'd never tell anyone this stuff but then again, no one normally ever wanted to know anything about her except if she could help them fence a couple of car stereos.

'If I had a pound for every model that told me that story, I could afford another pair of Gucci loafers.' Ted laughed, putting his briefcase down on the table and snapping it open. 'Has anyone bothered to show you the pictures they took in Moscow?'

Ted was leafing through a clutch of glossy snaps, pulling out three, which he fanned out on the table. Irina was more interested in the one croissant left in the basket that she hadn't managed to eat yet. But out of the corner of her eye, she could make out the jutting curve of a cheekbone.

She peered a little closer and wrinkled her nose. It wasn't even her in the picture but some proper model; all big eyes and pouting lips and with blotchy freckles scattered over her face. Irina snagged the picture with her finger and dragged it nearer.

It was her. Except it wasn't. There were all the separate pieces of her face that she hated, but added together and put in front of a camera, they became something else entirely. It was like everything had rearranged itself a few degrees, so that what looked odd in real life now looked a little more wild, a little more angular. Her grey eyes had transformed to liquid silver, the bony protuberances of her face looked elegant and ethereal, and her mouth, her stupid big mouth, balanced everything out.

'I don't look like that,' she said wondering, tracing the arch of her eyebrow.

'We get so used to our faces that sometimes we don't see them any more,' Ted murmured, which didn't make any sense, but then it kind of did. 'Do you want to be a model, Irina?'

It was the first time that anyone had actually asked her that. They'd all been too busy prodding at her and going on about visa applications.

Irina shrugged. 'Never think about it before.' She thought about it now, but only for a second. She liked what she'd seen so far: the money, the pretty clothes, the compliments. 'I guess being a model would be OK. Better than working in a factory.'

'You need to learn how to pose. You need to have a proper beauty regime, facials and exfoliations and loads of other treatments that Sofia will help you with, and we need to teach you how to walk.'

She could already walk, but Irina nodded dutifully again and finally snatched up the croissant. 'My mother think I have no ambition, but I want to make lots and lots of money. And I want to live in America. America is cool.'

'Well, aren't you goal orientated . . .' Ted began, but Irina wasn't finished.

'You keep all the money for me,' she said firmly. 'I need enough for pizza and I save the rest. I want to buy my mother a house in the Golden Triangle . . .'

Ted raised his eyebrow questioningly.

'Is the part of Moscow where all the rich people live,' Irina explained. 'And I buy her a house there and she all be crying with . . . how do you say? Gratitude. And then I remind her that she thought I was useless, then when she's sick with guilt I move to New York and never speak to her again,' she finished triumphantly.

'Well, that's a little harsh . . .'

'And that's why I'm going to be the most successful model ever.'

Ted got a little quiet after that, as if using revenge as a motivational tool was wrong. He talked her through the next two days of shooting for a big chain of sports shops who were using Irina to model their autumn range. The ads would appear in their shop windows and in magazines, even on buses. And for that they were going to pay her £10,000 less her agency fees and commission. Apparently when she wasn't fresh off the plane, she'd start to get paid even more.

Sweet.

★ ★ ★

It was one thing for people to constantly rave on about what a great model Irina was going to be when all they'd seen were some OKish Polaroids. It was quite another for Irina to get in front of a camera and be good at something for the first time in her life. No wonder that she'd spent the night before her first shoot throwing up pizza in her en suite bathroom. It didn't taste as good coming up as it did going down.

She was still weak-kneed and trembly the next morning when a car came to pick Irina up and drive her to a huge warehouse by the river in a place called Docklands. She inched slowly into a massive room covered in complicated-looking lights, flight cases and a huge table covered in the best selection of food Irina had ever seen. Someone got her a plate laden with scrambled eggs and smoked salmon, which she wolfed down while hordes of people crowded around her, dressing her, doing her hair and smearing make-up on her. And when they weren't doing that, they kept showering her with compliments about her bone structure and how beautiful her body was. They even asked her what music she liked, and soon Snoop Dogg and Eminem were blaring out of the sound system while they shot the pictures.

It turned out that modelling was as easy as breathing. Irina didn't know what all the fuss was about or why she'd wasted a night fretting and sweating. They'd built three different sets to resemble a gymnasium in the year 2108.

There was a sci-fi rock-climbing wall, and a futuristic tennis court and a space-age exercise bike. All Irina had to do was brandish a tennis racket in a purposeful manner, pedal furiously or climb up stuff.

The photographer told her not to smile, which worked out really well because she didn't like smiling anyway. And then he told her to look moody. There wasn't much that Irina had a natural talent for, but when it came to looking moody, she was a world champion.

'Keep your face tilted down and don't blink,' he'd say.

Or, 'Hunch your shoulders slightly and point your leg so I can see the muscles.'

Even, 'Pretend you're running towards the camera but stay still.'

And she was getting paid for this?

But the best was yet to come. At the end of the second day, the stylist told her that she could keep all the clothes they'd shot and even the ones she hadn't. There were two rails of tracksuits and T-shirts, hoodies, flippy skirts, swimsuits, and even socks and underwear. Plus a pile of trainers and two holdalls, which was cool because Irina's bin-liners were falling to pieces. The creative director was so pleased with the pictures that he biked over an iPod as a thank you present and the photographer's assistant had uploaded loads of tracks on it for her. Irina didn't know anyone who had an iPod, though Sergei had tried to steal one from an American tourist once. Though he could rot in hell anyway. When Irina had told the gang that she was going to England to become a model, he'd crowed with laughter.

'What are you going to model? Paper bags? You're so full of shit, Irina,' he'd scoffed before insisting that she was lying and that really she was being packed off to Vyasma.

Well who was laughing now? Irina was, and if she'd known that modelling was about doing nothing then getting paid ridiculous sums of money and having presents foisted on her, she'd have signed up years ago, she decided as she sat in her dressing room having her make-up taken off. Her gloating was only interrupted when Sofia walked in.

'Ted couldn't come so he sent me,' she said in Russian and Irina realized that it had been two days since she'd heard her native language. 'You're a very lucky girl.'

Irina couldn't help but agree. 'I know. People keep giving me stuff for free. I just got all this make-up.'

She never wore make-up, but she liked the glittery stuff they put around her eyes.

'I mean Ted,' Sofia sniffed. 'He's the senior booker. He never works with new girls. I work with the new girls.'

'He says that I'm going to be famous.' Irina squinted at her reflection, which still looked the same to her. 'Apparently I have a unique look. Y'know, whatever. And I love the English breakfasts and also KitKats, Doritos and Burger King.' Irina looked down at her stomach, which was still as flat as a board. 'And, like I said, they keep giving me presents.'

Sofia jiggled her bag. 'I have presents too,' she said, unzipping and delving inside. 'Mobile phone – don't lose it. Travelcard for the tube and buses. And these are your house keys.'

Irina's attention was riveted on the tiny, silver phone until Sofia jangled the keyring in her face. She looked up and shook her head decisively. 'No, I want to stay in the hotel.'

'But the hotel's expensive,' Sofia informed her grimly. 'And this flat won't have any Russian girls in it.'

'Where are the girls from?' Irina asked half-heartedly.

'The three of them are moving in today too. One's from England and the other two are from America. They're famous,' she added, but she didn't have to bother as Irina felt her eyes widen like she had no control over them.

'America,' she breathed. 'I love America.'

'And it's in Camden. There's a Burger King and a McDonald's one minute away, a big Sainsbury's, lots of clubs. And you get your own room—'

'I want my own bathroom and TV,' Irina interrupted because she deserved them. Or at least, she'd got used to having them.

Sofia gave a bark of laughter. 'Yeah, dream on. You can buy a TV – they're really cheap here – and if you can't kick the other girls out of the bathroom when you want to use it then I underestimated you.'

She had a point. And two of the girls were American so they could give Irina the lowdown for when she went to live in New York. 'I thought there were no spare rooms,' she said grudgingly because she still wasn't completely sold on the idea.

'We shifted someone around. An Australian girl was going to live in Camden, but now she'll have to share with Oksana and the others. She has a black belt in karate, I'm sure she'll be fine.'

Irina grunted. 'Well even if she isn't, it's not my problem.'

Chapter Four

37 Bayham Street didn't have a garden or a little white trim above the door. But it did have big red London buses whizzing past, some graffiti tags painted on the wall next door, a zebra-crossing opposite and a pub on the corner. Irina loved it – it was right in the centre of things.

The door was open, which was odd, because she thought that British people were more security conscious than that. But then she saw two men struggling up the stairs under the weight of several suitcases adorned with skulls and crossbones. They paused to let Irina climb over them, the smell of fresh paint catching at the back of her throat.

The door to the flat was open too and Irina rushed inside, intent on her mission to score the biggest room. The showdown with those vile Russian bitches had been a crash course in flatmate etiquette. If she had the biggest room, staked her claim first, the other girls would respect her. Even if they *were* American.

Hovering in the living room was a tall brunette. Irina barely glanced at her. Instead she walked down a hall and began peering into rooms.

There were two tiny rooms, one empty, one crammed

full of boxes and more pink crap than Irina could look at without feeling as if her eyeballs were being singed. And there were two big rooms. There wasn't much difference in the way of square footage, but one of them had a chest of drawers and the other one didn't. Soon, she'd have a lot of free clothes to put in the chest of drawers.

Decision made, Irina walked in and looked around. The windows looked right out on to the street, she could even hear the beeping from the zebra-crossing, which was a plus. She was used to a lot of noise. She was all ready to throw down her holdalls and bin-liners when she saw the leopardskin coat slung over the bed. Damn! Someone had picked this room first. It was no big deal, she could have the other large room at the end of the hall . . .

'Hey! *Hey!* What the hell do you think you're doing? This is my room!' There was a tiny girl standing in the doorway, face scrunched up and index finger pointing aggressively in Irina's direction. 'First come, first served.'

She was American and oddly familiar with her porcelain skin and inky-black hair. Like the Russian dolls that all the tourists went mad about. Unlike the Russian dolls, she had a working voicebox and wasn't shy about using it.

'Get out!' The girl shouted, like she could go for volume over manners and people would do what she wanted. Irina was so over being pushed about by bitchy flatmates.

'I not understand,' she said slowly, thickening her accent. 'Is my room.' And just to make sure that the other girl got the message, Irina flung herself down on the bed, making sure to dislodge the coat so it landed on the carpet too. There were some things that transcended the language barrier. Like actions that said very plainly, 'I'm bigger than you and if you try and physically remove me from this room, I will hurt you in ways that you never imagined possible.'

The girl stalked in long enough to snatch up her coat, then let loose with a string of expletives that Irina could barely follow. She hated her on sight, but she had to respect someone who could swear so fluently.

'Are you deficient or something? I already said it was my room!'

Yap. Yap. Yap. It was like Mrs Stravinsky's dog from next door. She disappeared out of the door and Irina followed the screeching back into the lounge, where the first girl she'd seen was still standing.

'Tough shit,' Irina snapped, folding her arms and turning to stare at flatmate number one, who still hadn't said a word. 'You know this girl, huh?' Now she'd started with the thick Slavic accent, it seemed like a good idea to run with it until she knew what she was getting herself into.

Yap! Yap! Yap! CRASH! The mini-Yank finished her temper tantrum by hurling something at the wall so that one of the pictures hanging there fell off its hook in an explosion of broken glass. It was really unnecessary, Irina thought, as her newest enemy began to harangue the guys still hauling in the rest of her luggage.

With a quick glare to make sure that the tinpot dictator was putting her stuff in the *other* big room, Irina followed the mute girl into the kitchen, where she was making a cup of tea.

'Milk, three sugars,' Irina prompted. She'd been running on Coca Cola for the last three days because she hadn't figured out where to buy tea. She decided that if this girl smiled or did anything that was even a little bit friendly, then she'd return the favour.

'I'm Laura,' the girl said. Her accent was flat and nasal and hard to understand.

'Irina.'

'So, are you from Russia or something?'

Irina definitely caught the word 'Russia', couldn't make out the rest, and decided to reply with a 'whatever'.

It didn't really matter though. Because the girl was pretty and she was doing what pretty girls always did; staring at Irina like she'd just crawled up from the depths of the gutter. Like Irina wasn't fit to breathe the same air as her.

They looked at each other for a long moment. Laura was as tall as Irina and as beautiful in the flesh as models were supposed to be. Her skin was flawless and creamy with a delicate pink flush to her cheeks, she had huge, green eyes and a lush, rosebud-shaped mouth. She tossed back a waterfall of straight brown hair, then turned and carried on making tea as if Irina had been judged and found sadly lacking.

In Irina's experience, this was standard pretty-girl behaviour. They didn't make any effort because they didn't have to. They were used to people kowtowing and being all deferential and shit just because their faces were pleasing to look at. It was pathetic.

Irina glared balefully at Laura's back, noting the way her jeans clung low on her curvy hips and the cute little red jumper that hugged her impressive chest. Irina could never get away with clothes like that, not because they didn't sell clothes like that in the markets that she frequented, but because she didn't have curves. Her body went straight up and down with no variation.

So far, her flatmates were a big disappointment. And also, strangely familiar, because she had a feeling that she'd seen Laura before too. Maybe all Western girls looked the same, with their perfect clothes and perfect hair and perfect way of fitting into every situation like they had a God-given right to be there.

'Want one?' Laura cut through Irina's reverie by pushing a mug of tea towards her and holding out a plastic container full of sweet-smelling, sticky squares. Food! Irina was almost faint with hunger – it had been hours since she'd decimated a bowl of chilli and rice at the shoot.

She grabbed a handful of whatever Laura was offering and took a huge bite of something oaty and syrupy sweet.

'*Spasibo*,' she mumbled. Her mother would have killed her for talking with her mouth full. 'Fucking starving.' If she didn't kill her for swearing first, Irina thought, before someone knocked her arm so that the mug of tea almost went flying.

It was that stupid American girl trying to get in on the tea-drinking. 'What's your name?' she demanded of Irina, her chin sticking out and just asking for it to make contact with someone's fist.

Irina stared at her without blinking and carried on stuffing Laura's oatcake things in her mouth. Nope, she wasn't going to give an inch and also she was really trying to remember where she'd seen them both before.

'Irina, Candy. Candy, Irina.' Laura was doing the introductions. 'Candy is . . .'

Even the name was familiar. Candy. Candy. Candy . . . It was Candy Careless, star of this MTV reality show that she'd been watching. Candy lived with two people from a rock group, who couldn't possibly be her parents because they acted like they were both fifteen. Candy had lost her temper every five minutes. It was possible that she was completely unhinged.

And while Irina was thinking about TV shows, her mind scrolled back to the *Make Me A Model* marathon she'd watched the night before, where a girl who looked just like Laura had won . . .

'You on TV,' Irina fired at Candy and then at Laura, 'You

too. Weird.' No wonder they were both so full of themselves. Irina swung out of the kitchen so they could bond over their ratings or talk about mascara or whatever pretty-girls talked about.

Back in her room, she bounced luxuriously on the huge bed and tried to get her thoughts in order. Did everyone get their own TV show? Was there a waiting list? She'd have to ask Ted.

Chapter Five

Another girl had arrived later on that evening while Irina was sorting out her new clothes from her old, dirty clothes. She'd been en route to the kitchen to try to work out how to use the washing machine, her arms full, when she'd bumped into this vision of blondeness who'd squeaked in surprise, said 'I'm Hadley' and scurried out of the way.

Irina had known who she was immediately. Hadley Harlow was famous even in Russia. Irina's younger sister, Elisaveta, had even had a knock-off Hadley doll. And when their TV had still worked, *Hadley's House* was always on, dubbed into Russian though, so it was weird to hear the real Hadley, eight years older and with a completely different nose, talking in a breathy American accent. But it was proof that everyone here was famous.

Irina was down with that. She wouldn't mind being famous too. Though being stinking rich was her number one priority. And Fierce seemed to want her to be stinking rich too.

Now, although it was nine a.m., Ted had already phoned her and told her that she had appointments, or go-tos, where she'd meet people who'd book her for photo shoots.

'Wear something pretty and try to act interested when people talk to you,' he'd advised.

Irina was wearing one of her new tracksuits. It was pink. Pink equalled pretty in her book, though she wondered whether it made her skin look more sallow than normal. She was fairly sure that trainers weren't pretty, so she slipped on a pair of ballet flats that had been part of her haul from the sportswear shoot and dabbed some of the glittery eyeshadow on her lids.

She was just rummaging in the fridge for food when Candy sashayed in.

'Are you going out like that?' she asked Irina doubtfully, like it was any of her business, especially when she was wearing a dress over her jeans. Pick jeans, or pick a dress, but don't wear them both together.

Irina took her time replying. The time it took to drink some milk straight from a carton that wasn't hers. But tough, property was theft – unless it was Irina's property. 'Are *you* going out like that?' she countered.

'OK, in the developed world this is, like, what we call a vintage dress,' Candy informed her snottily. 'And this is my signature style. I call it my fifties librarian-gone-bad look.'

Irina didn't even have to fake the confusion, just the thick accent. 'I not understand,' she said blankly. 'You look like crazy.'

She'd already learnt that it was best to make an exit while Candy was still gasping in outrage, and by the time

Irina was at the front door, Candy only had time to choke out, 'Did you hear what that bitch just said to me?' at Laura.

Figuring out the tube was worse than solving algebraic equations. By the time Irina had translated the place names into Russian letters in her head and cross-referenced them against her *AtoZ* and the different coloured tube lines, ten minutes had flown past. Hundreds of impatient people bumped into her as she stood by the train indicator board, debating if she wanted to go via Bank or via Charing Cross. Everything about London was royally pissing her off today.

Including the long line of girls snaking out of the door and down the stairs as Irina got to her first appointment.

The only thing different about each one of them was their eye colour. Apart from that, they could have come from some mail-order catalogue where willowy, elegant girls with blemish-free skin and shiny hair were standard issue. There were a few isolated titters as Irina joined the end of the line and stared unblinking at a spot in the middle distance so she wouldn't have to look at all the girls in their super-tight grey jeans and skimpy little tops. Though she'd never admit it, even under intense interrogation, maybe Candy had been right about her outfit.

Or maybe not. Half an hour later, when Irina finally made it to the front of the queue and got ushered into someone's office, the three people sitting around a big glass table fell on her with excited little cries.

'Tracksuit *and* ballet flats? Awesome!' exclaimed a girl with a shaved head.

Her male colleague agreed. 'My God, it's so chav-chic.'

'Russian, right? Straight off the plane,' surmised an older woman, not even waiting for Irina to reply because obviously she was too dumb to know what they were saying. 'I love her. She's so raw. The Little Match Girl meets Ingrid Bergman. I need her to walk, Paul.'

Paul was obviously the official interpreter. 'Have. You. Got. Some. Heels. With. You?' he asked Irina slowly and loudly like she was missing several million brain cells.

Ted hadn't mentioned heels. There were a lot of things Ted hadn't mentioned. Irina shook her head.

'Portfolio?'

That she did have. Sofia had given her a glossy black folder with some Polaroids from her sportswear shoot in it. And she'd also told her to tell them that 'I not have a – how do you say? – comp card yet.' The older woman was beginning to look towards the door as if she couldn't wait to completely patronize the next girl to walk through it. Then inspiration struck. 'Also, I not shoot Thursday as I do *Vogue* then.'

There was a moment of stunned silence. 'Well, what are you waiting for?' the older woman screeched. 'Book her now!'

Irina stopped at a shoe shop on her way to the next appointment to buy a pair of heels, but no one stocked anything larger than a 41. Not that it mattered in the end. The go-to idiots just raved about her tracksuit and ballet flats, made several borderline racist remarks about her cultural heritage, and got all giddy about her cheekbones. When Irina opened her mouth to address them in broken English, the stark-raving insane people who seemed to be employed by the British fashion industry just about peed themselves. Then they booked her.

And what made it the best day ever was the moment as she walked out of the last appointment.

'You're. Very. Beautiful,' the Creative Director shouted at her. 'You. Have. A. Big. Future. Ahead. Of. You.'

Irina stopped mid-scowl to see none other than Oksana heading towards them, and from the equally furious expression on her face, she'd heard every word.

'I come for the beauty story,' Oksana told the man stonily.

'Oh, you might as well turn around. It's already been booked, darling,' he said casually, before turning back to Irina. 'We're. All. Very. Excited. About. Working. With. You.'

Chapter Six

It took Irina three days to decide that actually modelling wasn't that much fun after all. She hated the stylists and their stupid clothes. The make-up girls who could talk about lipgloss for fifteen minutes without pausing for breath. The photographers who treated her like she was a fully poseable shop dummy, and the clients who patronized her and automatically assumed that she'd had a full frontal lobotomy before she'd got on the plane.

And Irina decided that she hated London too. London was harsh lighting and no shadows where she could hide, especially in the bright white interiors of a photo studio. London was standing in her underwear while people tugged at her hair, prodded at her skin and pinned the back of everything she put on so it hung better. London was people talking at her, never to her. And when they didn't talk, they just smiled. That was the hardest thing to get used to. Irina couldn't understand why everyone smiled all the time and said 'sorry', even when she was the one who'd knocked into them. In Russia people didn't smile or say sorry unless they had a damn good reason to.

And now, Irina hadn't even cleared the arrivals lounge of

Tokyo Narita International Airport before she decided that she *hated* Japan too.

Just getting to grips with English money and her new mobile phone had been enough to deal with, without being sent to Tokyo. Ted had given her one day's notice and the pithy advice that 'the Japanese are really big on manners, Irina, and they're not used to dealing with stroppy Russian teenagers. Do not piss anyone off.'

It was six in the evening and she'd lost an entire day during the twelve-hour flight. But even allowing for severe sleep deprivation, Tokyo still sucked. And so did every single Japanese person who stared at her like they'd never seen a girl who was five-foot eleven inches in her stockinged feet. Two women even pointed at her, their faces incredulous, as if Irina had escaped from a zoo or a maximum security prison.

There was yet another driver holding up yet another sign with her name on it as she cleared Customs after being barked at in a language that bore no resemblance to any language that she'd ever heard before. Irina settled into the back seat of the car for the ninety-minute drive to the Shinjuku district.

Irina thought that the lull of the car engine would help her to nap, but outside the windows everything was so shiny that it hurt her red-rimmed, dry eyes. There were a million neon signs all lit up and glowing in Japanese letters that resembled intricate doodles. And how so many bustling people could fit together in one single city, she didn't know. It should have been exciting, but it wasn't. It was scary and alien and if they made her take the train to her jobs, she'd get lost and have to spend days wandering the Tokyo subway system before she found a tourist that spoke English.

It was a relief to get inside the hotel and check in. Except it was full of thousands of hotel staff in pin-neat black uniforms and they didn't just smile, they bowed, as Irina was ushered to the reception desk and then the lift and finally her room, unable to understand anything that was being said. Laura's Manchester accent was bad enough, but English filtered through Japanese made as much sense as Martian.

Her stomach was growling relentlessly as Irina tossed a fax on the floor from the Japanese model agency who wanted her at their offices by eleven the next morning. The room was sleek and stylish, dominated by a low, large bed covered in crisp white linen; there was also a huge TV and, after opening a few cupboards, Irina found the minibar.

Two packets of peanuts and some weird Japanese rice crackers, washed down with a can of Coke (which didn't taste the same as British Coke) just made her stomach protest even more that it was hungry and it wanted food, proper food, now. Irina stared out at the fluorescent sprawl twenty storeys below her, searching in vain for the familiar golden arches of a McDonald's.

In the end, a huge wave of exhaustion drowned out the sound of her belly rumbles and Irina collapsed face down on the bed. One night without bothering to do her new skincare regime wouldn't kill her.

Four hours later, Irina was wide awake and mindlessly channel-hopping. It didn't matter that her body ached with tiredness and that the clock on her bedside table informed her that it was one in the morning. Her head was still on London time, where it was ten a.m. and way past getting up time. Why had she had that can of Coke? Because she was an ignorant bitch who'd never suffered from jet-lag before, that's why.

And Japanese TV was another item to be added to the gigantic list of all the things that already sucked about Japan. It was full of people quacking in Japanese and doing bizarre workout routines in garish leotards that made even Irina wince. Or martial arts movies. Or music shows with squeaky-clean teenage girls warbling in a pitch only audible to bats. Even *The Simpsons* was dubbed into Japanese.

The battery in her iPod died at three-thirty a.m. and the plug on her charger didn't fit the socket. Irina thought about banging her head against the wall a few times to knock herself out, then ate a bag of funky-tasting Japanese sweets from the minibar in the bath. After that, there was nothing to do but lie back on the unyielding mattress so she could stare at the ceiling and listen to the hum of the air conditioning.

She must have fallen back to sleep eventually because she was woken by the telephone. Apparently, and she wasn't entirely sure about this, there was a car waiting to take her to the Japanese modelling agency. There was just time to haul on the skinny jeans that Laura had left in the washing machine and a jumper and scrape back her hair so everyone could see her cheekbones. Hadley had told her that icy-cold cans of Diet Coke were the best thing for piggy eyes so Irina grabbed a couple on her way out.

When she got to the modelling agency she would smile. And then she'd ask them for food. Proper food. And once her belly was full, she wouldn't feel like she wanted to punch the next person who bowed at her. Well, that was the general plan.

But when Irina got to the modelling agency no one could see her smile because they were all too busy bowing and calling her 'Miss Ilina'.

'I have breakfast now?' Irina asked hopefully, and they smiled and showed her into a little room. Irina sat down on a floor cushion (they didn't seem big on sofas in the land of the rising sun) and waited expectantly for a basket of pastries and some coffee. Hell, she'd even eat fruit.

Instead, a girl came in, bowed, and then shoved a DVD into a little slot on the big TV in the corner. 'You watch,' she told Irina, before bowing and backing out of the room.

The DVD was an instructional film on how to model in Japan. Irina watched in amazement as a perky girl with a bouncy ponytail and a perma-grin performed a series of numbered poses.

One was a standard three-quarters profile to the right.

Two was a standard three-quarters profile to the left.

Three was a front-facing, head-and-shoulders shot with a big, peppy smile, and by pose number four Irina was grinding down hard on her back teeth and wondering what the tatami mats on the floor would taste like.

Irina sat there for half an hour after the DVD ended because she was too scared to stick her head out of the door and demand food. Well, not scared, but all the bowing and polite manners were beginning to freak her out. Eventually another girl came in, with a white bikini, and indicated with a series of hand gestures that Irina should put it on.

It was far too small. It was obviously designed for the tiny little Japanese girls she'd seen from the car window. It barely covered Irina's bum and there was just enough material left once she'd stretched it over her chest to tie the ends together. If Laura had been wearing it, with her big boobs and fat arse, she'd be practically naked. As it was, Irina adjusted the bottoms so they didn't completely disappear and walked out.

Everyone bowed again and this time she didn't even attempt to smile but folded her arms to make sure she wasn't flashing her nipples and inclined her head a mere fraction of a centimetre.

'Photo,' someone said, producing a camera, and Irina stretched her limbs into a pose that might have been number ten, though it could even have been number twenty-three, and stared at the lens.

That took fifteen minutes and then someone said, 'Walk,' as everyone cleared a path for Irina to strut her stuff.

Her walk hadn't really had a public outing yet. Although she'd diligently studied the runway shows on the Fashion Channel, Irina found herself doing her shoplifting walk from the time not so long ago when she'd had to head for the exit with things stuffed into her coat pockets, hoping that she wouldn't attract the attention of a security guard. Her steps were slow, like she had all the time in the world, but with an insolent swagger to give the impression that she wasn't a girl to be messed with. When she'd walked at go-tos, the clients told her that she had a feline grace, but Irina wasn't sure what the Japanese would make of it. They were all chattering away excitedly and the fucking camera was still taking picture after picture. If she fainted with hunger, it would serve them all right.

Back in her own clothes, she was given a typed itinerary, thankfully in something that vaguely resembled English.

'Shoot tomorrow, tonight dinner with client – important men – and we come to hotel at . . .' the Japanese booker wrinkled her nose as she searched for the right word. 'Eight.'

'What do I do now?' Irina asked, looking at her piece of paper, which didn't provide any clues.

'Day off.'

'How do I get back to the hotel?' She couldn't even remember the name of it.

The girl smiled. Always the smiling. 'Taxi. I write address in Japanese for you.'

'And how do I get food?'

'Food at hotel, yes.'

'But English food, ja?'

'Good food at hotel.'

'Like pizza or burgers or steak?'

'Yes. You go now. Goodbye, Miss Ilina.'

Chapter Seven

After she'd managed to order a cheeseburger and fries from room service, Irina had passed out in a deep sleep, like falling headfirst into a pile of feathers, and woken up with only half an hour to get ready for the dinner with the big important clients.

Irina had spent two hours in a restaurant wearing a Lanvin dress she'd been given by a stylist, that she'd only packed as an afterthought because she'd never worn a dress in her life. The conversation had jabbered around her while she'd picked at an elaborate dinner, which had arrived at fifteen-minute intervals on ornate lacquered plates and contained gross things that she refused to put in her mouth. Irina knew that for the rest of her life she'd have nightmares about the pickled red fish eggs. She swore that some of them were still moving.

In the end, Irina had given up on pretending to be interested in what people were saying and had sat there, tearing at an edge of the paper placemat, until it had been time to leave.

When she'd got back to the hotel and ordered another cheeseburger and fries from room service, they hadn't been able to understand her accent and sent up a bowl of rice and some cubes of fish instead. So she'd gone to bed hungry. Hadn't slept. Then slept too late. There was a definite, sucky pattern emerging. Irina still couldn't figure out the deal with breakfast. Did she order it in her room? Was there a special place to get it? Could she find someone to ask who spoke slowly and could actually pronounce their 'r's?

Luckily, when she got to the studio for a cosmetics shoot, there were the remains of a breakfast buffet just being cleared away. Irina didn't even bother to say hello to the little coterie of people who looked at her as she walked in, just snatched two glazed buns from a platter that was being carried past and took a huge bite before anyone could demand them back.

Then she walked out again, so she could stand in a corridor and wolf down the pastry so fast that it got stuck in her throat and she had to dislodge it with frantic gulps from a can of Diet Coke. Hadley had been bullshitting because they'd had no impact on the bags under her eyes, which were large enough to use as carry-on luggage when she flew back to London.

Irina stalked back into the studio to meet Aaron, the photographer, a grizzled, middle-aged American who spoke with a deep drawl. There was also an interpreter who twittered so softly that Irina barely understood the introductions to ten (ten!) suits from the cosmetics company whose names all seemed to end in 'san', and a nervous woman from the modelling agency who kept fluttering her hands. Irina decided to cut her losses and bowed to each of them in turn, even managing a smile, though she was sure she had bun dough stuck between her teeth. Ted would be so proud of her. When she said, 'Mushi-mushi' like she'd heard the hotel staff greet each other, they all sighed dreamily. What a bunch of suckers.

Irina tried to be on her best behaviour, she really did. Even when they dressed her in a barely-there wisp of chiffon that just skimmed the tops of her thighs. And for people that were spending a lot of money on a shoot to advertise their make-up, Irina didn't know why they insisted on sprinkling her face so liberally with yellow, pink and green glitter and drawing butterflies across her brow with liquid eyeliner. Like, whatever. It wasn't her problem.

'They want a lot of movement and youthful energy so I'm going to put you on a trampoline and have you jumping up and down,' Aaron told her. 'But I want ballet movements, lots of control, point your fingers and toes and watch your facial expressions. OK?'

Irina nodded. 'Ja, like jêtés and arabesques and shit.'

He grinned. 'Yeah, you got it, honey.'

Irina let the photographer's assistant help her on to the trampoline and bounced up and down on her toes just to get a feel for it. This could be fun, and if she worked off some of her energy then she might actually sleep tonight.

She waited for Aaron to give her a cue, but he was deep

in discussion with the interpreter and one of the suits, before the younger woman detached herself and hurried over.

'Mr Yakamoto-san he say like swan in winter,' she explained helpfully. 'And lots of pose number seventeen.'

And pose number seventeen was? 'Like swan in winter?' Irina repeated because something had got lost in translation.

'Yes, swan in winter and seventeen.' The interpreter bowed and went back to the huddle, while Irina tried to remember what pose number seventeen was.

In the end it didn't matter about pose number seventeen. Because every time she jumped, she didn't even have a chance to land before Mr goddamn Yakamoto-san decided that he wasn't happy and sent the interpreter over to deliver even more word salad about 'flowers unfurling their petals with intensity' and 'shooting stars that are in the sky'.

Lunch was delivered and they still hadn't shot one roll of film. Irina watched with rapt attention as the dishes were unpacked. What was the big deal with all the fish and rice? But there was also a huge bowl of noodles, a tray of fruit and more of the sticky buns, which had been all right though the red paste inside them had been kind of gritty.

Irina crouched down so she could vault off the trampoline, but was stopped by the photographer's assistant. 'Aaron says that you have to stay on it,' he ordered in a tone that was far too bossy for her liking. 'They're always like this, but they'll calm down in a while. It's a very big campaign for them and Mr Yakamoto has to be seen to be involved with—'

'I hungry,' Irina snapped because she didn't need to be patronized by someone's assistant. 'And yo, have you charged up my iPod yet?' She'd told him to do it hours ago, even snapped her fingers, but he'd just loped off with it in his hand like he had more pressing things to worry about.

She could tell that he wanted to shove her iPod somewhere that it would hurt, but he was way lower down on the fashion food chain than her. 'Stay on the trampoline,' he repeated mechanically in a soft, lilting accent, that Irina couldn't place. 'And just chill out, I'm only trying to help you.'

'Whatever, go away now,' Irina said brusquely, waving her hand in his startled face as she muttered in Russian under her breath. It was useful being able to vent in her mother tongue, and by the time another two hours had passed, lunch had been cleared away and Irina was hissing out the worst swearwords she knew every time she leapt in the air. It was either that or burst into tears, and crying was what whiny-ass girls like Laura did.

At least they'd progressed far enough that Aaron was managing to get a couple of shots in between interruptions, but it was very hard to throw athletic, beautiful shapes when she needed to pee and eat and do something about her itchy make-up. In that exact order.

'Miss Ilina, number four pose,' the interpreter called out. 'Now, jump.'

Irina jumped, her legs stretching out in a perfect arabesque, her arms arched behind her and her face turned to the camera with an intense stare.

'Miss Ilina, can you smile with eyes?'

Miss Ilina had had enough. 'Screw this shit,' she shouted, leaping off the trampoline and striding towards Mr Yakamoto-san. 'What is the problem?' she shouted, as he held his hands up in protest. 'Why are you getting all up in my business, ja?'

'Miss Ilina! Miss Ilina!' The interpreter and the woman from the modelling agency were shrieking in unison, the Japanese were barking like demented sea lions, and Aaron calmly put down his camera, seized Irina around the waist and carried her off to the dressing room.

'Put me the fuck down!' she shouted, before unleashing a volley of the worst swearwords she knew in Russian, French and English. By the time she ran out of curses and was gasping for breath, the woman from the modelling agency was there, wringing her hands and tweeting frantically. There were actual tears starting to roll down her face. Irina knew exactly how she felt.

'Miss Ilina, you have disrespected Mr Yakamoto-san. We very angry with you,' she conveyed via the interpreter, who was standing by the door as if she wanted to put as much distance between herself and Irina.

'I not a machine,' Irina yelled. 'All day, do this, do that. But we not do anything! Five freaking hours on a trampoline!'

'OK, you need to lose the attitude right now, little missy,' Aaron advised her, his soft Southern drawl sharpening. 'You're wasting everyone's time and you're *this* close to being put on the first plane back to England.'

'Good! I not care! I hate this country and the food is crap!'

But Irina was shouting at a closed door. Everyone had walked out and left her alone. Alone and hungry and still needing to pee. Well, she was damned if she was going back in there, even if it was to use the bathroom.

What she really wanted to do was scream and shout a bit more and hit someone. Preferably Mr Yakamoto-san. Instead, she settled for picking up a handful of his stinking eyeshadows and hurling them at the wall, where they shattered and sent an arc of multi-coloured, iridescent powders spilling everywhere.

She'd been seething for a good half hour when Aaron came back in with his little toady to find Irina lying on the floor with her legs propped up against the wall.

Irina acknowledged their presence with a twitch of her toes, then ignored them. She had backache from that damn trampoline and if she'd slipped a disc then she was going to sue them.

'I'm going to cut you some slack because you don't

know the ropes,' Aaron informed her, straddling a chair. 'But if you throw another snit, I'm going to make sure that you never book another modelling job again.'

He sounded like he meant it too.

Irina sat up and scowled. 'They treat me like I have no feelings,' she complained as Aaron and his assistant shared an amused look, which made her itch to slap it off their faces.

'You're a model, get used to it.' Aaron grinned, before his expression grew more serious. 'It's three days' shooting. You got the itinerary, honey. That means we put up with a lot of corporate bullshit today and we get the pictures shot later on in the week.'

'No one tell me that,' Irina said sulkily.

'Well, you're being told now.' Aaron jerked his head in the direction of the door. 'They think your grandma just died, but you're going to put on a coat and some sunglasses and Javier's going to take you across the street so you can buy some flowers and think of an apology that's both convincing and sincere.'

It was on the tip of her tongue to tell them that she never apologized, but Irina reined it back in. Especially as Aaron continued, 'And if you're mean to Javier again, then I've given him permission to beat you.'

Irina wasn't entirely sure that Aaron was joking, so she stalked out in silence, making sure to bump Javier into the doorframe as they went. Javier's name had been on the call-sheet but Irina hadn't realized that the J was pronounced as an H, not that Irina ever intended to say it out loud.

Instead, once they got outside, she turned to give Ha-vee-ay (or however you said it) the most filthy look that she'd ever achieved. It was really quite spectacular. 'In Russia we don't like sneaks,' she hissed venomously. 'We push them into the canal in the middle of winter!'

When Irina returned, her arms full of delicate spiky flowers, she cornered the interpreter first, who looked like the softest of touches. The fact that she was visibly terrified of Irina also helped. Either way, she accepted the apology and was happy to spend ten minutes giving her an impromptu lesson in Japanese.

When she approached Mr Yakamoto-san, his lips thinned and his little minions tried to block Irina's path. Clutching the blossoms, she bowed so low that her head almost touched the floor before advancing on him.

'I regret my behaviour,' she said in what she hoped was passable Japanese. 'I've been bereft over the death of my grandmother. Please find it in your heart to forgive me.'

Both her grandmothers were still alive and she sincerely hoped that God wouldn't wreak his revenge by striking one of them down as payback. Especially as Mr Yakamoto-san was all sunny smiles now and even reached up to pat Irina's head, which would usually have been her cue to try and detach his hand from his wrist.

'Mr Yakamoto-san say your apology almost as beautiful as your face,' the translator beamed as the minions all smiled and bowed.

The apocalypse had been averted. Irina let the make-up girl apply even more glitter and climbed back on the trampoline.

She ignored the gnawing pangs of hunger and the cramp in her left foot and jumped, posed, then waited for Mr Yakamoto-san's next instruction.

It was hours before they wrapped for the day with a measly two rolls of film in the can.

Irina couldn't wait to get her make-up off and change into clothes that didn't flash her knickers to the world. She walked back out into the studio to find Aaron and Javier packing up their gear.

If she didn't apologize on principle then saying thank you came a close second, but it was good to get the photographer back on side – before he could make any calls to Ted.

'That tip you give me about the flowers was good,' she said casually. Aaron ignored her and continued to pack his camera lenses back in their case. 'So, like, we friends again, ja?'

'Not right now, sugar, no,' he bit out. 'You think you're something special because you've been booked for a few jobs? Well, you're not. You're just another jobbing model who might still be around in a few months' time. And if you pull a stunt like this again with me, I swear to God you'll be back in Russia in a heartbeat. Now scoot!'

Chapter Eight

Irina was still trembling with fury when she got back to the hotel. It was the kind of rage that she'd used to quell by either breaking stuff or hurling things into the canal behind their block of flats. There didn't seem to be any canals in Tokyo so Irina picked up the wastepaper basket and smashed it against the wall until it was nothing but wood chips. It didn't make her feel remotely better. In fact, it made her feel worse. Like she wanted to smash herself against the wall, until *she* broke into tiny pieces. Then she could put herself back together again into a prettier, happier, less screwed up version of Irina who belonged in the world and didn't feel like an outsider everywhere she went.

It wasn't really an option. And chucking loo rolls around was just pathetic. It was only once she'd torn her lilac tracksuit to shreds that Irina felt calm enough to run a bath and wash off the glitter.

She was just towelling off her hair, still vibrating slightly, when there was a knock on the door. She hadn't ordered any room service, as she'd planned to hunt out one of the hotel restaurants and draw a picture of a pizza if she had to, so who the hell was knocking?

Rubbing a hand over her throbbing forehead, Irina opened the door.

'What do you want?' she demanded as she saw Javier standing there. Talking hadn't been a good idea because her voice wobbled alarmingly.

'You left your iPod behind,' he said easily, like she wasn't giving him a face full of wrath. 'Here, take it. I was passing the hotel anyway.'

She snatched at her MP3 player, but the annoying boy was side-stepping past her so he could walk into the room and survey the chaos she'd managed to create by flinging the contents of her holdalls around.

'Was there a hurricane in here?' he asked in an amused voice. 'Do you know how to put clothes away?'

'Russian girls never put their clothes away,' Irina snapped, slamming the door behind him because there might be yelling soon. 'I not invite you in!'

'Are you worried about Aaron telling your booker about the little scene?' Javier enquired gently. 'I'm sure he won't. He was probably just trying to scare you into behaving.'

Irina tried to look as if she didn't care one way or another. She eyed Javier warily, best to keep him on side until she had her iPod back, then she'd kick his arse. 'Are you from America?'

Javier glanced out of the window at the brightly lit cityscape, the dark shadow of Mount Fuji looming in the distance. 'Brazil originally, but I've lived in New York for the last five years.'

She processed that information. His accent was musical and soft, totally unlike her harsh way of biting words out.

'Why are you so angry, Irina?' And he said her name like it was a poem.

She shrugged. 'Not angry. Just the way I talk, is all.'

'Well, if you're OK . . .'

She was OK. A-OK. But if she spent another night in this hotel with no one to talk to, trying to order food that wasn't what she wanted and watching TV that she couldn't follow . . . 'I'm hungry! All the time I'm hungry and they not understand my accent and I not understand theirs and they keep giving me fish and I hate fish,' she burst out. 'And everyone stares at me like I'm the giraffe and they bow and smile all the time and they always so polite and it's just bullshit!'

'And you get cranky when you're hungry?' Javier smiled faintly. 'My aunt is just the same.'

'My tummy hurts and is all I can think about,' Irina said, her throat starting to feel tight and swollen again. She sat down on the bed and stared up at Javier. He was a real pretty boy; tall and slender with glossy, dark brown hair falling around a sculpted face. Not her type. She liked muscular blondes like Sergei who were handy in a fight. Javier looked like he'd cover his face with his hands to protect his cheekbones and his girlish mouth if someone wanted to step to him.

There was a moment of silence which stretched on far too long and Irina suddenly felt embarrassed about her balled fists and her blotchy face. The make-up today had covered up most of her freckles. 'If you tell anyone what I just say, I have you killed,' she declared in her most menacing manner. 'I know people.'

Javier didn't seem too bothered, but he shuffled towards the door at a brisk pace. Then he paused and turned. 'I'm meeting up with some friends now, you could hang out with us if you like,' he offered. Irina had the feeling that he regretted the words as soon as they left his mouth,

Tough luck, pretty-boy. 'Give me five minutes to get dressed.'

The first thing Irina wanted to do was hunt down the nearest McDonald's and order everything on the menu except a Filet-O-Fish. But Javier refused to be a party to it. 'You can't eat McDonald's in Japan,' he protested, as Irina stood on a street corner and stared frantically in all directions. 'You should explore the local culture.'

'Does the local culture have chicken nuggets and French fries and cheeseburgers?' She was starting to drool or else she just looked wild-eyed and deranged, because Javier sighed in capitulation.

'Compromise,' he said. 'We'll go to Mos Burger; it's like the Japanese McDonald's.'

Mos Burger was way cooler than McDonald's. Irina had

found the food in Britain a little bland for a girl who'd grown up on sauerkraut and gherkins. She demolished a spicy cheeseburger and fries, then as Javier looked on in amazement, she ordered a teriyaki chicken burger, another portion of fries and an apple pie for dessert.

Javier had a rice burger with something called black root, because he was a vegetarian. Irina had never actually met a vegetarian before, but it confirmed all her suspicions. What kind of man didn't eat meat? It was unnatural and she'd told him as much.

'Do you blurt out every single thought and opinion that you have?' he asked her thoughtfully.

Irina nodded firmly. 'I hate people who are double-faced, or whatever. My flatmates pretend to be all open and talk about their feelings, but they never really say what they mean.' She pointed at herself. 'I say the truth.'

'Your version of the truth,' Javier pointed out, resting his arms on the table. He had beautiful hands; his fingers were long and tapered and he gestured constantly with them as he talked. 'Some people might see things differently and some people might get upset when you're so . . . um . . . frank.'

Irina didn't buy that for a second. 'Then they pussies,' she mumbled through a mouthful of fries. 'I only get angry when people give me the bullshit.'

Javier had the nerve to pinch one of her fries, though as he'd paid for the food, Irina decided not to smack him.

Also, she still needed to ask how to get some yen. 'OK, I'll be honest with you,' he said with a challenging grin. 'You're the rudest person I've ever met and I think you have a tapeworm.'

'You getting the hang of it,' Irina grinned back. 'Now why do you have friends in Japan? Is a long way from Brazil, ja?'

'I've worked here a lot. I used to be a model,' he added quietly, like it was something that he was ashamed of – and quite rightly. There was something very wrong about guys being models, and not eating meat too. Possibly he was a gay.

'Are you a fag?'

Javier winced like he was in deep pain. 'No, Irina, I'm not a fag, and that's so offensive. Just say, "Are you gay?"'

'I learn a lot of English from rap tapes,' Irina said crossly. 'I don't care if you are a gay.'

'Just gay, and I'm not, and have you any more deeply personal questions that you want to ask?'

He'd got all stiff-backed and defensive like a cat with wet fur. People were so touchy. 'So, I shouldn't call anyone a ho or a pimp or a muthaf—?'

'Oh my God, what is wrong with you?' Javier exclaimed sharply.

Irina stood up and nudged him with her hip. 'I'm joking! Do people in the fashion industry not joke? Now you come and show me how to get yen.'

Chapter Nine

Irina followed Javier down a flight of stairs and into a curved grey room with clusters of white plastic sofas and armchairs. It was like being in a spaceship. Javier headed for a group of people lounging at the back near the bar and Irina had no choice but to follow him like a devoted dog. She sincerely hoped Javier's friends wouldn't be all up themselves like the fashion people she'd met so far.

'This is Irina, she's Russian, we're working together,' he shouted. 'Irina, this is Charlie, Hisae, Maia, Bill . . .'

It was like the United Nations of friends. There were trendy little Japanese girls, Australians, Germans, Americans, French . . . Irina sat down in the space they'd made for her and pulled out a handful of yen, which she thrust at Javier. 'I buy, we drink.'

It was the best way she knew to break the ice.

Irina had been drinking neat vodka since she was twelve. Her mother would mix it with pepper when she had a cold. Vodka was the fuel of life in Russia. On big family occasions they'd have meals that lasted for hours, each course accompanied by a shot of vodka. It wasn't about getting drunk (though her cousin Nikolai begged to differ) but about sharing a drink with friends or family, toasting their health and enjoying their company.

Drinking wasn't like that in this new world. And the bottles of Japanese beer were something else entirely. But Irina happily clinked one against the sides of the other bottles being raised and called out a quick '*Budem zdorovy*' before she took a careful sip. There were no snacks within sniffing distance and she didn't want to get drunk in front of Javier and his friends. He'd already seen her mere moments after a monumental temper tantrum and that was bad enough. But one bottle of beer and a long conversation about the new Batman movie, which Irina had seen on the plane, left her feeling pleasantly buzzed.

Javier suddenly flopped down on the seat beside Irina and asked if she was all right as if the answer actually mattered to him. Irina groped frantically for an answer that would keep Javier's big, dark eyes fixed on her but she needn't have bothered. He was only too happy to start jawing on about the ex-love of his life, Beatriz, a Brazilian model, who sounded like a vain, spoilt bitch from way back, as far as Irina could tell.

'She was so beautiful,' he sighed, and he obviously wasn't as used to alcohol as Irina because his head kept lolling as if it was an effort to hold it upright. 'We grew up together in Sao Paulo. I took her first pictures; man, she had legs all the way up to her armpits and her body . . .' He sketched out a figure eight with his hands, while Irina rolled her eyes. Men were so damn predictable – they always got sidetracked by curves. 'And she got me my first modeling job . . .'

Irina tuned out as Javier reminisced about the loft apartment in New York and travelling the world with the beautiful Beatriz until she dumped him for a Hollywood action hero and he ran away to Japan. 'These are good people,' he announced, waving his beer bottle at his friends. 'They pulled me out of my funk and helped me get some work behind the camera. And then I made an important decision . . . do you know what it was?'

Irina didn't, and she didn't particularly care either, but she liked listening to Javier's lilting voice. 'Knock yourself out.'

Javier leant in even closer so his warm breath tickled her ear. 'I never get involved with models. They're bad news.'

Irina didn't know whether to feel insulted that somehow she'd managed to have 'bad news' stamped on her forehead yet again or flattered that Javier wasn't lumping her in with all the other models that he didn't get involved with, because the solid warmth of his arm was currently slung around her shoulders. 'You're drunk,' she informed him disapprovingly. 'Real men hold their drink.'

'I'm not a real man then,' Javier announced woefully, reaching out an unsteady finger so he could brush it against her cheek. 'I've never seen freckles like yours.'

They weren't freckles. Freckles were faint little marks

that looked cute on girls like Laura. Irina had dark splotches all over her face like someone had waved a brown paintbrush about. 'You're drunk *and* you're talking shit.'

'Freckles are like little sun kisses,' Javier insisted. '*Beijos de sol*,' he added huskily in Portuguese, so Irina felt an actual shiver ripple down her spine because it sounded like he was running his fingers along her skin.

The beer was evil stuff – normally Irina didn't have a romantic bone in her body. Javier almost fell off the seat when she slid out from under his arm. Without his Irina-shaped prop he almost slid on to the floor, but Irina pointedly ignored him and started talking to Maia and Hisae, who were planning a trip to a karaoke bar the next evening. 'You should come, Ilina. It's your first time in Japan so you have to make a fool of yourself at karaoke. And we can go out for pizza first.'

Irina scrutinized their faces carefully to make sure that it wasn't just a joke that Japanese people liked to play on impressionable foreigners. Not that pizza was something she ever joked about. But they were looking at her expectantly so she pulled out her phone and handed it to them. She still hadn't worked out where to put people's numbers. 'Tomorrow I shoot vodka commercial, then we go out,' she agreed hurriedly, inwardly high-five-ing at not being confined to the hotel again. Then she cast a resigned look at Javier, who was slumped lengthways across the seat. 'Come on, pretty boy, I get you back to the hotel now.'

Javier was a very amiable drunk, happy to lean against Irina as she flagged down a green taxi and handed the driver the scrap of paper with the hotel address written on it. She didn't know where Javier was staying, so she had no choice but to drag him up to her room, noting that having a drunk boy in tow meant that the bows from the hotel staff were a little less effusive than usual.

Irina left Javier propped on a chair with a bottle of water close by while she got into bed, and listened to his deep, even breathing until she fell asleep.

He was gone when she woke up, just a note scrawled on hotel stationery on the pillow next to her. *Thanks for taking care of me last night. Hope your shoot goes well today (don't do the diva thing). See you soon, J.* Irina sniffed contemptuously, then went to check that he hadn't thrown up in her bathroom.

Chapter Ten

Although it got decidedly hairy at times, Irina behaved like an angel on the vodka shoot. Maybe a fallen angel whose wings had got clipped on the dismount, but pretty much an angel.

She kept her mouth tight shut when she was handed a fur bikini and a Cossack hat so she could advertise a Japanese brand of vodka that claimed to be filtered over ice imported straight from Siberia.

She gritted her teeth when she was introduced to her co-star, an ageing Japanese movie heart-throb, who she spent most of the day straddling while he tried to put his hand down her bikini bottoms.

She willed her mind to a tropical beach even though she was posed on her hands and knees on a block of ice, which actually wasn't that hard when you'd lived through seventeen Russian winters. Still, Irina was grateful that one of the camera assistants was there to blast her with a hairdryer every few minutes to make sure she didn't develop hypothermia.

But the most arduous task was not voicing her opinions on the vile taste of the vodka when a bottle was ceremonially opened so they could toast the success of the shoot. Irina took one mouthful and almost gagged because it tasted like pond scum.

'Miss Ilina, you like?' The interpreter asked anxiously, as if she was expecting the mother of all tantrums.

Irina sent up a silent prayer of forgiveness and held her glass aloft. 'Tastes as good as Russian vodka,' she declared, as she firmly but surreptitiously slapped away the actor's hand, which was edging towards her arse again.

The minute that Irina left the studio, she had to let loose a long stream of vitriol which she'd been bottling up all day. This time she couldn't really blame anyone's shocked stares, because it wasn't every day they saw a freakishly tall Russian girl, blue with cold, barking out curses.

Back at her hotel, Irina surveyed her crumpled clothes and tried to assemble an appropriate outfit for a karaoke/pizza double bill. Javier's friends all had an effortless cool – their jeans hung just so and they did these artful little things with accessories; a flower brooch pinned at the hip, a woolly beanie hat over pigtails. One of the boys had even held up his jeans with an aeroplane seatbelt. Irina knew that she'd never figure out the fashion thing as long as she lived. It seemed like a gigantic waste of time and effort.

She pulled on a freebie, tight black dress, knotted one of her vests over the top of it and shoved on a pair of tennis shoes. She preferred the big boxy trainers, but Candy had told her in no uncertain terms that they were strictly gym wear. Irina didn't trust Candy as far as she could throw her, but she made fashion pronouncements with the air of a girl who knew what she was talking about. It was almost time to meet Hisae and Maia in the hotel lobby, so Irina quickly twisted her thick hair into a top-knot and stared at her face.

Ted had made her have a lesson with a beautician so she could do her own make-up before go-tos, but she usually ended up looking like Bozo the Clown. The phone started buzzing as she swiped at her mouth with a tube of lipgloss and hurried out of the door.

She'd been worried that Hisae and Maia would take one look at her and realize that their friendliness the night before had been a terrible mistake. But they gave little bows and smiled at her like everything was cool. Irina stretched her lips in return and hoped that the evening wouldn't turn into one long, uncomfortable silence. She never usually hung out with other girls, but if she spent one more night in that hotel on her own . . . she'd probably destroy all the fixtures and fittings from sheer boredom.

Hisae and Maia took her to a pizza place called Shakey's, in the Harajuku district, that Gwen Stefani was always going on about. Irina was appalled to find seaweed and pickled ginger on a pizza base, but they also did ham and cheese so she didn't complain too much. All this restraint was exhausting.

When the last slice was gone and Irina was licking her

fingers, Hisae stood up. 'Now we meet the boys at the karaoke place.'

Boys? There were going to be boys? Were they the same boys from the night before? And would that include Javier? And how did she feel about that? There were many questions rattling around Irina's brain, but she was already being tugged out of the door, and every time she tried to ask exactly who they were meeting, her attention was distracted by something in a shop window, like a pair of nose straighteners or a display of sweets that looked like petrified kidneys. The Japanese were crazy bastards.

The karaoke parlour proved that once and for all. Irina had been expecting another trendy bar with a stage, a TV screen and a microphone. What she got was a *whole building* of private karaoke rooms. They took the elevator up to the seventh floor and were shown to their room, which was entirely enclosed in glass so they could look out at the dazzle and glare of Shibuya's Center Gai District.

The first thing Irina saw and heard was Charlie bellowing out the words to *Crazy In Love*. He sounded like a cat being choked. Irina tried to walk straight back out again but Hisae grabbed her wrist. 'It will be fun,' she insisted, but a new item had just been added to the already gargantuan list of all the things Irina didn't do; singing in public was straight in at number three.

Hisae and Maia were already squealing over their song selections as Irina sat and looked around for . . .

'Javier's turning up late,' Bill told her. 'He was shooting in Osaka today, getting the bullet train back.'

'Whatever,' Irina shrugged, peering curiously at the wooden square boxes that people were drinking from. 'Did they run out of glasses?'

'Haven't you tried sake yet?'

Irina decided that she liked sake. Not as much as vodka, but it had a creamy sweet taste that went down surprisingly well. She stopped after one of the little wooden boxes, which were called *masus*, but she was feeling unusually mellow. Mellow enough that she climbed on to one of the benches so she could jump up and down on it while she shouted the words to *The Real Slim Shady*. Shouting didn't count as singing.

Javier walked in just as she lost her place and squinted at the TV screen. They'd bleeped out the swearwords, which had totally thrown her off.

'*He could be workin' at Burger King, spittin' on your onion rings . . .*'

Irina tugged down her dress, which had ridden up her thighs, and wished that she hadn't chosen the longest song in the world. She managed to get to the end, to the accompaniment of many cheers and an off-key group singalong on the chorus, before she climbed off the seat and happily relinquished the microphone.

Javier had dumped his heavy bag in the corner and was slowly working his way around the group so Irina could affect a studied nonchalance by the time he got to her and pressed a quick kiss on her cheek. 'Hey,' he said sheepishly. 'About last night . . .'

'Is nothing,' Irina assured him tightly. 'But, yo, you have no head for alcohol.'

Irina watched with interest as Javier flushed slightly under the trucker's cap he was wearing. Boys shouldn't blush, which was just another mark against him. 'Getting the bullet train with a hangover was not fun,' he shared dolefully. 'And the sushi for lunch was a really bad idea.'

Irina felt a small pang of something. He sounded so woeful. 'Don't have the sake then,' she pointed out helpfully. 'Is almost as strong as vodka.'

'Don't mention spirits,' he begged, and then he was sitting down next to her, even though there were other roomier places to sit.

They spilled out of the karaoke bar a couple of hours later, with a vague, drunken plan to go to another bar and drink even more sake, but Javier shook his head firmly. 'We have an early call time,' he said, pulling Irina away from Hisae and Maia. 'Like seven a.m. early. We're going to take a cab back now.'

Irina frowned. It hadn't said seven a.m. on her itinerary.

'Aaron wanted to make an early start,' Javier explained once he'd bundled her into a cab. 'He said he was going to text you.'

Irina's phone was always beeping and ringing, much to her annoyance. 'I not sure where my hotel is,' she said as she'd lost the crumpled piece of paper with the address on it.

'Don't worry, I've got it covered. And I'll drop you off first,' Javier said hastily, like Irina needed reminding that he wasn't her type. And even if he had been, guys that looked like Javier didn't go for girls who looked like Irina, even if she was a model by some freakish set of occurrences which she still didn't properly understand.

But then she thought about being on her own in that sterile, minimalist hotel room. And how cute Javier looked when he got flustered and red in the face. How she liked to hear him say her name.

'You can come back with me, if you want?' she offered casually.

Javier went very still so his face looked like it was carved of marble. Then he started fidgeting with his bag strap. 'You're very beautiful, Irina, but we're working together and so dating would get really complicated.'

'Who said date? We drank together, we friends, now we hook up,' she explained patiently, because in her head it all sounded so plausible. 'Is really not such a big deal.'

'It's that simple?' Javier sounded doubtful. 'Shouldn't sleeping together be a big deal?'

He was such a pussy. Back home, they'd all paired off at the end of the night. Irina had always hoped that she'd end up with Sergei, but he would take first pick of Lilya or some other giggly girl with an elfin face. Not Irina. She'd have to wait until everyone else had disappeared into dark corners and made do with what was left, which was usually Vlad, who had acne, bad breath and had never been that happy with the arrangement either.

'I'm not going to force you,' she gritted, rejection making her voice sound harsher than usual. 'You not want to sleep with me? Fine, is your loss.' And just to show him what he was missing and because she'd been dying to do it all evening, Irina leaned over and kissed him.

Usually she just stuck her tongue in because boys liked that, but Javier reared back and her mouth crash-landed on his ear. His hands gripped her shoulders, maybe to hold her off, but Irina found herself being pulled closer so Javier could kiss her.

Irina had never really liked kissing that much. But then Javier's lips moved gently, unhurriedly against hers, and made her feel shivery and hot at the same time. Every time she tried to kiss her way, with a lot of fervour and tongue, he would distract her with something sneaky like trailing his fingers along her neck or kissing her nose.

By the time the cab drew up outside the hotel, Irina was reeling from kisses that had turned her inside out and then right way round again.

The kissing had obviously sealed the deal because Javier followed her into the hotel without any more silly excuses.

He even tried to hold hands while they waited for the lift, but Irina's palms were sweating so she swatted him away.

But the moment the hotel room door closed behind them, she turned to him. 'Get your pants off then.'

'Could you try and be a little more romantic, Irina?' Javier suggested softly. 'Let's set a mood here.'

She thought about it for a second, before yanking her vest and dress over her head. 'OK, I show you mine if you show me yours.'

Javier pulled a grouchy face, but he was unbuttoning his black shirt. He had a much nicer body than Vlad, who'd been skinny but with a sizeable beer gut. In fact, Javier didn't compare in any way. It was like asking someone to spot the difference between a television and a washing machine.

All his skin was the same rich teak colour as her mother's sideboard and, as he slipped off his shirt, she could see the muscles in his arms ripple. Not body-builder muscles but like the statues of the saints she'd seen in churches. He also looked like he'd be much handier in a fight that she'd given him credit for.

Irina realized that she'd been standing there, staring at Javier, with her mouth almost hanging open. Like, she couldn't actually believe she'd been able to trick a guy so beautiful into coming back to her room. She needed to play it cooler than this, so she toed off her sneakers and sat down on the bed.

'Come here now,' she demanded, flicking her hair back in what she hoped was a flirtatious manner.

But Javier wagged a reproachful finger at her. 'Stop being so bossy,' he grinned. 'You beautiful girls think you get to run the show, but if we do this, then I get to have a say too.'

It had been much easier with Vlad, who'd followed Irina's lead because she threatened to smack him if he didn't. And he didn't feed her any 'beautiful' bullshit either.

Javier was pacing towards her like a big jungle cat, which made Irina want to inch back to get away from him. Instead she forced herself to lounge on the bed like she didn't have a care in the world.

'Oh, stop glaring at me and give me a kiss,' he teased, before pouncing on Irina so unexpectedly that she heard herself shriek like a girl.

'What the hell do you think you're doing?' Irina snarled when Javier tried to snake his hands around her waist.

They'd done it. It had been nice. Actually it had been better than nice. It had been sweet and tender and other words that Irina never usually associated with sex. Javier had kept asking if she was all right and telling her that she was sexy. That was when he wasn't kissing her. He'd kissed her deeply and frequently so many times that she'd lost count, and there'd been hair-stroking and even hand-holding.

So they'd done it. Now it was time for him to get out of bed, put his clothes back on and get out. But Javier was trying to *cuddle* her. What the hell was wrong with him?

He managed to resist all her attempts to wriggle away, and wrapped his arms tight around her. 'It doesn't just end because you went to Happyland,' he whispered in her ear. 'Now we just chill out and enjoy being with each other. Tell me about Russia.'

It was dark and Javier was kissing the suddenly sensitive patch of skin between her shoulder-blades, so he couldn't see Irina's extravagant eye-roll. At least he hadn't asked her to talk about her feelings. 'What do you want to know about Russia?' she asked sulkily.

'What do you miss about it?'

She didn't miss anything. Not one miserable thing, but Javier made an impatient '*tsk*', and haltingly she began to talk.

She told him about how everyone thought Russians were rude, but that was only with strangers. When it came to family and friends, you'd do anything for them – well, unless it was *her* family they were talking about. And that made her think about how much she missed sharing a bed with Elisaveta because they'd spend hours talking about what they'd do if they won the Sportloto. How she missed drinking tea with black cherries in it and her mother's blintzes. How magical everything looked when it snowed and the turrets of St Basil's Cathedral were like something out of a fairy tale.

Irina traced the tribal tattoo that banded around Javier's arm. 'Is so cold in winter that it feels like millions of little needles piercing into your skin, like when you had this done, ja?'

Javier shivered against her. 'I don't like the cold.'

'You cover up as best you can, but the wind stings your eyes so you not even see where you're going.' Irina yawned sleepily. It wasn't cold here, cocooned against Javier's chest, the thin quilt pulled tight around them. 'You get used to it though and my mother always has a pot of soup on the stove. Or if she gets paid we have hot chocolate with cinnamon and ginger, lots of vodka too.'

'I thought you didn't miss Russia,' Javier mumbled and he sounded like he was half asleep too.

Irina didn't miss it, but right now she wished she was back there so she could show Javier the Arbat with its cobbled streets and souvenir stalls, or take him to the bath-house, which would make him cry when one of the attendants forced him to plunge into the cold pool after the sauna.

'Is not so bad there,' she conceded, just before she fell asleep.

Chapter Eleven

Javier was meant to be gone when she woke up the next morning, not on the phone ordering breakfast. Or telling her to take a shower because they were already running late to start shooting the stupid cosmetic ads again.

And he wasn't meant to wait for her after they were done shooting, holding the door open for her and trying to carry her bag.

Irina could see Aaron looking at them with amusement as she clung on to the strap of her tote. 'I hold it myself. I'm not helpless,' she insisted. This was not how pretty boys were meant to act. Not that Irina had really met that many of them, but generally she understood that they'd popped out of a similar mould to pretty girls.

And pretty girls acted like they didn't give a damn about anyone else. The world was at their feet, so all they had to do was continue to look decorative. Maybe it was slightly different with pretty boys. And maybe stuff had changed now they'd slept together. Because Javier stayed glued to Irina's side, only going back to his hotel to get some clean clothes.

But it wouldn't last. And Irina was an expert at making do with what she had. They wrapped up the two-day cosmetics shoot by going out for a meal with Aaron and the stylist. Luckily, the translator had begged off, as Irina couldn't take any more, 'Miss Ilina, Miss Ilina . . .'

After a strange meal that they were meant to cook themselves using special steamers that had arrived on the table, she and Javier wandered back to the hotel. He tried to hold her hand again, but it was going to be hard enough to say goodbye without giving in to the strange urge to do all the mushy stuff she usually sneered at.

But when she woke up the next morning, their fingers were tightly entwined. Javier was still asleep, so she could trace her finger along the bridge of his nose while she tried hard not to look at her packed bags sitting by the door.

Javier was snoring gently, which shouldn't have been so cute, as she zipped her wet toothbrush into a side compartment and checked her pocket to make sure that her passport hadn't vanished overnight.

The car was going to be here any minute and there was no time for niceties or pretending that this was anything more than what it was. 'Hey, pretty-boy, I'm going,' she said loudly, one hand already on the door handle as Javier slowly stirred. 'I'll see you around maybe.'

Javier sat up and wiped the sleep out of his eyes before stretching tiredly so the sheet slipped down and Irina got one last look at his beautifully defined stomach muscles. It had suddenly got rather hot in the room. 'I'll call you,'

Javier mumbled vaguely, already collapsing back on to the pillows. 'If I'm in London.'

At least he'd pretended like he actually wanted to see her again, Irina thought as she shut the door quietly so she didn't wake him again.

She was just checking in at the airport when her phone rang. It was a long shot but maybe it was Javier calling to say that he'd rethought the whole not-getting-involved-with-models thing and that he was already bereft without her. Irina allowed herself a tiny secret smile as she pulled her phone out of her bag.

It was Ted. 'Sweetie, thank goodness, I caught you in time. Change of plan. You need to stay on for a few days. You've been booked for *ELLE Nippon* and a fashion show. Have you still got your luggage?'

'Yes, but is not possible, I—'

'Just grab it and take a cab back to the agency. They've cancelled your ticket and they're going to try and re-book your hotel.'

Irina was already wheeling her suitcase out of the queue. 'Not the same hotel,' she declared quickly, imagining Javier still there being all tanned and adorable on the snowy white sheets and the dismayed look on his face when she suddenly reappeared, like she couldn't live without him. 'Another hotel, but one that does cheeseburgers on the room service menu.'

'Well, you're going to get paid £10,000 to strut down a catwalk, so I guess I can swing the hotel,' Ted chirped. He was in a seriously good mood. 'And then you'll be back in London long enough to do some laundry before you fly out to New York.'

'New York?' Irina breathed incredulously, all thoughts of avoiding Javier and the inevitable 'It was good while it lasted' speech he'd give her, flying out of her head.

'Yeah, little city, big attitude. You'll love it, sweetie – and you've already been optioned by *Harper's Bazaar* for a beauty story.'

It was too much to take in. 'But—'

'Gotta go, Irina, my other line's beeping. We'll talk later about the hissy fit you threw at the cosmetics shoot on your first day. Ciao!'

Chapter Twelve

It was probably the moment that the dodgy-looking guy tried to convince her that his clapped-out car was an official taxi and a $100 drive into Manhattan was a bargain, that Irina felt like she'd come home. She could totally respect a guy with an eye to making a quick buck out of an unsuspecting tourist. She'd been there herself after all.

But she actually fell head in heels in love when she was finally in an official New York taxi crossing over the Hudson River and saw the city laid out in front of her, a glittering urban sprawl of jagged skyscrapers all lit up like a Christmas tree. The taxi dropped her off at a hotel overlooking Central Park and then she was standing on a genuine New York sidewalk breathing in hot muggy air that caught at the back of her throat, eyes darting this way and that because she didn't want to miss a thing.

Candy had said New York was tiny. She'd kept talking about villages, East Village, Greenwich Village, *The* Village, so that Irina had an impression of tiny clapboard houses around a duckpond, but actually it looked just like it did on TV.

The buildings stretched up to the sky and the streets were so long that you could look down the road to see it disappearing into the distance but never ending. Irina couldn't get over the steam rising up from the manhole covers or how the subway stations all gave off the same strange, flat smell. And it was hot: a damp humid heat, so as soon as Irina stepped out of the air-conditioned hotel on to the sidewalk, she started dripping with sweat. But if New York was hot and smelly, then mostly it was noisy: on every corner people shouted and music blared, car horns tooted. And New Yorkers were almost as rude as Russians. On her first day, she'd come to a grinding halt as she consulted her map and some man had screamed in her face, 'Screw you! Get the hell out of my way.'

If she could make it here – she could make it anywhere.

But first she had to convince Erin, the senior booker from the high-end women's board at Fierce New York, who'd barely looked at her, just shoved a bikini in Irina's hands and told her to get changed. *Plus ça* bloody *change*.

When Ted rolled up, Erin was critiquing Irina like she'd never been critiqued before and showing no signs of stopping any time soon. 'You have a really strong jaw, too strong, and you need to have some definition to your hair. It's so flat and brown and blah,' she complained. 'And you have weird knobbly bits on your hipbones – that's going to be a problem for swimwear. Also your posture is appalling, why do all you tall girls hunch over so much? You're tall, get over it . . . Oh, hey Ted – You bring me some British chocolate?'

'What do you think of my little protégée?' Ted asked, nodding his head at Irina. 'Have you seen the gap in her teeth? It's so "early Madonna".'

Erin frowned. 'Her head is almost freakishly too big for her body.'

Irina had also got used to people talking about her like she wasn't even in the same room with them, but she couldn't do anything about the way her eyes flashed with annoyance.

'And she's got an amazing walk,' Ted enthused, prodding Irina in the ribs. 'Give us a twirl, sweetie.'

Irina did her usual shoplifter's swagger up and down the length of the agency and returned to the pair of bookers. 'You could say hello,' she pointed out to Ted, waving her hand in front of his face. 'And you think I have no manners. *Pffft!* Whatever, dude.'

Erin looked excited for the first time. 'She's got such attitude,' she exclaimed, clapping her hands in glee. 'And that walk; it's so butch but kinda feminine too. We should definitely put her up for the big Bryant Park shows at Fashion Week and not bother with the smaller designers.'

Ted and Erin hadn't paused for breath yet and Irina wriggled in annoyance because she'd only had a Hershey's bar for breakfast. American chocolate was horrible, but they had other foodstuffs that made up for it. Irina never thought she could love any food as much as a four cheese pizza, but that was until she'd discovered American diner food, which consisted of bacon so crisp she could snap it between her fingers, hash browns and these fat, fluffy pancakes that she liked to smother in maple syrup. Her tummy growled in sympathy but Ted didn't notice, even though he'd promised her brunch before they went on go-sees together. Go-sees. Not go-tos. Irina had learnt that the hard way after Laura had laughed about it for a full fifteen minutes. Whatever, that dough-faced bitch hadn't had a single booking yet.

'Marc always loves the really edgy girls, though he tries to fob them off with last season's clothes instead of paying them. But it's a high profile gig,' he was saying and Irina gazed around the room to check out the other girls. That's when she saw Javier talking to one of the other bookers, his hands gesturing extravagantly.

Irina's eyes flitted over him hungrily. Javier's face was in profile so she could admire his bone structure, which was almost as exotic as her own. And he'd smiled just like that, a little crooked, a little lopsided, when she'd told him that her brothers and sisters were total pains in the arse but she still sort of missed them. In fact, he'd been the only person she'd met since she left Russia who treated her like a normal girl instead of a beautiful freak or an ugly freak. Either way, most people treated her like a freak. And Javier hadn't. And he was pleasing to look at and he kissed like people kissed in the movies. God, she really didn't want to be standing in a bikini with the weird knobbly bits of her hipbones on display.

'I change now,' she announced. 'Then we go for brunch before I starve to death. Please,' she added as an afterthought because she wanted Ted in a good mood so he'd forget that he'd pencilled in a discussion about her little snit in Tokyo.

She didn't wait for permission, but with one eye on Javier who was now leafing through a portfolio, Irina skirted the edge of the room, then dived for the loo.

'Usually I order the bacon as a side,' she told Ted as they waited for the lift. 'Once it came in an omelette but it taste like crap. And once I ordered home fries but they weren't proper fries.'

'God, Irina, do you ever eat anything with vegetables in it?'

'No, she really doesn't,' said a soft voice behind them. 'I tried to make her eat seaweed in Tokyo and she punched me.'

Irina whirled around to see Javier standing there looking like something out of a Tommy Hilfiger ad in his simple white T-shirt and a pair of dark blue jeans.

'Oh, hey,' she said, affecting surprise. 'What's up, bitch?'

'Sweetie, we don't call Aaron Murray's assistant a bitch,' Ted remonstrated, holding out his hand. 'Javier, good to see you again.'

Of course Ted and Javier would have to be all friendly. Any minute now he'd invite Javier to come along for brunch so Irina would have to sit there squirming.

'Irina learnt some of her English from rap songs,' Javier explained. 'It's cool. When I was learning English, I watched *Sesame Street* all the time.'

The lift came and the three of them got in. 'How have you been?' Irina heard herself ask, which was dumb because normally she'd never ask that or listen with interest to the reply.

'Good. Just had my first shoot published in *Nylon*,' Javier said. 'How long are you in New York? You should have called.'

Yeah, she could have and then Javier would have thought that she was some clingy stalker chick. Besides, Irina had smashed her first phone in a fit of rage after she'd had a row with Candy and lost all her numbers. 'I been really busy,' she said in a offhand manner. 'But maybe we can hang if I get some free time.'

'There's a film festival in Williamsburg, if you're around for the rest of the week,' Javier said, just as casually.

Ted looked on fondly while Irina and Javier exchanged details. 'I think that young man's sweet on you,' he sing-songed as they watched Javier walk down the street. 'About time you got yourself a boyfriend.'

Irina started pulling Ted in the direction of the diner she'd seen on her way there. 'Boys are not into me in that way,' she scowled because next she'd be talking about her feelings. All these stupid fashion people were rubbing off on her. 'They not want to get in my pants.'

'I should think not. You have to let them treat you like a lady. Take you out to dinner, buy you presents. Of course, in return you have to be charming, which I know is a bit of a stretch for you.'

'I don't do charming,' Irina insisted stubbornly. 'Charming is for pussies.'

'Why haven't you called me?' Irina hissed at Javier as soon as he picked up the phone. She hadn't been planning to, but there was nothing on MTV except a *Real World* marathon she'd already seen and the more she thought about Javier, the madder she'd got until she was calling his number as if her fingers were acting independently of her mind.

'Oh, hey Irina. I had a job come up,' Javier said lazily, his voice muffled. 'Hang on . . .' She hung on, silently fuming. It sounded like Javier was in the middle of a train station. But then his voice came back, sharper and clearer. 'I'm just developing some pictures. So, what's up?'

'Nothing.' And wasn't that the truth? Irina kicked her legs out in annoyance and heard the sheet rip underneath her. It was obvious why she was calling, but he was determined to make her say it. 'So, I have dinner with Ted tomorrow, but then we go to a club?'

Javier sighed so heavily that Irina swore that she could feel the gust of air down the phone. 'You want to go dancing?'

'I don't dance,' she said quickly.

'You didn't sing in public either but I've got your karaoke performance saved on my phone,' Javier pointed out and Irina made a mental note to find it and destroy it. 'OK, we'll go out, I'll teach you how to mambo.'

Irina imagined her head on a giraffe's body as Javier tried to lead her through a quick two-step. 'Maybe,' she hedged. 'You pick me up at Balthazar at ten, ja?'

Although Javier didn't sound too happy about her being so assertive, Irina made him repeat the instructions back, until she was satisfied enough to hang up.

Chapter Thirteen

The 'no' pile on the floor of her hotel room got larger and larger. Irina didn't do pastels. Or frills. Or flounces. Or anything with a floral print. There were the new jeans she'd bought, but Erin had taken one look at the crystals sewn on them and declared that they were so fashion backwards she was getting a migraine. In the end, all that was left was a deep green, empire-line smock which showed a lot of leg. That was fine with Irina. She'd rather people looked at her legs than anywhere else and the blisters on her feet from tramping the sidewalks in heels all week made the decision to wear sneakers an easy one. The one fashion trick she'd learnt was that as long as you wore your clothes with attitude, everyone automatically assumed you were cool. Fashion people were such tossers.

'Sweetie, you're working it tonight,' Ted cooed when she arrived at the restaurant. 'Very "Zac Posen".'

Ted always used designers' names as adjectives. Irina sat down, before he could kiss the air above her cheeks, and fell on the bread basket. 'Why is the table laid for three?' she asked suspiciously. 'Do I have to be polite all evening?'

'Eventually, polite will be your default setting,' Ted replied hopefully. 'And there is someone who's dying to meet you who'll be here soon.'

'They' weren't here soon. After Irina had exhausted all her conversational topics, which were mostly about rap stars whose videos she'd like to be in, she had to force Ted to order food. The clock was edging towards eight, Javier was turning up at ten, if he knew what was good for him, and no way was she not dancing on an empty stomach. She was also trying to ignore the determined glint in her booker's eyes. It reminded her of her mother and conversations that started with the words, 'We need to talk,' which never lead anywhere good.

'So . . .' Ted began. 'I've been hearing good things about you from the Japanese agency.'

Irina smiled serenely. Apart from the Mr Yakamoto-san-sponsored fit, she'd been on her best behaviour the rest of the time. The effort had nearly killed her.

'I also had an interesting chat with the photographer, Aaron,' Ted added casually and he didn't sound like friendly, avuncular Ted any more. Not with ice coating every syllable. 'I ever hear about you pulling something like that again, and you'll be back in Russia so fast that you'll bounce all the way there.'

Irina wished that someone would come up with a new threat, because that one was getting really old. 'I had jet-lag and I apologize,' she said in an aggrieved tone, because she had and Aaron was a pig to tell tales on her. 'It only happen the one time!'

'It shouldn't have happened at all,' Ted insisted grimly.

'I'm trying,' Irina said sulkily and for one second she contemplated telling him to shove his modelling business right up his . . .

'Aaron also said that you got on *very* well with Javier,' Ted continued in a lighter tone, leaning forward eagerly. 'I knew something had happened between the two of you. Tell Uncle Teddy all about it, sweetie.'

Where the hell was the mystery dinner-date? Irina shuddered with irritation. 'When do I get the proper, big fashion campaign?' she asked brusquely, more to change the subject than anything else. 'Because the Japanese modelling agency say that's where the big money is. Like, millions!'

'If you're nice to clients and they decide to put you in their runway shows for Fashion Week, then the next step is being considered for their campaigns.'

Irina nodded. That made sense. She would be so nice that they'd beg her to do their shows. 'That bitch Oksana from the flat in Archway, is she up for campaigns? She's got a face like a horse on its way to the slaughter yard.'

Ted spat iced water over the table. 'You can't say that.'

'I just did.'

'And I can't possibly discuss another model's bookings with you,' he said primly. 'But when we go to Milan, I'm

107

taking you to meet the guys at House of Augustine, who are launching their first fragrance. But, honestly? They're looking for a very feminine girl.'

Irina mock-pouted like Laura did when she was feeling mopey, which was ninety-nine per cent of the time, and stuck out her chest for good measure. 'See, I can do feminine too,' she deadpanned and eventually Ted smiled. He still didn't know when she was joking. 'Is no problem. When I meet them, I'll knock their socks right off their feet. You're always moaning to me, Ted, but when it comes to a million bucks, I be anything they want me to be.'

Ted looked like he wanted to argue the point, but he just picked up his fork and started prodding at his egg-white omelette instead. The empty place setting was still there, though Irina was now convinced that the mystery guest was going to be a no-show. But just as her *steak-frites* arrived, there was a commotion at the door and Irina looked up from her laden plate into the face of the most beautiful person she'd ever seen in real life.

'Teddy-bear!' the vision cried in a broad Cockney accent. 'Sorry I'm late, the traffic was bloody murder.'

Ted stood up so he could genuflect more effectively. 'Caroline, so glad you could make it. This is Irina. Irina, this is Caroline. We used to be with the same agency. I was the junior booker and she was on the New Faces board when we first met.'

'And then I got really famous and jumped ship,' Caroline cackled. Irina had just shoved a handful of fries into her mouth, so she waved and mumbled a greeting while her eyes scanned the other girl. She didn't have hair. She had this corn-gold silk sheet streaming down her back. She was tall and her features, the big blue eyes, the generously curved mouth and tip-tilted nose, were so perfectly proportioned that all Irina wanted to do was stare and stare. Then stare a little bit more.

And she might be some ignorant girl from the wrong side of town – she might *personify* the wrong side of town – but Irina still knew a supermodel when one was sitting down gracefully in the chair next to her and casually shaking out her hair so it rippled in the candlelight.

'I've seen some of your test shots,' Caroline chirped at Irina. 'And Steven Meisel was raving about you when I bumped into him in Milan.'

'I see you on the Fashion Channel,' Irina muttered. Caroline had one of those prancey walks like a dressage pony. Ted kicked her under the table. 'Also your Versace campaign, you looked very beautiful.'

Caroline beamed. Though she must have known that she looked beautiful. She probably looked beautiful even when she had flu. If she got run over by a bus and had blood streaming down her face and one of her arms hanging off, she'd still look beautiful.

Irina demolished her steak, one eye still on the clock, as

Caroline and Ted swapped fashion gossip about people that Irina didn't know.

'. . . she needs to work on adjusting her attitude,' she heard Ted say. 'And she needs to learn to look in the mirror and realize that she's actually stunning.'

They were both staring at her. Irina brushed her hand over her mouth to make sure there weren't any stray blobs of ketchup. 'What?' she asked defensively. 'Stop looking at me.'

'See what I mean?' Ted sighed and Caroline reached over to pat Irina's white-knuckled hand.

'I hope you don't get that arsey with clients,' she said. 'And you need to lose the piss-and-vinegar face.'

'Is not like I make people cry or anything,' Irina protested half-heartedly. Which wasn't strictly true. She'd managed to squeeze a few tears out of Laura when she'd eaten her last chocolate muffin, but Laura cried if the wind changed.

'Like, when you're on a shoot, you have to smile and suck up to people,' Caroline advised. 'Doesn't matter if the photographer's a tosser or you're jet-lagged and feel like ten tons of crap. Teddy's here to unload on if you're pissed off about something.'

Teddy didn't look too delighted at the prospect of being Irina's punchbag, but he was nodding slowly.

'And it doesn't matter how well you photograph or how good your walk is, if you get a rep for being a diva, no one's going to book you,' Caroline continued. 'I was a mouthy little girl from Hackney when I started out, but I soon wised up after I lost a few jobs because I got gobby with the wrong people.'

They seemed to be waiting for Irina to say something. She got what they were saying, she really did, but she'd spent almost eighteen years being told that she looked like a freak. Almost eighteen years of avoiding mirrors. Almost eighteen years of wishing that she was pretty in a way that everyone understood and not just the delusional people who inhabited Planet Fashion. You couldn't just shake that stuff off overnight. But the big hand on the clock was inching towards the hour, so she stretched out her mouth in a vague approximation of a smile. 'OK, I try harder.'

'There's my girl,' Ted beamed. 'And Irina, you need to lose the insecurities. That uncertainty shows on your face when you're being shot and it's not going to work for much longer. You need to look at that camera with confidence, not like you want to smash it.' He stood up. 'Be back in a minute, ladies.'

There were still a few stray fries on her plate that Irina doused in ketchup. Caroline clicked her fingers at a drooling waiter and ordered a glass of wine as soon as Ted was out of earshot. Then she turned to Irina with a malicious smile. And just like that, her beauty faded away. 'Love Teddy to death, but he's a dickhead,' she purred.

'Always trying to get me to do the big-sister routine with his latest girl.'

At least she was honest; Irina could respect that. 'I not need a big sister.'

'Good, because it sure as hell ain't gonna be me. Face facts, darling, the whole Eastern European look is going to be over in a few months and then you'll be scrabbling about for catalogue work. Haven't even got the tits to do glamour,' Caroline spat.

'I knew you were a bitch,' Irina smirked, enjoying herself for the first time. She might be new to modelling and all its endless nonsensical rules, but when it came to facing down some uppity skank, she was an old hand. 'You know you look beautiful, so why waste your energy on dissing me?'

That shut her up. Caroline narrowed her eyes, but her forehead didn't move and Irina had watched enough TV with Hadley to know what that meant. 'I not have big tits but at least I not need the Botox.'

She half expected to get Caroline's wine flung in her face, instead it was drained in one angry gulp. 'That stuff I said about being nice to people? Not true,' Caroline confessed with a glittering smile. 'I'm the biggest bitch you've ever had the misfortune to meet, and you'd better stay out of my way if you know what's good for you.'

And actually Irina didn't need a campaign to make her feel beautiful. Having a supermodel (a goddamn supermodel) declare war on her was making Irina feel pretty beautiful right at that moment. Caroline must be feeling threatened if she was making such an effort to point out how worthless Irina was.

'I not think we run into each other again,' she declared. 'I'm on the way up and you on the way down.' Ted was threading his way through the tables. 'Is so lovely to meet you, Caroline,' she simpered as Ted reached them. 'Thank you for all your advice, is given me a lot to think about.'

'Don't mention it,' Caroline said tightly, and Irina knew that she wasn't going to say anything to Ted. Didn't want him to think that she was anything other than Princess Perfect.

'I knew you two girls would get on,' Ted said smugly. And he was a good booker and Irina knew that he'd do his best to make her famous, but Caroline was kinda right. He was a dickhead too. He saw beauty in everything but couldn't see the ugliness that lurked just beneath the surface. Maybe that's why she gave him a sudden fierce hug, which made him go rigid in her arms before he gave Irina a proper little squeeze. She looked over Ted's shoulder to see Javier was standing by the front desk. Irina wriggled free. 'Got to go now. Get off me.'

Chapter Fourteen

Javier gave Irina a strained smile as she walked towards him. He'd pulled his hair back into a little ponytail so she could see the emotions flickering over his face like a slideshow. Relief, wariness, even something fleeting like he was pleased to see her.

As she got within touching distance, he grabbed her hand. 'Let's go.'

Irina let herself be tugged so Caroline and Ted would think that Javier was totally panting to be on his own with her, but the moment they got outside, he let go of her hand and shuddered with revulsion.

'Was that Caroline Knight?' He didn't wait for Irina's confirmation. 'I *hate* her! She's the closest I've ever come to pure evil.'

At least it wasn't only Irina who thought so. 'She gives me the tips on modelling.'

'Whatever she said, do the opposite,' Javier advised, taking her hand again as they crossed over Broadway. 'I did a shoot with her when I was modelling, which was bad enough. She tries to screw all the male models, but when I did a shoot as an assistant, she treated me like utter crap.'

'She tell me I'm over in a few months,' Irina said, and if

she didn't sound bothered, it was because she wasn't.

'That's not true!' Javier exploded all over again. She didn't know he could be this emotional. It had to be exhausting for him. 'Her looks are so vapid. There's always a beautiful blonde who makes it big out of every crop of models, but you have something unique. You're one of a kind, bet she couldn't stand that.'

Irina's face heated up; it had nothing to do with the humidity and everything to do with Javier's praise. Not what he said, but how he said it, like her uniqueness was a simple fact that couldn't be denied. 'She get pissed when I tell her she on her way out and I could see the Botox.'

'For real? You said that?'

'You think I not have the stones to say that?' Irina said haughtily. 'And anyway, she start it. I finish it.'

Javier and Irina were meant to be friends who'd hopefully hook up at some stage tonight, but he kissed her right then on the middle of Thompson Street, as they were buffeted by the late-night crowds. His hands cupped Irina's face gently even as his mouth swooped down hard on hers.

'I've never met a girl like you,' he said throatily, when they came up for air. 'You're so . . . so . . . There's nothing fake about you. I hope you don't change.'

Irina ducked her head and stared down at her greying sneakers. 'Don't go mushy on me,' she grumbled. 'Is not manly.'

For a few seconds, Javier looked as if he wanted to take

back what he'd just said about Irina never changing and book her an intensive course at the nearest charm school. But then his usual lazy grin returned. 'I'm going to teach you to dance,' he said. 'And if you cry when your feet start bleeding, then bonus.'

Irina's feet didn't bleed, which she was grateful for. It seemed that they already knew how to dance, though the rest of her had a little problem with all the twirling that Javier insisted on. It was hot and sticky in the hole-in-the-wall dive that he'd taken her to on the Lower East Side and his face glistened from the exertion, his tongue poking out of the corner of his mouth as he concentrated on leading her through a set of simple steps.

Irina couldn't help the grin that stuck on her face as the beats of the music got faster and faster and the trumpet guy jumped down from the tiny stage so he could wind his way through the dancers.

And it was even more fun when the music slowed down and the crowd on the dancefloor reached critical mass so Javier and she had no choice but to wrap their arms around each other and do a shuffle and grind that didn't stop even when they got back to her hotel.

It felt like she'd spent the whole night in Javier's arms – from the instant that they stepped on to the dancefloor to the moment that she woke up, the beep of her wake-up call chasing her out of dreams.

'So do you wanna go to that film festival this evening?' Javier whispered in her ear as Irina tried to persuade her eyes to open.

'I not even got out of bed yet,' Irina yawned and rolled over. 'I order breakfast, ja? They do these great muffins . . .'

'I don't want muffins.' Javier yawned. 'I just want to know if we're going to hang out later.' He scratched his head thoughtfully. 'I'm going to be in London at the end of the month too.'

'Whatever,' Irina said, like she wasn't bothered one way or another. Inwardly though, she was punching the air in triumph at Javier's throaty insistence that he wanted to see more of her. Maybe they could be friends who hooked up in different cities around the world? She could roll with that. 'But I tell you now, the girls I live with are morons. Just so you know.'

She was saved from having to go into further details by the frantic buzzing of her phone.

'Change of plan,' Ted barked, when she picked up. 'Get your bags picked, you're flying to Milan to do a shoot for *Vogue Italia* and I'm going to get you in to see Donatella, Giorgio, Miuccia and Zilli and Costello while you're there.'

Irina realized that this was meant to be a big deal but all she really wanted to do was stay in bed and trace her fingers over every inch of burnished Javier-skin that she could reach. 'But I have go-sees,' she reminded Ted plaintively. 'And I'm doing a shoot for *Radar*.'

'We'll rearrange,' Ted snapped. 'This is the big time, kid. *Vogue* bloody *Italia* and the chance of fronting a huge perfume campaign for Zilli and Costello that will propel you right to the top of the league table.' He paused for some much-needed breath. 'And if you even think about acting like a diva . . .' He let the sentence hang menacingly in the air so that Irina could supply the missing words about being unceremoniously booted back to the former Soviet Union for herself.

'I'm never going to throw another tantrum ever again,' she told Ted loudly so Javier could hear every word and beam approvingly at her. 'I'm going to work really hard and be all nice to people even though they're idiots. I absolutely promise.'

Chapter Fifteen

Six months later

'Take all the crap off my face and start again!' Irina screamed at the make-up artist. 'Why you use a yellow-based foundation that makes me sallow?'

'But Irina, darling, we need to start shooting now before we run into overtime,' the photographer cajoled from behind her. 'You look gorgeous. Doesn't she look gorgeous?'

The small, anxious collection of people gathered around agreed vigorously as Irina perched on a stool and glared at them in the mirror. 'I look shit,' she insisted. 'And I not have my picture taken when I look shit.' The make-up artist still wasn't moving so Irina picked up the pot of cold-cream herself. 'You take it off or I do. Your choice.'

Irina couldn't remember the last time she'd had a day off. She worked every day. Sometimes two shoots a day. Even weekends. There was barely time to eat, sleep or do her intensive skincare regime. This morning she'd woken up with a headache after five hours of sleep because she'd had a late shoot the night before. All the hot water had been used up and breakfast had been a couple of stale Pop Tarts. Who could blame her for being cranky?

But right now, Irina had to take all the work she could get because the end of her glittering career was so close that she could taste it. And it was all Laura's fault.

At the thought of Laura, Irina hissed loud enough that the make-up artist took a frightened step back. Laura! That fat, talentless cow! It wasn't enough that she'd stolen the Siren campaign out from under Irina's nose with her simpering, suckass ways. No, she'd also had to bring curves back, so every magazine that Irina picked up had Laura's puffy face pouting out from the pages. And she had a cosmetics contract too. And now she was up for an international print and TV chocolate campaign. It wasn't fair.

Irina had worked her butt off for that Siren contract; had elocution lessons, laid waste to the competition – she'd even made one girl fall off the runway in Milan just from shooting her the evil eye. Months of working towards one goal and then Laura had waddled in at the last moment and snatched it away from her. Because Laura was *pretty* in this cookie cutter way that was so obvious and didn't need words like 'edgy' or 'striking' or 'savage' to describe it. Girls like Laura always got what they wanted with minimal effort, and it was so unfair that Irina suddenly scooped up her iPod and threw it at the wall as the make-up artist squealed in shock. It was the fifth one she'd destroyed in a month.

Laura was moving up and Irina was stuck exactly where she was six months before. Laura was setting the trends and being called a freaking supermodel and Irina was just another jobbing model working every day for a lousy £5000 base rate for editorial. OK, Irina had got two high-end campaigns: bags for Dior and sunglasses for Versace, while Viktor and Rolf were keen for her to front their autumn campaign. And Mr Yamamoto-san loved her so much that he'd locked her into a two-year contract so she couldn't advertise cosmetics for any other company in Japan. But big bloody deal. If she hadn't got those campaigns and done some lucrative runway work, why, she'd practically be destitute.

Even Hadley's career had finally taken off again after a few false starts and lots of shocking stories in the tabloids. Not only was she in a movie, a proper movie, she was in love with Reed, Candy's half-brother. It was hard for Irina to remember that she actually liked Hadley when she was wearing an ear-to-ear smile and telling Irina how much she loved Reed every five minutes.

She'd even suggested that Irina and Javier double-date with them, but Irina had laughed bitterly at the suggestion. Javier was her non-boyfriend, and non-boyfriends didn't do dates. They just hung out or hooked up. Like last month when they'd been in Barbados on separate jobs, Irina had insisted that Javier take her clubbing. But it hadn't happened because they met on the beach and Javier had decided that there was nothing better than just 'chilling out and watching the moonlight reflect on the water'. What was the point of *that*? Irina had made her feelings on the subject perfectly clear and then she'd stormed off in a huff and hadn't heard from him until this morning, when she'd had a text message like nothing had happened. IN LONDON NEXT WEEK. ARE YOU FREE TO HANG? J. It was deeply unsatisfying.

Irina flinched as the make-up artist almost jabbed her eye out with a cotton bud. She thought about throwing another temper tantrum but her heart really wasn't in it. Because her heart was currently bruised, battered and dried up in her chest cavity like a pickled egg. The one bright spot on her dark and cloudy horizon was that Candy was more miserable than Irina. The emotional fall-out, simply because Reed had dared to give Hadley the starring role in his movie, had ended with Candy sobbing into a paper bag after hyperventilating for hours. If she ever found out about Hadley and Reed dating, then Irina planned to emigrate. Luckily Candy mostly stayed in her room and sewed more outlandish clothes on this big machine she'd bought. Last night Irina had had to bang on the wall because the *clack clack clack* and Candy's swearing when she puckered a seam kept waking her up. No wonder she had a headache.

And now she was at a shoot where the clothes had been designed for a girl who actually had breasts and hips. They'd had to sew her into them, and the stylist had kept pricking her with a needle. That had been bad enough until she'd been presented with a dreaded pair of rubber chicken fillets and told to stuff her bra with them. Then Irina had seen the Polaroids for the first shot, caught sight of the colour of her face and had justifiable reasons for pitching a fit. That was another useful phrase she'd picked up from Candy.

'I look like I have . . . the disease of the bile,' she spat at her reflection as the photographer walked back in to see how the touch-up was going. 'The one that makes you yellow.'

'Jaundice?' someone suggested.

'Ja, jaundice.' Irina folded her arms. 'You take these pictures, is not going to be good for any of us.'

'I could put a different coloured filter on the lights,' the photographer offered. 'And maybe we could tone down the base a little bit.'

The make-up girl bit her lip. 'Well, I guess I could.'

'We'll change the white backdrop to something warmer.'

'And why doesn't someone get Irina a can of Coke and something to eat?'

'I only eat two slices of green apple and two hundred and fifty grams of cashew nuts a day,' Irina said, because no one here knew that she'd stuffed her face with pasta for lunch. 'And the slices must be exactly the same size.'

As the make-up girl carefully began to take off her base and replace it with bronzer, Irina watched everyone rushing around with only one thought in their heads: to please her and jolly her out of her bad mood so she'd perform in front of the camera. They were never so obliging when she was trying to smile and say please and thank you. She still didn't look like a model, just a sullen, gawky girl. But she knew how to act like a model, and that would have to do.

After an exhausting day of having her make-up taken off and put on again until she looked less of a plague victim, the last place Irina wanted to go was back home. She'd had enough of Laura's fugliness staring down at her from billboards, without having the real-life version on the sofa. Also, the flat had divided into two camps: Irina and Hadley versus Candy and Laura, though Irina suspected that if Hadley didn't hate Candy quite so much she'd have happily joined forces with Laura.

Either way the atmosphere was really toxic, and she had friends now. Well, not friends exactly because they were all models, which meant they'd stab her in the back with a pair of scissors if it came down to it, but at least she had some people to bitch with in Russian.

When she got to Troija, the little Russian restaurant in Primrose Hill, where they all hung out, Famke was already waiting for her.

'*Pri'viet*,' she said glumly, staring at a steaming plate of cheese blinis in front of her. 'Sofia says I need to put on some weight.'

Irina could only nod in sympathy. The angular Eastern European look was so very over. 'We just hold tight for a season or so,' she said with more confidence than she felt. 'Curves can't be in for ever.' But even so, she started looking at the menu for any dish doused in cream. As it was, she was averaging six meals a day and still hadn't put on any weight.

'She's your flatmate,' Famke said bitterly. 'You have plenty of opportunity to put rat poison in her tea.'

Irina smiled limply because if she thought she could get away with it, then she'd have done it weeks ago.

'I'm not joking, Irina!' Famke stabbed one of the blinis with her fork.

It was funny that she and Famke hung out now. Like, they'd bonded over how much they hated Masha and Oksana when they did a shoot together in Ibiza. There'd been much glaring at each other across the airport baggage carousel until Famke had marched over. 'You staying at Los Jardines de Palerme, right? You want that we share a cab?'

Irina had dropped her laundry bag (she'd still been waiting to hear from her financial advisor if luggage counted as a legitimate business expense at that point) so it just missed the other girl's foot. 'You share taxis with peasants?' she'd asked icily.

Famke paused in lighting a cigarette. 'Oksana is a bitch,' she'd said matter-of-factly. 'You think she was bad that day, you try living with her.'

Even Irina had felt a tiny pang of pity. But . . . 'You get all up in my business again, then we have a problem,' she'd said, as they shuffled further up the line. And then she'd had to ask. 'Oksana – what the hell is her problem?'

Famke had taken an angry drag of her cigarette. 'She made a big fuss that I trained with the Bolshoi Ballet, but before that, I live in a small town in Siberia and my father is a caretaker at a school. And she acts like it's something to be ashamed about. I hate her.'

There was nothing like some mutual hatred for a common foe to bring two girls closer together. 'I hang out in Troija in Primrose Hill with some other girls, maybe you can come too,' Famke had offered casually as they'd flagged down the next empty cab – and that had been the beginning of a beautiful friendship. Or, like, keep your enemies close enough that they couldn't make any sudden movements towards any sharp implements.

The rest of the girls trooped in with matching expressions of discontent and, by the time the table was covered with empty plates and drained glasses, they'd all convinced themselves that they'd be back in Russia before the new season started.

'Those curvy girls are too fat for runway,' someone grumbled. 'Clothes look better on thin girls.'

There were various mutterings of dissent from the ranks. 'All the designers are obsessed with nipped-in waists,' Katja, a glacial blonde girl, pointed out. She pinned Irina with a disapproving look. 'If you'd got the Siren campaign this would never have happened.'

Irina was sick of the word 'Siren'. And she was sick of being blamed for Laura's domination of the fashion world. 'When I do the shows, I'll make sure she's wearing six-inch heels and then push her down some stairs,' she snorted. Five pairs of eyes looked at her expectantly. 'I'm joking!'

'At least you're booked for the shows. I'm going to New York with some options, but I have no bookings,' Famke said. 'I'm finished unless I can put two inches on my hips in the next three weeks.'

There was a flurry of activity as menus were snatched up and desserts were ordered. But Irina knew that it would take more than a double portion of cheesecake to get her career back on track. She needed a plan. She needed a strategy. Or else she needed to take out a hit on Laura.

Chapter Sixteen

Four weeks. Four different cities: New York, London, Paris, Milan. It might be February and the shops were already starting to fill up with dainty, flower-sprigged spring fashions, but the world's most famous designers were busy showing women what they'd be wearing that winter. Irina had finally figured out that when it came to anything fashion-related the wrong way round was usually the right way round.

Irina was over ninety-five per cent of her strop now. New York's Olympus Fashion Week had been a kick; she'd booked all the major shows after scoring a Missoni campaign that had been promised to a Hollywood actress who'd then got arrested for drink-driving. That had created one hell of a buzz. And that buzz had seen her through the London and Paris Fashion Weeks too. Laura might have been everywhere that she turned, but Irina had done more shows. And that was what counted.

Irina surveyed the crowded backstage at the House of Augustine show as a stylist teased her hair into a gravity-defying bird's nest. There were lots of new girls this season. Lots of girls with the new look, which was softer and prettier and, God damn it, curvier.

She stared down at her almost flat chest in dismay. She'd put on two pounds in the last month, but it wasn't as if anyone had noticed.

'Hey, what are you looking so sulky about?' said a soft voice in her ear, before there was a fleeting kiss pressed against her shoulder.

Irina swivelled around to see Javier standing behind her with a camera, which he clicked and pointed at her as she tried not to look too pleased to see him.

'What are you doing here?' she asked carefully, ignoring the little burst of happiness at the sight of him. She also ignored the urge to reach up and touch him; stroke the tight muscles of his arm, plant a little line of kisses across his cheek.

'I've been booked to take some backstage shots,' Javier told her proudly, aiming the camera at her face again. He looked excited, his eyes shining, and Irina wasn't sure if it was because he was being paid to stand in a room full of beautiful girls in their underwear, or simply because he was in a room full of beautiful girls in their underwear.

'Great,' she said flatly. 'You take one more picture of me without make-up on, I break your camera.'

'Fair enough,' Javier conceded, with a tiny shrug. 'You wanna hang out after? I got tickets to the Versace party.'

Irina glared at Karis from Texas as she walked past in her knickers, the lush curves of her breasts jiggling slightly. 'Sure, whatever,' she said in a bored voice. If Javier took even the sneakiest peek at them, she'd stab her fingers in his eyes. She really would.

'Are you maybe a little bit pleased to see me?' Javier asked, tucking a strand of hair behind his ear.

That would infringe all sorts of unspoken rules. Like, girlfriends would be pleased to see their boyfriends if they turned up suddenly. But girls who were only good to sleep with on a casual basis were meant to feign mild interest.

'Maybe just a little bit,' Irina deadpanned, before turning away. 'I get ready now, see you later.'

Javier's attention had already disappeared in the direction of the corner where her arch nemesis was holding court. 'Yeah. Cool. I should get some shots of Laura,' he said vaguely. 'Oh, they're fitting the wedding dress on her, better get over there.'

At least Irina got to wear a gauzy dress without a bra, which guaranteed lots of flashes from the scrum of photographers amassed at the end of the runway. Her nipples totally trounced Laura galumphing down the catwalk in a white dress.

She stared vengefully at the other girl as two fitters extricated her from the metres and metres of silk organza.

'There she is, our little Siren,' Zilli, the designer, cooed at Laura as he entered the backstage followed by a crowd of hangers-on. Irina was almost mown down in the rush to get to Laura and 'mwah mwah' her fat face.

'Loved the collection,' Laura simpered. 'It was so pretty.'

'You can have your pick of any of the dresses,' Zilli said. 'Nothing but the best for our beautiful Siren girl. Come and find me after you've got changed, I want you to meet some of our backers.'

He swept off, pausing to give Irina a distracted smile, like they'd only been introduced once before and not spent hours together talking about how she was the front runner to advertise their stinking perfume, which smelt worse than horse manure.

Irina was still seething about that as she gathered up her belongings and stuffed them into her new Fendi tote.

'Nice bag,' Laura said, coming up beside her so she could peer at her face in the mirror. 'You enjoy the show?'

'Piss off,' Irina suggested. 'The sickly sweet routine does not fool me and is getting really old.'

Laura folded her arms and stuck out her chin. 'And your sulky act is beyond tiring. Would it kill you to drop the attitude and start acting like a human being?'

It really would. Irina could already see herself dropping dead from a sugar overdose if she was forced to be nice to losers who didn't deserve it. 'Avoid the pasta while you in Italy,' she advised the other girl. 'The cellulite is starting to come back.'

Laura twisted around and craned her neck so she could see the backs of her thighs in the mirror. 'No it's not!' she gasped. A belligerent look glanced across her insipid features. 'You know, Irina, this is why Ted didn't want you to get the Siren campaign. Because you're already the biggest bitch anyone has ever met and no one at Fierce could have coped if you reached new heights of bitchdom. But congratulations, looks like you managed anyway.'

Irina stared at her dumbly, her snappy comeback nowhere to be found. It was possible that she'd misheard because Laura still sounded like she had mud in her mouth when she spoke. 'Ted would not pull a stunt like that,' she stated firmly. 'He was my booker first. You're lying.'

'Don't dish it if you can't take it,' Laura sneered, tossing back her stupid hair which was far too short to be tossed back. 'Bottom line is, I got the Siren gig, you didn't, now get the hell over it.'

'Say that you were lying,' Irina insisted, taking a step forward so their noses were practically touching. She might not be as big as Laura, but she had the looming thing down to a fine art.

Maybe Laura realized that she was one word away from having her face rearranged. Or maybe she felt guilty for opening her big mouth. Either way, she bit her lip like she'd already said too much. Way too much. 'Have it out with Ted, not me,' she said, waving frantically at someone on the other side of the room, like she needed rescuing. 'Though you ever thought that maybe I got the job because I was the best girl for it?'

In all her theorizing and teeth gnashing about not

getting the Siren campaign, Irina hadn't let that possibility cross her mind. 'I *hate* you,' she spat at Laura. 'All the Russian girls hate you.' It was the truth. She hated Laura for stealing the Siren campaign but she hated her for a lot of other things as well. For the doting parents who arrived regularly with Tupperware containers full of cake. For calling house meetings like she owned the place. For having everything she wanted just fall into her lap while Irina still spent hours of her free time practising poses with a mirror and a Polaroid camera. Even being a bloated whale of a girl worked out just fine for Laura, who was already wriggling away.

'Bothered,' she drawled. 'Like I could care any less.'

Then she had the nerve to walk off and get swallowed up by a crowd of gushing admirers. Irina scanned the room and saw Javier putting rolls of film into his bag as he joked, no, *flirted* with blonde twins from Australia. God, now they were breeding them in multiple units.

Irina was nipping that in the bud right away. She marched over and grabbed a handful of Javier's T-shirt. 'I not want to go to the Versace party,' she announced, shooing the girls away with her free hand. 'We leave now and go back to my hotel.'

Javier shook free of her grip. 'I need to go to the party,' he said quietly. He could pack a pretty resolute punch when his voice got all low and growly like that. 'It's a great networking opportunity.'

Irina tried to stare him down, but he was getting much better at not flinching. 'If you don't leave with me right now, then you not "network" with me ever again, pretty-boy.'

For one awful moment, Irina thought that Javier was down with that, but he sighed in defeat. 'Fine, whatever. But, Irina, please just chill out and stop being so bitchy.'

'I am not a bitch,' Irina hissed as she started dragging him towards the exit. 'I just stand up for myself.'

Chapter Seventeen

They shared a cab back to the hotel in a tense silence. Javier sat hunched over in one of the over-stuffed armchairs that all hotel rooms had as Irina ordered a vat of fries and some cheesecake from room service. And when she put the phone down and turned to him, he looked away.

Javier's grumpy moods never lasted long – which was just as well because Irina's did. And it was time for her to get sneaky. She rummaged through her bag for an envelope. 'I have photos of my family, if you want to see,' she said. 'They arrive the other week.'

It was the magic combination to put a sunny smile back on Javier's face. He loved hearing stories about Irina's life back in Russia, though she couldn't imagine why because they all sounded like an episode of *EastEnders* scripted by Dostoyevsky. And he was always nagging her to show him photos and wasn't entirely convinced by her excuses that only oligarchs could afford cameras.

He'd already shown her pictures of his family. There were hundreds of them. Brothers, sisters, cousins, aunts and even an ancient great-grandmother, all taken at the annual family football match in Sao Paulo where they ate loads of food, drank beer and kicked a ball around for hours. And now that she was ready to return the favour, the last of his bad temper melted away and he was joining her on the bed so she could show him the pictures her mother had sent (along with a snotty letter asking why she hadn't written in eight months).

'Elisaveta's the pretty one, Piotr's the clever one, and Yuri's the baby,' she said, pointing at their grinning faces.

Javier held the picture up so he could peer at it more closely. 'And which one are you?'

'The rude, difficult, ungrateful, always-in-trouble one,' Irina replied, snatching it back before Javier could see the peeling wallpaper and the plaster saints and icons in the background. There were some things that he didn't need to know about. And before he could protest, she played her other joker. 'You wanna watch football?' she asked casually. 'We can get the sports channel on pay-per-view.'

Actually it wasn't just a sappy girl tactic to keep Javier on side. Irina liked watching football too. Or she liked laughing at Javier as he shouted at the TV, his English becoming more and more accented until he let loose a string of Portuguese curses at the referee who was blind. In fact, the best time they'd ever had was in Milan a few months back when a fashion company had given her VIP tickets to see AC Milan play Juventus. He'd just about wept tears of joy. And on the way back to the hotel after the match, they'd bumped into a bunch of

Swedish tourists and had an impromptu game of football in one of the town squares. It hadn't been romantic but it had been fun.

Not as much fun as making out under the covers after Javier's team had won three goals to nil though.

'I'm glad we didn't go to the Versace party,' Javier mused, as they took a breather in between the kind of kisses Irina would remember when she was ninety.

'It would have been full of wankers,' Irina murmured, propping herself up on her elbow so she could gaze down at Javier and the *GQ*-esque picture he made lying on the white sheets. 'And there would have been no fries.'

'Or football. You're so cool, Irina,' Javier yawned.

There was no point being modest about it. She *was* cool. As non-girlfriends went, she was the very coolest, and she was just about to point this out to Javier before they got horizontal again when she realized he was fast asleep. Normally Irina liked watching Javier asleep: sprawled on his back with one arm tucked under the pillow. She didn't even mind the breathy grunts he made, as she'd sit up and marvel at the fact that she'd managed to keep getting a boy like this into her bed for six months now.

But falling asleep while they were still fooling around was not of the good. It was a sure sign that he didn't even find her attractive enough to stay awake and have sex with her, and sex was the cornerstone of their entire relationship. Hmm, though maybe 'relationship' wasn't the right word as it implied actual dates to cinemas and restaurants, which wasn't Javier's strong point. And holding hands, which actually Javier was really good at (the finger-squeezing and the wrist-stroking in particular), while Irina let the side down.

When Javier slept, nothing could wake him up that didn't involve glasses of cold water and screaming right in his ear. It left Irina free to explore all her favourite places: the little line of freckles creeping down his back, the raised indentation of his tattoo and the little scar on his finger from where he'd accidentally shut it in a taxi door when they were in Paris. Irina had had to run into the nearest bar and grab an ice bucket, and Javier, when he could form words again, had said it was the sweetest thing she'd ever done. And then he'd kissed her and said that it was the only thing that was keeping his mind off the throbbing pain. Yeah, the little scar on his finger was definitely her favourite part of Javier.

The dark shadows were starting to fade as the early-morning sun crept through the gaps in the curtain. Irina hated the times that she couldn't sleep while it seemed as if the rest of the world was tucked up and slumbering. Bad thoughts seemed to chase around her head; 'the mean reds' Irina and Hadley called them, after they'd watched *Breakfast at Tiffany's* one Sunday afternoon.

Irina gave a frustrated sigh, jostling Javier with her elbow, but he barely stirred. Sleep was just not going to happen, so she crawled out of bed and into the bathroom so she could wreak havoc with the free tissues and cottonwool balls supplied by the hotel. It didn't work as well as smashing stuff and she never did that with Javier on the premises. He'd seen her hurl her vanity case down a flight of stairs once, and hadn't been too impressed. But shredding loo roll really wasn't scratching the itch and, in the end, Irina gave up and plopped down on the floor, back against the bath tub and started thinking all the thoughts that she'd been trying to avoid.

She'd travelled the world, made a ton of money and had a whole raft of fashion bods quaking when she pulled on her fight face, which wasn't bad for a girl who'd got thrown out of school and had never been able to hold down a job for more than two weeks. There were worse fates than to only last less than a year as a model.

Except she wanted more. One taste wasn't enough. You couldn't just give a girl a glimpse of a better life and slam the door in her face. At the thought of it, of going back to the housing project and the disappointed look on her mother's face, of not ever seeing Javier again and hearing him say her name like he loved the sound it made . . . Irina started a new attack on a defenceless copy of *Vogue Russia* which she'd been reading in the bath.

It was really late now and the bathroom floor was cold and uncomfortable. Irina made one detour via the minibar before she got back into bed so she could lie there not sleeping and holding rapidly melting ice cubes against her face so she wouldn't be puffy-eyed for the next day's shows.

Irina must have fallen asleep eventually, because suddenly she was woken up by a hand stroking down her back. 'Your skin looks so beautiful in the morning light,' Javier murmured in her ear as he spooned up against her. 'Like warm syrup.'

She opened one eye to peer at the clock in disbelief. She had to be at her first show in half an hour. 'Get off me,' she grunted, rolling away from Javier's gentle hand because it made her want to roll in the other direction, straight into his arms.

Getting out of bed was hard when Javier was in it. Also, she was so tired that her legs were about as steady as a newborn foal's. Irina snatched up a pair of jeans from the floor and began to haul them on.

'I'm going to be in London again next week,' Javier said. 'You want to get together?'

Irina dragged a brush through her hair. 'Yeah, if you can stay awake this time, sure.'

'I'm paying for some studio time,' he continued, ignoring her pointed remark. Normally her pointed remarks should lead to shouting, which should lead to fighting, which should lead to passionate kissing and rolling about on the floor while they made up. But no, Javier just soldiered on regardless. 'I'm doing a test shoot. Fancy being my model?'

Typical! Javier only got proactive when he wanted something. Men were all the same.

'I not work for free,' Irina informed him haughtily. 'Ask Laura.' Even though Laura was making so much money that Irina felt sick with envy, she still did occasional test shoots for her friends. The fat bitch really was a gigantic loser.

Javier was out of bed now and padding over so he could try to pull her stiff body into an embrace. When that didn't work, he kissed her forehead. 'But it's a favour, baby.'

'*Niet*, I don't do favours.' Irina pushed him away. 'You got £5000, I do a test shoot. If not, cosy up to some other girl.'

She was almost at the door when he yanked her back by her jacket collar. 'Jesus! Can't you do me a favour out of the kindness of your heart or would that mean that you have to admit that you actually have one?' he asked softly, in a way that was completely at odds with his hands tightly gripping her shoulders

'Don't talk shit.' Irina slapped his hands off her. 'Is not like we're anything more than casual friends.'

'What the hell do you call this then?' Javier gestured at the messy room and the two of them standing in the middle of it in fight stance. Finally she'd made him drop the laidback act.

And it was a really good question. 'This' was so she

didn't have to be on her own in another hotel room in another foreign city. 'This' was snatching a few more hours with a boy who was going to wake up and smell the coffee, and realize that he was hooking up with an ugly, skinny Russian girl when he could have his pick of anyone. 'This' was as good as Irina was going to get.

She glanced over at the clock on the bedside table. 'I'm going to be late now,' she said accusingly. 'I not have time for this crap.'

'Fine,' Javier sighed in defeat because he always let her have the last word. He dug into his wallet and pulled out a crumpled pile of Euros, while Irina recoiled in horror. He always did this and it was beyond boring. 'For my share of the hotel room.'

'Don't be an arse,' she told him brusquely because she hated this as much as he did. 'One of the designers pay for the room.' They didn't, but £10,000 a show, less agency fees and commission, was still about fifty times more than Javier got paid.

'Bullshit they are,' he snapped, because he'd been in the fashion business far longer than Irina. 'I'm paying my share.'

She was officially late now. Officially about to lose it in a really spectacular way. Irina cast a dismissive look at the money that Javier was trying to thrust into her hand. 'That not even cover the room service,' she told him pretty gently, all things considered. The only thing Javier got really touchy about was money. He insisted on at least paying half

146

when they went out, even though Irina had told him a million times that it wasn't necessary. 'Is not a big deal, don't make it one.'

'So you refuse to donate half a day of your time to do a test shoot, but you won't let me pay for the hotel room?' Javier clarified dully, though his eyes were flashing every which way. 'And I'm never to give you presents, apart from a crappy Polaroid camera because I was going to chuck it out anyway—'

'Work is totally different. Sides, I get loads of shit for free and you not get paid very much—'

Javier didn't let Irina finish protesting the present issue but carried on, his face red with anger as his voice got louder and louder until it could technically be classed as shouting. He never shouted. He didn't mind calling her out when she was being difficult and always telling her to chill, but Javier rarely shouted. And suddenly Irina didn't think that getting him finally to lose his temper was a good thing. She had a feeling this wasn't going to end with passionate kissing and rolling about on the bed. Not even close. 'In fact, all I'm allowed to do is wait for you to call and order me to come round and service you as your schedule permits it. Well, I'm over it and I am so over you and your constant need to create drama when there doesn't have to be any!'

Irina forced herself not to gasp or cry or show any other signs of emotion, though her nails were digging into her palms so hard that they had to be drawing blood. How could they be over, when they'd never really started? She cast one longing look at the bathroom door because there had to be something in there that she could break. And then she cast an even more longing look at the thunderous expression on Javier's face, trying to memorize every freckle, every shape his lips made when he smiled, the way his hair constantly flopped into his eyes and was pushed back with an impatient hand.

'Whatever,' Irina said, steeling herself to sound unmoved. It had been her decision to pretend that she understood the rules of the game they'd been playing, so there was no point in quibbling over the small print. If she started getting upset, or worse, crying, then Javier would start to get suspicious. And it would all come spilling out because she couldn't hold it in any longer. She'd confess that she was in love with him because he was beautiful and funny and kind and a whole bunch of other things that Irina never knew boys could be. And even though Javier would be secretly horrified at the truth when he'd just wanted a no-fuss, no-muss shagbuddy, he'd be really sweet about it, because that's what he was like, and his sweetness would just about kill her. So Irina said the only thing she could in the circumstances. 'I see you around, I guess.'

Then she walked to the door with her eyes forward, because she was sure that if she dared to look at Javier, she'd turn to stone.

Chapter Eighteen

Irina turned up at the tent in the Rho-Pero fairgrounds still shaking, but a black-clad minion merely ticked her name off a list without a word. No one cared that Irina was fifteen minutes late or that her heart was broken into a million jagged pieces. They just plonked her down on a stool at a make-up station so her hair could be grabbed by someone who wasn't too concerned that it was still attached to her scalp.

The backstage was buzzing even more than usual. There were people milling about wielding hairdryers, clipboards and huge Styrofoam cups of coffee. And the noise was deafening. Over the pre-show soundtrack of ear-splintering techno were frantic calls for shoes that had gone missing or models that hadn't turned up yet. But underpinning it all was an expectant hum as everyone waited for Caroline Knight to put in a guest appearance. She was jetting in at great expense, because runway was too beneath her these days, to spend five minutes sauntering down the catwalk for the designer who paid her £2,000,000 a year to model his dresses in glossy magazines.

Someone peered at Irina's face and then shoved a frozen eye mask at her to get rid of the puffiness. Irina watched with a sneer as Laura swept in with her little gaggle of model friends. It was sickening the way they called themselves The Breakfast Club because they met for toast and tea whenever they were in the same city. Though Laura seemed to think it was unbelievably cute.

Irina glared at Laura and had it returned with interest as the other girl flicked through her clothes rail. Then she saw Ted come in and wrap Laura in a bear hug. He was never that affectionate with Irina. OK, she'd squirm away and swear at him if he tried, but that really wasn't the point.

The point was that he was all about Laura. Irina was yesterday's news and he'd totally sabotaged the Siren campaign for her.

'If you pull my hair one more time . . .' Irina growled at the hairdresser, letting the threat of retribution go unsaid, as another make-up artist hurried over.

'Jeans off,' she instructed tersely and, once Irina had kicked herself free of the denim, starting slapping foundation on her legs while someone applied thick white gloop to her face.

The tugging and the slapping and the pushing was seriously getting on Irina's nerves. Now Javier had arrived and was hugging and kissing far too many models for her liking, and when Caroline finally made her grand entrance in a squashy fur coat and shades, only ten minutes before the show started, Irina realized what was happening. It was some fiendish plot to put everyone she hated in one room so they could make her explode with rage.

'Outfits now! Irina, move!' someone screamed in her ear, which was her cue to jump down from the stool with her Kabuki make-up completed and run for her clothes rail. But someone had beaten her to it.

It was one of Laura's little friends. An American girl called Danielle, with a thick, treacly accent and vacant blue eyes. 'Can I swap this with the red dress then?' she was asking the creative director as she snatched a black fitted suit off the rail. 'It's all wrong for my skin-tone.'

Irina was there in a blink of one thickly lashed eye to snatch it back. 'Piss off – *my* rail.'

'We're changing the order,' the creative director said. 'The designer wants Danielle on first.'

If the most coveted spot was the wedding dress or big showy frock at the end of the show, then the second most coveted spot was going first, when the lights went down and the music started and the audience gasped as the first model stepped on to the runway.

'I go on first. Is agreed,' Irina protested. 'Take your hands off my clothes.'

Danielle didn't budge an inch, just looked uncertainly at the creative director, who was consulting a clipboard. 'Nope, order's changed. Come on, Danielle, get into the suit. Irina, you're down to wear the red dress on Danielle's rail and you're on fifth.'

Irina gave a tiny hiss of anger, which made the two of

them eye her warily. She was so fed up with people trying to walk all over her and act like she didn't matter. 'I don't swap,' she bit out. 'I go on first, so get your grubby hands off the suit.' And just to make sure that Danielle got the message, Irina gave her a good hard shove away from the rail.

'Don't push me!' Danielle squawked indignantly, rubbing her arm like there were already bruises.

Irina pointed at Danielle's rail. 'Go over there and get the hell out of my face,' she shouted, grabbing the suit.

'Two minutes!'

The creative director threw his hands up in despair. 'It's too late to argue about this now. Irina get into the damn suit, Danielle, you'll just have to make the red dress work.'

'But I'm meant to go on first,' Danielle whined.

Irina was already easing into the narrow pencil-skirt. There was no way it would have fitted Danielle. 'Sucks to be you,' she grinned, teetering on one sky-high heel as she groped for the other with her foot.

'You're a bitch,' Danielle spat, whirling around so the ends of her blonde hair whipped against Irina's face.

But if she was a bitch, then she was a bitch who was going on first, Irina thought as she was pushed through the white gauzy curtain into a melee of faces and flashbulbs. She strode with long, stabbing steps, her face defiant because she might not be modelling for much longer or be able to charm people with her sunny disposition, but she could still tear up the runway with her walk.

The other members of The Breakfast Club were vocal in their support of Danielle. As Irina rushed through her outfit changes, she kept hearing the phrase 'The Moscow Mule' cropping up time and time again. So, they'd given her a totally unfunny nickname? Was she meant to run from the tent in tears? Never going to happen.

Irina stepped out on to the runway for the third and final time and began the long walk down. Usually she just blanked out so she saw nothing, felt nothing but the air rush around her as she walked like an Amazon. But as she approached each member of The Breakfast Club she distinctly heard the word 'Bitch' hissed at her. Irina got to the end of the runway, held her pose for a count of five, then slowly turned so it didn't even seem as if her feet were moving.

She headed for the curtain only to see Danielle gliding towards her and wiggling her hips like she was the star act in a strip show. As they got level, she heard it again: that unmistakable five-letter word. But they couldn't even begin to imagine just how much of a bitch she could be. Maybe it was time that she showed them. And as soon as she thought it, Irina angled her body so her shoulder hit Danielle hard enough that she wobbled on her heels.

It was only a fraction of a second, but it seemed to last for ever. Danielle teetered, arms freewheeling to keep her balance, before she gave an unearthly shriek and landed in a spreadeagled heap on the polished white surface. Irina calmly stepped over her and carried on walking, as Caroline stepped out in an intricately beaded, white fishtail dress and pointedly ignored both Irina and Danielle, who was trying to scramble to her feet.

Irina had one second backstage to catch her breath then she was surrounded on all sides by members of The Breakfast Club, including a tearful Danielle clutching her ankle melodramatically.

'You're a bitch!'

'Who the hell do you think you are?'

'What is your problem?'

'We're going to tell our bookers that we refuse to work with you!'

'Piss off!' snapped Irina, as a dresser unzipped her. 'I not work with amateurs anyway, so no loss.'

'If my ankle's broken, I'm going to sue you,' Danielle wailed, while Laura simultaneously glared at Irina and comforted her friend.

Everyone was staring at their little corner, rather than the designer who'd come backstage to be fawned over. Out of the corner of her eye, Irina could see Javier looking at her in disbelief, disappointment, dismay, and many other words beginning with D.

'What you looking at?' she shouted at him as Ted hurried over, accompanied by Caroline and an older women in dark glasses.

'Teddy-bear,' Caroline was saying in her shrill, piping voice. 'Haven't you taught your ducklings to play nice with each other?'

Teddy-bear had the look of a man whose fur had been seriously ruffled. 'What was that about?' he asked Irina, his voice positively murderous to match the flinty look in his eyes.

Irina didn't even get a chance to speak.

'She pushed Danielle!'

'And she pushed me against the clothes rail before we even went on. And I've sprained my ankle. Look!'

They all stared down at Danielle's ankle, which was already reddening and swelling up like a monkey's arse.

Ted whistled under his breath. 'Can we get some ice over here?' he called out.

Irina folded her arms. 'Is not my fault if you can't walk in heels and a tight skirt,' she said loftily. 'Though maybe if you concentrate on walking instead of calling me a bitch, you not fall over.'

'Or maybe she wouldn't have fallen over, if you hadn't pushed her,' Caroline remarked with a cat-like smile. 'I saw it when I came out. She really bashed into her. Are you all right, darling?' she cooed at Danielle, who bit her lip like the brave little soldier that she really wasn't.

And Irina was meant to be the biggest bitch in the room? Ted obviously thought so because his hand was already wedging under her armpit so he could drag her through the gawping onlookers and out into a chilly backroom where the catering staff were pouring out glasses of champagne.

He spun Irina round to face him so fast that it was nearly her turn to go crashing to the floor. Instead she planted both feet firmly on the ground and narrowed her eyes. Irina would have preferred to do this when she wasn't wearing just a bra and thong, but whatever.

'She thinks that she just waltz in and steal my first outfit,' she burst out. 'No way!'

'Shut up, Irina. Just shut up!' Ted hurled back at her. 'You are treading on the thinnest of ice right now.'

She should have taken more notice of the tight, throbbing tone of his voice, like he was barely hanging on to the shreds of his temper. But Irina had more important things to think about.

'What are you going to do, Ted?' she taunted. 'Dump me from another campaign like you did with Siren? I know all about it!'

Ted didn't even bother to look embarrassed. 'You ruined your own chances by being arrogant and aggressive.'

'My pictures were perfect!' Irina yelled. 'Everyone say so. I even took fucking elocution lessons!'

Which hadn't been worth it because right now her accent was thick enough that she needed subtitles to be understood.

'So were Laura's pictures. It was *that* close. And you want to know what it came down to in the end?' Ted didn't wait for Irina's reply but rushed on. 'They dreaded the thought of two years dealing with you and your temper tantrums. They wanted to work with Laura, rather than some out-of-control little diva who thinks the world owes her a living because she's had a hard life. Oh, grow up, Irina!'

All Irina could do was gape as she brushed an impatient hand across her cheeks to get rid of the tears.

'No one ever dare to speak to me like this,' she rasped, which was a complete lie because her mother and her teachers and just about everyone else used to speak to her exactly like that. 'I not put up with this shit.'

'Then what do you intend to do about it?' asked a cut-glass voice and Irina turned to see the older woman Ted had been with before standing behind them.

'This is Mimi, she's the owner of Fierce.' Ted stepped back, breathing deeply as he made a visible attempt to calm down.

But Irina had left calmed down about three hours ago. And some posh woman looking down her nose at her was the last thing she could deal with right now. 'I not need your crappy agency,' she sneered. 'I go somewhere else and they have me like a shot.' She snapped her fingers in Mimi's face, though she didn't even blink. 'They even bother to get me proper campaigns.'

Ted's shocked gasp was a good indication that Irina had officially gone too far. The story of her life.

Mimi stared at her long enough that Irina wanted to scramble away from the intimidating look which seemed to strip everything away so that the woman could see that, underneath the heavy make-up and attitude, she was just a stupid girl with a colossal deathwish.

'Book her out for two weeks, Ted,' she announced. 'Starting immediately.'

Irina felt goosebumps force their way painfully along her arms. 'You not book me out. I have five more shows.'

'Book her out,' Mimi repeated firmly. 'I need to see some people back in the tent. Come and find me later, Ted.'

She walked away as Irina was still working on her next protest.

'Go home, Irina,' Ted said grimly. 'I'll give you the tiniest amount of slack and admit that you've been working too hard. Go on holiday or go and see your mother, who's been calling me every week.'

Irina wiped away more tears. 'Why is she calling you?'

'Because you haven't had the decency to tell her that she's been cut out of your life,' Ted informed her. 'I want a new, improved Irina in two weeks or you can go and find another agency, though after today's sterling performance, I doubt anyone would want to sign you up.'

'Ja, they would,' Irina blustered. 'You just saying that. I make you loads of money and then you think you can throw me away like trash. Is not—'

'Oh, go home, Irina,' Ted said, like he'd never been more bored in his entire life. 'I don't even want to look at you right now.'

'But—'

'Later,' Ted snapped, turning on his heel and leaving Irina standing there with her world falling around her expensively shod feet.

Chapter Nineteen

By the time Irina arrived back in London, the shock had given way to this slow-burning anger that made her blood itch as it raced around her veins.

Slamming the front door behind her didn't really help, but if Candy was home, then at least Irina could take out her bad mood on her. She scrutinized the carpet for stray pins from Candy's DIY experiments in dressmaking so she'd have a justified reason for screaming at her, but for once there weren't any. She'd already thrown her agency phone out of the cab window on the way to the airport and now the TV was looking like a likely prospect. She'd always wanted to drop one out of a window and see it shatter on to the street below. Irina's destructo mission was interrupted by a muffled giggle coming from Hadley's room, followed by a deep rumbly voice.

Great. Double bloody great. Hadley and Reed were in there, probably trying to eat each other's mouths off their faces, which also meant that Candy was safely off the premises.

Irina put a wash on, ate a whole box of fondant fancies which she'd found in the fridge, watched an episode of *Ugly Betty*, and Reed and Hadley still hadn't emerged.

Which was a shame because it had given Irina time to come up with a cunning plan.

It was a plan that she wasn't too proud about, because she did like Hadley. Not enough to actually confess that her modelling career had suffered a setback. Or that she was besotted with Javier, even though they weren't officially dating. But they'd bonded over a common Candy-shaped foe, gone on winter expeditions to buy thermal underwear, and had their whole quid-pro-quo thing where Irina taught Hadley how to use various household appliances in return for fashion advice and pizza ordering.

So it didn't make what she had to do any easier, as Irina shouldered open the door of Hadley's room without knocking.

She'd been expecting some horrific scene of half-naked debauchery, not Reed and Hadley lying on the bed and peering at a laptop.

'Hey, Irina,' Hadley chirped, looking up from the screen with one of those smiles that were all blinding white teeth and pink gums. 'We're writing a screenplay together! Or Reed's writing it and I'm telling him what to put.'

'It's your story,' Reed demurred. 'I'm just adding in the camera angles.' He shot Hadley a look – tender, exasperated, a little bit awestruck. And Irina wished that just once Javier had looked at her like that. It hardened her a little for what she had to do.

'I need a part in your movie,' she blurted out in a rush. 'And if you say no, then I tell Candy you're dating.'

There was a split-second delay before Hadley's inevitable anguished squawk rang out. 'Why? Why would you do that? To me?'

Reed pushed himself up to a sitting position and regarded Irina with distaste. 'Yeah, Irina. Why would you do that?'

Irina shrugged. 'Is nothing personal,' she said tonelessly. 'I need to branch out from the modelling and you need my mouth shut. Supply and demand, ja? And you don't even need to pay.' Which was actually really big of her, not that either of them seemed to be appreciating that.

'We should just tell Candy anyway,' Reed said to Hadley, as Irina's heart plummeted all the way to the floor. Maybe she should have threatened to do something vile to Mr Chow-Chow, Hadley's freakishly small dog, who was currently trying to chew on Reed's shoelaces.

'No!' Hadley clapped her hands over her ears in horror. 'She'll kill me. And then she'll start on you. She's been an absolute B.I.T.C.H. just because I'm starring in your movie. If she knew we were in love, then she'd come at me with her pinking shears, and your producers still don't want anyone to know that we're dating.'

Reed's hand automatically reached out to stroke Hadley's hair back from her face. 'Don't stress out, baby,' he murmured throatily, even as he shot Irina a look of intense dislike. 'We've only got a week left of shooting.'

Which wasn't Irina's problem. 'Great,' she said, deliberately playing dumb. 'I free all this week and you not go through the agency. We sort it out between us.'

'We still have to film the nightclub scenes and the second unit stuff,' Hadley piped up. 'Maybe Irina could play one of the prostitutes?'

Reed didn't look too happy about it. 'We do need some extras—'

'*Niet*,' Irina interrupted firmly. 'I need a speaking part. I can lose the accent, is not a problem.'

'But you can't even act!' Hadley protested, forgetting that her future happiness lay in Irina's hands.

Couldn't act? For months she'd been playing the part of a beautiful girl in front of the cameras. Acting like she was ecstatically happy or sexy or absolutely in love with the outlandish clothes that she was wearing, depending on what the photographer wanted. She was such a good actress that she should have an Oscar.

'Is not difficult,' Irina pronounced airily as Hadley gasped in indignation. 'I can be good at it. I not want to look like an idiot.'

'Look, what is this really about?' Reed asked, his voice gentler now as he quit the filthy looks and tilted his head as if he expected Irina to unburden. 'Is everything OK?'

Irina rolled her eyes. 'Everything's cool. I not be a model for ever, I need to start the diversifying of my talents.' She

164

wasn't exactly sure what 'diversifying' meant, but neither of them was smirking so it must be the right word. Irina couldn't bear to stand there for another second with the two of them staring at her like she was something that had crawled in from the local dump and was giving off an unpleasant stink. 'I leave you to sort out the details and I work any day over the next fortnight.' She walked out of the room before she'd even finished the sentence. Mr Chow-Chow decided to come with her so Irina could curl up on her bed while he nuzzled against her as she softly stroked his wrinkled skin. Why couldn't he just have fur like a normal dog?

From the sound of it, Hadley and Reed were having the mother of all fights. She could hear them shouting through the wall, though it was quite hard to work out the specifics, until Hadley screamed, 'Well, she's not my friend any more! And if you're going to be mean to me, then you can do it somewhere else.'

Five seconds later, the front door slammed so hard that the whole flat shook. And fifteen seconds after that, the walls quivered again as Hadley slammed the bathroom door behind her.

She emerged three hours later, scrubbed pink and with suspiciously red-rimmed eyes. Irina was slumped in front of the TV, not watching a chat show, as Hadley stomped in and folded her arms. 'You know, if you wanted a part in the movie, all you had to do was ask,' she said softly. 'You didn't have to get all blackmaily about it.'

Irina hadn't known that Hadley could do quiet dignity; she was very good at it. And also, even more annoyingly, she was right. 'I have to cover all my bases is all,' she muttered, not looking at the other girl. 'Six months ago, you pretend to date a gay guy just to get in the papers, so no point being all pissy about stuff.'

Hadley drew herself up. 'I happen to have grown as a person in the last six months,' she informed Irina haughtily. 'And anyway, I was totally on the skids. You're a successful top model. You didn't need to be so ruthless.'

She really hadn't, but it was too late to back down now. 'Just get over it,' she advised Hadley harshly. 'Is not like is your problem. Now shut up, I'm trying to watch this.'

Hadley huffed a few times before flouncing out of the room with a majestic twitch of her dressing gown. She stuck her head around the door a minute later. 'You're not going to tell Candy, are you?' she asked anxiously.

Irina wasn't going to tell Candy anything, because Hadley had this way of worriedly gnawing on her bottom lip and drawing her eyebrows together, which made even Irina's heartstrings tug. She willed them to behave and for her heart to go back to its usual stone-like state. 'I get in the film and I even sign a piece of paper promising not to tell her,' she offered, like she was doing Hadley a huge favour.

Hadley obviously didn't think so. 'I feel very sorry

for you, Irina,' she said sadly. 'You have serious self-esteem issues.'

'Don't let the door hit you on the way out,' was all Irina could muster in the way of a witty comeback.

Irina had had a vague idea that she'd play a glamorous prostitute, until she arrived for the first day's filming and the make-up girl began painting track-marks on her arms. It took hours to achieve the desired look – that Irina spent all her time standing on street corners turning tricks, and didn't have an account with a spa in Bloomsbury and her own personal aesthetician. The wardrobe was a whole other exercise in extreme humiliation, and consisted of a neon-pink tube top and denim hot pants with knee-length white boots. But the worst thing about her first film role was taking direction from Reed.

He was mightily pissed off with her. Irina got that. But it wasn't until he talked her through her role as Anita, the Kosovan teen hooker, that she realized how much he really didn't like her. The good news was that she had four days' filming and a screen credit. The bad news was that Anita was a nasty, conniving crack-whore who had a screaming fight with her pimp before being thrown off the top of a ten-storey car park. Reed made it very obvious that he'd prefer not to use a stunt double for that scene.

Hadley wasn't happy with Irina's role either. 'It's not a very positive female portrayal,' she complained when she got the revised script. 'I'm meant to be a role model and it doesn't look good if my character hangs out with mean crack-whores.'

Reed's face went very red. And then he and Hadley had another fight, which wasn't actually Irina's fault though Hadley seemed to think it was. 'I'm never ordering pizza for you again,' she hissed at Irina as they were waiting to be called for their first scene.

As threats went, it was fairly tame so Irina ignored Hadley and concentrated on remembering her first speech, which started with the immortal line, 'I got picked up by the pigs last night.'

Reed shouted a lot through his megaphone, and it was really hard to lie on cold, wet tarmac and pretend to be dead, but Irina didn't mind suffering for her art. Or Reed's art. Or for the chance to be in a proper movie that might even come out on DVD. And she didn't mind going back to the flat each night and rehearsing her scenes until she was as perfect as she could be. All in all, she ended up being fairly successful at not sucking.

'You were better than I thought you'd be,' Reed grudgingly admitted when Irina wrapped her final scene. 'Kate Winslet isn't going to be having any sleepless nights, but you were OK.'

'I know,' Irina said simply. 'I always do good work.'

'Well, you're still one of my least favourite people in the world,' Reed sniffed, but then he smiled, and Irina understood why Hadley went all dreamy when she talked about him, even though he was a blood relative of Candy. 'You did a good job. And if you tell my sister about me and Had, I'll get someone to throw you off a ten-storey car park for real,' he added, but Irina was unmoved. Compared to Ted when he had his strop on, Reed was like the fluffiest of pussy-cats.

Chapter Twenty

Irina rotated aimlessly on one of the black leather chairs in the Fierce conference room as she waited for her first audience with Ted in two weeks. Obviously she was still in his bad books if he wasn't going to stump up the cash to take her out for breakfast.

Irina was still furious over the Siren thing. And she was still praying that curves would be resigned to fashion's dustbin along with bubble skirts and polka-dots. But if Ted wanted her to be all sweetness and light, then she would. Or she'd *try*. As long as no other girl got in her way.

'What part of "booking out" did you not understand?' Ted asked from the doorway, startling her out of her contemplation of a hangnail.

'I understood all of it,' Irina said, peering carefully at his face. His lips weren't all tight, but his eyes were very glarey behind his glasses. 'You not book me any jobs for a fortnight.'

'So why have I been hearing all sorts of things about your first film role?'

Not smirking required huge amounts of willpower. 'You not book me for that, I book myself,' Irina replied. 'And you not getting a cut on my wages either.' That popped out

171

before she could rein it back in, but she had only got £400 a day.

'You are unbelievable,' Ted groused, but his words lacked bite. 'Did you get an Equity card out of it at least?'

'What's an Equity card?'

Ted sighed and made a note on his Blackberry. 'I'll get someone in Film & TV to sort that out. And when you weren't expressly going against my orders, did you enjoy your time off?'

Irina hadn't enjoyed her time off at all. Back in Russia, if she'd had two weeks with a satellite TV package and as much food as she could carry home from Sainsbury's, she'd have been as happy as a pig on a truffle hunt. But these days her parameters of happiness were harder to define. Besides, there were only so many episodes of *Extreme Makeover: Home Edition* she could watch.

'Is all right,' Irina said diffidently.

'So do you want to get back to work?'

She wanted it more than anything, but Irina was damned if she was going to act all desperate and grateful. 'Yeah, I guess.'

Ted wasn't getting ready with call-sheets and itineraries, but folding his arms. 'If you do a job, you will turn up on time. You will be polite and pleasant to everyone on set, even if the junior stylist's nan puts in a surprise appearance. You will not argue about your make-up or your clothes or your direction. You will not slap, shove or intimidate the other models in any way, shape or form, and if I get one more complaint about you, sweetie, you are finished.'

Irina opened her mouth to plead her case, but Ted held up his hand because he wasn't finished cutting her down to size. 'And before you start singing that song about going to another agency, believe me when I say I'll be on the phone to every booker in town before you've even left the building. You'll be lucky to get a job giving out cans of dog food at Crufts.'

Props to Ted for being such a badass, Irina thought, relieved that she was staying dry-eyed and expressionless throughout the tirade. She could squirm later.

'OK,' she said evenly. 'I try to be on my best behaviour. But you were totally out of order to put Laura forward for the Siren job. She got the extra coaching.' Irina knew that for a fact because Heidi, Laura's old booker, had told Sofia, who'd told Oksana, who'd told Famke, who'd told Irina, so it had to be true. 'That would have been my biggest campaign, and now what? I have another six months left, then I'm finished.'

Ted raised an eyebrow. 'OK, noted. But at the risk of sounding dense, what happens in six months?'

Ted playing dumb was just the sort of thing guaranteed to make Irina lose her temper, but she managed to grit her teeth and count to ten. Well, five. 'Another bunch of girls come, or curves stay in, or I'm still too edgy and I only shoot the editorials and not get the commercial stuff,' Irina got out in an angry rush.

'Oh for goodness' sake, Irina, you have the kind of striking looks that never go out of fashion,' Ted snapped. 'Why do you think I get so annoyed when you pull stupid tricks like you did in Milan? That's what will finish your career, not your face. People will always want to look at you.'

'I rather be pretty than striking,' Irina whispered under her breath, and she was half relieved that Ted didn't hear her.

'So let's just move on and be friends again, OK?' he continued. 'I don't like having to ride you all the time.'

'Ja? I think you enjoy it,' Irina grinned, because having Ted on her side was better than having him on Laura's side. 'Yeah, we friends.'

Ted opened the black leather document folder he'd brought in with him. 'Good, because I only send my friends to New York for a few weeks . . .'

Usually when Irina went to New York it was for a few days, where there wasn't time to do anything but race from go-sees to shoots. But a few weeks was long enough to get a feel for the place that she was going to call home one day.

'Cool with me.' Irina craned her neck to try and read the piece of paper Ted was holding up.

'There are going to be a lot of go-sees and meetings with potential clients, so you have to be a little ray of bloody sunshine,' he warned. 'But you've already been booked for some amazing jobs. Here, look . . .'

Irina ran her eyes down the sheet of paper. There was a three-day shoot for a music video with some band she'd never heard of, a charity runway show, fashion editorial, fashion editorial, oh and another fashion editorial and then off to Paris for a beauty shoot for *Vogue* . . .'

All Irina could see was the photographer's name in big, black letters. 'This Paris shoot is with Aaron?' she clarified.

Ted smiled slyly. 'And his charming assistant, Javier.'

'That pansy ass little bitch!' During her time off, Irina had managed to totally not get over Javier, though he'd sent her a text message: HEARD YOU GOT BOOKED OUT. ARE YOU OK? She'd replied with a terse: DROP DEAD, WANKER.

'Irina, this might be the time to tell you that we want you to see an anger management specialist,' Ted remonstrated, though, no it would never be the right time to hear that. 'Anyway, I thought you and Javier were tight.'

'You thought wrong.' Irina couldn't help but pout a little. It was typical that even something huge and wonderful like a shoot with *French Vogue* came with something crappy attached to it. 'Not like I care. I too busy working to worry about stupid pretty-boys.'

'Is there anything you want to tell me as a friend?' Ted asked gently, but Irina could see the telltale flush of excitement on his face. Ted was a terrible gossip.

'No, we hung a little bit, but he's a very shallow person,'

Irina said blandly. 'No backbone, no balls.'

And that was all she had to say on the subject. Especially as there were far more important things to talk about, like why Ted should add a clause to her contracts forbidding people to ask her to stuff chicken fillets in her bra.

Chapter Twenty-One

As Irina was driven across the George Washington Bridge en route to the video shoot in New Jersey, she stared morosely at Javier's number in her Blackberry. It was odd to think that he was probably somewhere close by on this tiny island – although he might just as well be on the other side of the world. And it was also odd that Irina was feeling all sorts of things that their fling didn't warrant. Like she was missing him or something, which was just whacked.

Irina sighed extravagantly, then popped in her iPod's ear buds so she could listen to the track that had been biked over by the record company.

The band were called The Hormones and were everything she didn't like about music. The lyrics whined on about all sorts of random shit and the music didn't have a beat that you could dance to. She pulled out the press kit and flicked through the photos of the four Hormones, two girls and two boys, who were dressed all in black and staring sullenly out at her.

Great. She had to spend three days with these losers.

Midway through the second day of the video shoot, Irina

was ready to rip her ears off. That way she wouldn't ever have to hear that godawful song again or listen to The Hormones snap and snarl and bitch at each other. Compared to them, Irina would have made a convincing Miss Congeniality.

'This song is shit,' she told Bob, the make-up guy, as they skulked in the dressing room of the draughty warehouse. At least in here there were no Hormones and plenty of space heaters. Besides Bob always had lots of dirt on other models and a secret stash of chocolate, both of which he was happy to share with her.

Irina needed to keep her energy levels up. Lolling on a bed in some fancy underwear with a haughty expression while The Hormones' singer, Dean, flailed on the floor like he'd just been electrocuted, was very exhausting.

'I know,' Bob muttered darkly. 'And the lyrics make no sense. You can't rhyme "Cadillac" with "heart attack". I mean, *please.*'

'Is that what it was? I not make it out with all the yelping,' Irina sniped, warming to her theme, as she hopped up on the counter and swung her legs. 'And the bit in the middle sounds like someone scratching their nails on the blackboard. This band, ja, do they actually have any fans?'

'About five million, according to the sales of their last album,' said a furious voice from the doorway. Irina's head whipped around to see The Hormones' manager standing there, with Dean lurking behind him. 'Who the hell do you think you are?'

There really wasn't an appropriate answer that was going to pacify the very angry man, who spent all his time shouting at people, when he wasn't shouting down his phone. 'I talk about another band,' Irina lied hastily.

'Bullshit! You've just talked your way out of a job, is what you've done. I'm firing you.'

Ted was going to kill her. And then Erin would chop up her corpse and scatter the pieces all around New York. 'Please don't,' she begged, hating the whimper lodged in her throat. 'I really not mean it.'

'Tough,' the manager bit out. 'I'm going to phone your agency and make sure you never work in this town again.'

If that was the case, then Irina decided it would be all right to jump off the counter and smack the horrible man.

'You can't fire her,' Dean piped up. 'We've already shot half the video and I'm not spending even more time in this fucking freezer while we re-shoot it.'

'No one talks about you like that,' the manager insisted grimly. 'And not some two-bit model who can barely speak English.'

That stung. Irina spoke better English than he did, but Bob put a warning hand on her arm when she opened her mouth to tell him that. 'I very sorry,' she said demurely, head lowered. 'I promise it not happen again.'

The manager had already taken out his phone and

paused with his finger over the keypad. 'What's the number of your agency again?' he asked.

'Oh piss off, Paul,' Dean huffed. 'Stop being such a wanker. She's said she's sorry, and anyway the song *is* shite and we all know it.'

'The song is not shite,' Paul said stoutly, but he was tucking the phone back into his suit pocket. 'It tested really well in the focus groups. Very radio-friendly; will do well in the Asian markets.'

'Oh, well then, I stand corrected,' Dean sniped, but Paul's attention was already diverted by a hapless camera tech doing something that met with his disapproval.

'Jesus Christ!' he exploded anew, striding away. 'Is everyone here a flaming idiot?'

Bobby and Irina exchanged an amused look but said nothing, as Dean was still hovering in the doorway. 'Sorry about him,' he muttered. 'He likes to throw his weight around.'

Irina had fulfilled her trouble quota for the day so she picked up a magazine and made a noncommittal grunting sound. Which was not meant to encourage Dean to haul himself up on one of the stools.

Candy and Laura loved Dean. They loved him with a passion that bordered on creepy. They'd even pinned his photo on the kitchen noticeboard so they could plant lipstick kisses on his face. But he didn't really do it for Irina. He was too lanky, too scruffy, *way* too emo for her.

'It's cool that you say what you think,' he remarked casually. 'Because that song? It's like three minutes of toxic noise pollution. Our songs used to have proper tunes and choruses and a beat that you could dance to.'

'Maybe you should sack your manager?' she suggested quietly, in case said manager rushed back in.

'Yeah, well, I would do that, but I signed my life over to him many years ago.' Dean scrubbed the back of his hand across his eyes and gazed around. 'Is that Candy Careless?' He pointed at the cover of Irina's magazine. 'God, I hate that girl.'

'Really? She's my flatmate,' Irina said neutrally. Could there be more to Dean than tight jeans and too much stubble?

'Then you have my sincere commiserations,' he said without even a hint of embarrassment – and that definitely warranted putting the magazine down.

'She's hell to live with,' Irina confided. '*Yap, yap, yap* all day and she's so bossy and rude. And she makes the awful dresses that only the blind people would want to wear.'

Dean shuddered. 'I met her at a party once and she spent the whole night telling me what a burden it was to be famous, apart from when she was shoving me away so she could have her picture taken.'

His band might suck like lemons, but maybe Dean wasn't so bad after all.

Chapter Twenty-Two

The next day, after they wrapped the video, Dean asked Irina to go home with him. And she said yes.

The atmosphere in the warehouse had got more and more tense as the shoot progressed. Off-camera, the four Hormones kept as far away from each other as possible. Even Sandrine, who Bob said was Dean's girlfriend.

Sandrine didn't seem like Dean's girlfriend; she spent most of her time draped over their manager, Paul, wheedling for more camera time than the others. Then there had been the moment after lunch on the third day, when she'd pulled up her top and invited Irina to admire her new boobs. 'You can't even see the scars,' she'd said. 'Go on, give them a poke. They don't feel that hard, do they? You should totally get your tits done, you're flat as a board.'

Irina had put protective hands over her 34AAs. 'I never get into the clothes with two balloons on my chest,' she'd growled, but Sandrine had just laughed.

'Men love girls with curves,' she'd declared airily, before sauntering off to practically sit on Paul's lap and flick her hair around.

The other two, T and Tara, had sat on opposite ends of a sofa listening to their iPods, and Dean had hung out in the dressing room with Irina and Bob.

Then when the shoot wrapped, he'd got really panicked. Like he didn't want to leave. Which was when he asked Irina to come with him. 'I've got PlayStation, Nintendo DS, or we could watch DVDs. And there's a great Chinese place a couple of blocks away so we could order take-out. Or if you want . . .' He'd rambled on and on with all these different enticements, until Irina realized what his deal really was.

Dean was lonely. The big, successful rock star who had girls all over the world planting lipstick kisses on his pictures didn't want to go home on his own to an empty apartment. Irina could relate, she didn't fancy going back to an empty hotel room either. So that worked out fine. And if Javier didn't want her, then it looked like there were plenty of other guys who did.

Dean lived on the top floor of a warehouse development in the Meatpacking District, just a couple of blocks away from the Industria studio complex where Irina did a lot of her shoots when she was in New York.

They rattled up to the fifth floor in an old freight elevator and stepped out into a big, airy space that was all exposed metal beams and rough brickwork. Irina thought that the place would look more stylish and comfortable, with some shagpile carpeting and a big squashy sofa instead of the black leather and chrome tubing seats that looked as if they'd give anyone who dared to sit on them severe curvature of the spine.

'Make yourself at home,' Dean said as he padded over to the kitchen area. 'Do you want something to drink?'

Irina toed off her sneakers, sank down on a nest of cushions on the floor and slotted the Grand Theft Auto cartridge into the PlayStation. The next two hours were some of the best of Irina's young life. They jacked ambulances and got into fights with drug dealers, ate kung pao chicken and egg rolls, listened to the new Timbaland album and discovered that they had far more in common than a mutual loathing of Candy Careless.

'It's like everyone acts as if I'm something special because I'm in a band that by some strange fluke became famous, but I still feel like the same scrawny kid from Southport,' Dean said after his third bottle of beer. 'I always have this feeling that someone's going to tap me on the shoulder, point me towards the exit and say that they made a mistake, y'know?'

Irina did know. 'And you spend your whole life being told that you useless but then it all changes in a flash and you just have to deal. I earn more in a week than my mother does in a year. Is totally screwed up.' She still felt this vague sense of unease when she spoke about her mother, but Irina squashed it firmly down with a couple of egg rolls.

'I don't know,' Dean was saying. 'At least being famous is

better than when I used to work in McDonald's. Why are you staring at me like that?'

Dean had turned into a Big Mac before her very eyes. 'If I was not a model, then working at McDonald's would be the best job in the world. They give you free food, ja?'

'Yeah, but it didn't really make up for having to clean the griddle or wipe up kiddie puke from the play area after a birthday party,' Dean grinned. 'Oh, you've just shot up a cop car.'

Irina scowled as the sirens started blaring in surround sound. She made her character run into a handy field to hide behind a shack, before she paused the game and turned to Dean. 'So, we gonna get it on?' she said baldly.

'Well, OK, I guess . . .' Dean replied warily, putting down the controller.

He crawled over to where Irina was propped up against the sofa and, while she was still licking her lips to make sure there were no stray crumbs, he kissed her.

Dean was a good kisser, in Irina's limited experience. He knew how to do all the teasy stuff; lots of nibbling and sucking and shit. Irina was getting a crick in her neck so she slid further into the cushions and rubbed her hands up and down Dean's back. It was strange that there seemed to be absolute zero sparkage between them when they'd spent most of the day kissing for the cameras.

'Hang on,' Dean muttered against her mouth, before pulling back so he could tug off his shirt. Irina averted her eyes, he was very skinny and pale. Skinnier even than her, Irina could have easily counted each one of his ribs. Instead she pulled off her T-shirt, grabbed Dean's hand and clamped it to her chest, before she pulled him down again.

But it was like two sticks rubbing together, except there was no fire, just bones banging painfully, and the giddy, swirly feeling that Irina always got when she was kissing Javier was nowhere to be found. She was obviously doing something wrong, she thought, as Dean kissed the side of her neck. She ran through a mental checklist of moves, but she'd done everything correctly so it was a mystery why all the writhing and kissing was getting them nowhere fast.

In one last-ditch effort to get things back on track, Irina slid her hand down to check that Dean had everything in working order. Which he did, except . . .

'I'm not hot?' she demanded angrily, wrenching away from him so she could sit up and fold her arms. 'You not think I'm sexy?'

Dean dragged himself up to a sitting position and hugged his knees. 'Of course, you're hot,' he protested. 'You're really hot. You have insane legs and you're a model.' He shook his head violently like he was trying to dislodge a few brain cells. 'Look, it's not you, I must have had too much to drink.'

'You only had two and a half beers,' Irina reminded him icily, getting to her feet. She could feel every inch of her blushing, and normally she never went red. But being found severely lacking by a weedy guy with bad hair would do that to a girl. 'Is my tits – they're too small? My face is not pretty . . .'

'No, no, you're gorgeous,' Dean assured her hurriedly, before looking away. 'I can't believe this is happening.' And while Irina was deciding whether to get dressed or shout at him, he struggled upright so he could practically run to the bathroom and slam the door behind him.

Irina got dressed with jerky movements, kicking the side of the couch in frustration. By the time Dean emerged with a pale face, she was hopping on one foot and clutching her injured toes.

'No to worry, I go in five seconds,' she hurled at him, because it was obvious that he didn't want her there. And she wanted to be there even less. She'd been kidding herself that she could bag a successful rock star just because she was a model. Being a model didn't change anything. It hadn't changed her.

'It's not you,' Dean sighed, flopping down on a chair. 'It's me. Really. If I had any control over this situation we'd be hanging from the light fitting right about now.'

Irina glanced up at the spiky metal fixture, which didn't look like it would be able to hold their combined weight. 'Whatever.'

Dean clutched his head in his hands and muttered something that Irina couldn't catch.

'What?' she snarled. 'What do you say?' She'd bet her

new Nike trainers it was some mumbled aside about how she was flat-chested or ugly or looked like a boy.

Dean sighed again. 'I'm on antidepressants,' he admitted out of the side of his mouth. 'They kind of kill the urge. But you're so beautiful that I thought I could go through with it. I've always liked mouthy girls, y'know.'

No, Irina didn't. She looked around the apartment and all the expensive designer furniture and technical gadgetry. 'What the hell do you have to be depressed about?'

'Oh, not much. Just every single aspect of my life . . .' Dean stared at a knot on the wooden floorboard. There was something so still about him, so removed, as if she was looking at a picture instead of a flesh and blood guy. Usually Irina didn't do empathy and despised people who did, but Dean looked like a puppy who'd been abandoned by the side of the road.

'No wonder your songs are so whiny,' was what she heard herself say, but it made Dean raise a faint glimmer of a smile.

'You should have heard them before I started taking Prozac then,' he drawled, sounding a little more like the arrogant musician she'd seen at the video shoot when he'd been arguing with the director about his camera angles.

'Look, if it make you feel better, I not fancy you so much. But then I think I should, so I make the first move. And you kiss good, but I just wasn't feeling it either.' Dean should have been relieved, but his face got bleaker and bleaker, until Irina was worried that he might try and throw himself on a kitchen knife. The antidepressants obviously weren't working.

'Irina?'

'What?'

'You really don't fancy me?'

Irina cackled because now Dean was looking put out that there was a real live girl in his apartment who didn't want to jump his scrawny bones.

'You not so good-looking in the flesh,' Irina told Dean because someone had to. She sucked at comfort, but maybe he needed someone who did the straight-talking instead. 'Your nose is crooked and your features are unbalanced and your hair smells funny.'

Dean's lip curled. 'And you just don't get me horny, even when we were kissing, though that could just be a medical side-effect. If I kick the drugs, maybe we could have another bash at it?' He leered at her long and hard until Irina was forced to pick up a leather cushion and hit him over the head with it.

'No, you have one chance to get in my pants and that's it,' she said firmly. 'Now we be friends instead, ja? Cool?'

'Yeah, I think it would be cool if we were mates,' Dean said, and now his smile wasn't so worn around the edges.

Irina rolled her eyes. 'I already tell you that. So we friends now, that means you give me the last egg roll.'

She didn't wait for his reply but snatched it up and

stuffed it in her mouth. Dean stood up and brushed down his jeans for imaginary crumbs. 'I think we need more beer,' he said, then hesitated. 'You won't tell anyone about the drugs or my, um, performance problems?'

It was a little bit insulting that he even had to ask. 'We friends,' she pointed out again. 'I don't rat out my friends. Ever.'

Dean tried to look convinced, but he wasn't doing a very good job of it.

Irina tried again. 'When I get back to London, my agency make me see an anger management specialist,' she sniffed, because she didn't need to see anyone but Ted wouldn't let it go. 'Everyone is fucked up in their own way. You're not special.'

Dean shot her a smile that might be one of the reasons why the sun came up and there were stars in the sky. 'Thank you for that,' he said quietly, and Irina looked at him and he looked back at her and yeah, they totally got each other.

Chapter Twenty-Three

It wasn't until later, when Irina was standing in the middle of Gansevoort Street, trying to flag down a cab, that she decided the whole friend thing was just a result of too much beer, loneliness and egg rolls.

Dean was in a band, which Candy said made people automatically cool, even if their music sucked. Unless they played Country and Western, in which case all bets were off. And he had a girlfriend, even if Sandrine was a huge skank with fake boobs. In short, Irina would never hear from him again. But if they bumped into each other at an airport, then she'd say hello. Irina smirked to herself as she climbed into a taxi. She was getting so classy.

But the next day, as she was sitting on a fire escape drinking Coke and waiting for the photographer to stop dithering over coloramas, Dean rang.

'Hey Rina,' he said. 'There's a launch party tonight for some lame-o club on the Lower East Side. Shall I put your name on the door?'

It was a hard decision. Stay in her hotel room watching pay-per-view movies, go out with the Russian girls and hear about their latest lame attempts to bag investment bankers, or go to a hip club opening with her new best friend. 'Yeah, text me the deets.'

'Cool.'

'Cool.'

And then he was gone. The whole exchange had taken less than a minute. It was so different from the times she'd steeled herself to call Javier and ask him if he wanted to hang. He'd hardly ever called her. And when she finally did get him on the phone, he'd hum and hah and basically make her work really hard for a few hours of his company.

Irina was so much better off without him.

The first thing Irina saw when she stalked into Real on Avenue A was Candy, with a camera crew in tow. She had a weird pink creation perched on top of her head that might possibly have been a hat in another life.

Irina watched with interest as Candy greeted various hipsters who were all cheekbones and skinny jeans. She wasn't one to give Candy credit, but what the girl lacked in inches she made up for in pure charisma. Even if you took the camera crew and the outlandish headgear out of the equation, she lit up the room. It was odd. Irina was so used to Candy being an annoying and very loud presence in the flat, she forgot that she had this other life, the details of which were a little foggy.

But that was just how Irina liked it, so giving the other girl a wide berth, she did a quick sweep of the club. People still stared at her, but it wasn't like the old days when her clothes were shabby and she looked like a gangly freak. Now she still looked like a gangly freak but she was wearing an Azzedine Alaia grey tube dress and had a $1000 bag over her shoulder, so people naturally assumed she was a successful model.

'She's signed with Fierce,' Irina heard one girl enviously mutter to her friend as she walked past them. 'How long are her legs?'

It was just the little pick-me-up she needed as she searched in vain for Dean. She thought she caught a glimpse of him by the DJ decks, but she was stopped in her tracks by a dishevelled blonde woman who seemed vaguely familiar.

'You look like a Slavic Penelope Tree,' she informed Irina, before she took a good slug of her cocktail. 'You really have the most beguiling eyes. Candy never said—'

'Moth-er, what the hell are you doing?' With Candy suddenly popping up like a demonic Jack-in-the-box, the resemblance was clear. 'I told you not to talk to anyone.'

This was like Christmas, birthday and her saint's day all rolled into one. 'You must be Bette,' Irina said politely, which was a huge stretch. 'Candy never shuts up about you.'

She hadn't said anything directly to Irina, but there had been long, obscenity-laden diatribes about Bette's plastic surgery, her failings as a role model, and her complete and utter stupidity, that Irina couldn't help but overhear.

Bette beamed. She wasn't too shabby for an old woman and, back in the day, she must have been a stunner. What a pity Candy hadn't inherited her looks or her pleasant personality. 'She has?' she asked Irina eagerly.

'Yeah, she never stops.' Irina ran an assessing eye over Bette's delicate features. 'I not think the surgeon botched your nose at all.'

'Go fuck yourself, Irina,' Candy snarled, one hand on her mother's wrist as she tried to drag her away. 'She's Russian, she doesn't understand half the crap she comes out with.'

'When you get to my age, sometimes you need a little helping hand,' Bette said, as if Candy hadn't even spoken. 'I know that rock stars aren't meant to do Botox—'

'Dad's the rock star, you're just the hanger-on, Mom . . .'

'But all those late nights playing grimy clubs have taken their toll,' Bette continued. 'And I used to smoke forty a day, really gives you lines around the mouth.'

Candy was huffing and puffing so hard, Irina was surprised that she didn't float off the ground. 'You look fabulous,' she said, and it wasn't even to piss Candy off. Though it did, which was a bonus. 'My mother is only thirty-eight, but she looks really old. Really, really old.' And her mother had pointed out every frown line and grey hair and told Irina that she was responsible for them.

Bette preened a little. 'Before we did the TV show, people used to think Candy and I were sisters.'

'No they didn't. Could you be any more deluded?'

'I would never go clubbing with my mother,' Irina mused. 'They never let her through the door anyway. But if she look like you, then it not be a problem.'

'You're adorable and so beautiful. How long are you in town, because we should do lunch?' Bette was already pulling out her Blackberry. 'Give me your digits, darling.'

Irina hadn't even got the first three numbers out before Candy was yanking Bette away. 'Why do you always do that?' she yelled, as Irina wriggled in delight. How could the night get any better?

Half an hour later, after she'd chatted with a Polish model she'd met at the Dries Van Noten show and told a girl from *Ugly Betty* where she'd got her shoes, Irina realized that she was still having a good time. Though she could have done without the steady stream of guys trotting up to her, like lemmings trying to hurl themselves off a cliff. Each one had a worse chat-up line than the last, but they all started with the same thing: 'Are you a model?' 'Are you a total moron?' was the only suitable response. It didn't matter *who* Irina was, just *what* she was. A £5000-a-day clotheshorse suddenly made her a prime candidate for skeevy guys who needed a girl to slime over.

The fifth guy was more persistent than the others. He only came up to Irina's chin, but he dogged her footsteps and wouldn't take 'piss off' for an answer. 'So I launched my first internet start-up at sixteen,' he droned over the music.

'And I sold the company when I was in my second year at MIT. Made ten mill, but I kept my stock options and…'

Then she saw him. At first she thought it was just another hipster with a tribal armband tattoo and a beanie. But the lights suddenly flickered and Irina saw that lazy smile and the slight shuffle that he always did when they were playing a song he liked. The lights flashed again so Irina could see the two beautiful girls he was talking to; one arm looped around a tall brunette's shoulders, as he smiled at a blonde girl in a tiny pair of shorts and a stripy halter top. The three of them looked like a magazine page come to life. Irina felt dingy and resolutely substandard with her grey clothes and her grey past. Maybe she'd have a sunnier outlook if she'd been brought up in a hot climate.

She was still beetling her brow when Javier looked up and their gazes collided. He didn't smile, didn't do much of anything, but then the brunette girl tugged at his T-shirt and he couldn't wait to stop locking eyes with Irina.

'Hey, been looking for you,' said a voice in her ear – and hallelujah! She was saved . . . and not a moment too soon.

'Dean,' Irina hissed out of the side of her mouth. 'Don't be funny about this, but put your arms around me.'

'Why?' Dean needed to replace the perplexed expression with something a little more loving and tender.

'Arms – around me now!' Irina barked at him and he snapped to obey.

'Ma'am, yes ma'am!' Dean pulled her closer. At least he looked like he was enjoying himself. Hopefully, not too much.

Irina tugged Dean around so they were standing right in Javier's line of vision and reached up to cup his face in her hands. 'I still not fancy you but I'm going to kiss you now,' she said by way of a warning and then mashed her lips against Dean's for a count of five.

It was no good. She couldn't see if Javier was looking, so she yanked Dean ninety degrees to the left. 'Mind telling me what this is all about, Rina?' he enquired casually. 'Or is this a Russian thing?'

Irina came up with a few answers, discarded them instantly and decided to go with the truth for once. 'There's a guy over there who dump me for no reason. And he's all over two girls and I not want him to think that I'm not getting any either, OK?'

'OK, you should have just said,' Dean drawled and, before Irina had time to catch her breath, he dipped her backwards and resumed the kissing.

It was a pity that they had no chemistry. Because Dean did things with his lips that would have made Irina come totally undone if she was one of those girls who got sappy and pathetic just because they'd gone to first base with a boy. As it was, she was one of those girls who had to resort to lame tricks to make a boy jealous.

But was Javier jealous? 'There's a guy in a dumbass

woolly hat striding towards us,' Dean whispered in her ear. 'I think he wants to kill me.'

Irina struggled out of Dean's embrace and pulled at her dress, which had ridden up in all the excitement. Even in the dim light of the club, she could see the blazing lines of fury etched into Javier's face. Finally, she'd got him to feel something! Irina licked her lips in anticipation of how she'd kick him to the kerb. Then she'd stamp up and down on him for good measure.

Which was a really great plan. Except it was derailed by Candy suddenly clutching Irina's arm and making it plain that she wasn't planning on going anywhere else. Snogging Dean was one thing but doing the lesbian routine immediately after was just overkill.

'Get off me!' Irina tried to shake Candy free, but she was clinging on for dear life.

'Why do you always have to be such a bitch?' Candy demanded, and Irina was just about to tell her exactly why, when Candy did something Irina wasn't expecting.

Candy Careless, second generation punk princess and scourge of 'airbrushed airheads everywhere', burst into tears.

It didn't matter anyway. Javier had been waylaid by yet another girl who looked like she mostly preferred to live in a bikini, and Dean was staring at Candy and edging away. 'She's crying,' he muttered in an appalled voice. 'This is not in the friend contract. You deal with it.'

Irina was just about to point out that she wasn't friends

with Candy either, when Candy collapsed on her shoulder. 'I hate you,' she spluttered between sobs. 'I hate you more than any person I've ever met, and I've met a shitload of people in my life.'

'Gee, you must be so proud,' Dean grinned as he waved a hand in a mocking salute before disappearing into the throng, and Irina was left with a weeping girl who'd better not be getting snot on her dress.

'Stop crying,' she ordered, but since when did Candy do anything she was told? 'Stop it right now. You look like a loser.'

And Irina was being tarred with the loser brush too. A little crowd had gathered to point and gawp at the really tall girl and the really tiny girl locked in an awkward embrace.

There was no other option but to drag Candy into the bathroom, where she bodily prevented a pink-haired girl taking the one free cubicle by barring the door.

'Don't even think about it,' she growled and the girl fled, because the poncy fashion world hadn't totally busted Irina's balls. She slammed the toilet lid down, pushed Candy on to it, grabbed some loo roll and shoved it at her. 'Wipe your eyes and stop with the awful noise,' Irina said, leaning against the wall. 'Christ, always with the noise.'

Even with sticky eyes and a red nose, Candy could pull off a malevolent glare almost as well as Irina. 'You,' she mumbled indistinctly. 'You . . .'

Irina raised her eyebrows. 'What about me?'

'You don't repeat things I said about my mom to her face! It's just fucking rude.'

'*Niet*, fucking rude is talking trash about your mother so everyone hear it,' Irina snapped. 'She seems like a nice lady. Maybe we do lunch . . .' She'd only said it to get a rise out of Candy, which was never that hard, and what a surprise, it was working.

'You're not going anywhere near her. It's bad enough that Hadley's with Reed all the time working on that goddamn movie but you're not getting in on the act and taking my mom away too.'

'You not even like your mother . . .'

'I do, she's just embarrassing, like going to the same clubs as me and talking to my friends like she's the same age. God, she's a train wreck that gets beamed into the nation's living rooms at nine o'clock on Thursday evenings.'

'At least she want to hang out with you,' Irina said, because whether she liked it or not, she was stuck with talking Candy down from her snit.

'Why do you care? You haven't spoken to your mother since you left Russia. Everyone at Fierce knows that!'

'None of your business, little girl,' Irina bit out and clenched her hands behind her back so they didn't separate Candy's head from her neck.

'I'm just saying that you don't know shit about me or my life. It's not like it is on TV. No one knows what I have to put up with or what I've been through and if they did, then maybe they'd—'

'Oh, spare me the Western-girl privilege,' Irina spat because it was time for the pity party to end and all the guests to leave. 'You not know how good you have it.'

It shocked Candy out of her tears at least. 'Excuse me?'

'You always have the food to eat, clothes on your back, central heating, ja?'

'Well, yeah, but that's not the point. I'm talking about—'

'Well, I didn't. And when you in the broken bed that you share with your younger sister and you not sleep because your stomach aches with hunger, then you can bitch and moan about how crap your life is. Until then, find someone who cares, because I don't!' Irina took in a few much-needed breaths, which Candy thought was her cue to start whining again.

'Jesus, melodramatic much! I'm talking about, like, *emotional* hunger!' Candy was back to her usual scathing, psycho self. 'And that Little Matchstick Girl routine, Irina? Bor-ing! I don't care how much cabbage soup you had to eat in Russia, you were a stone-cold bitch from the minute you walked into the flat.'

That wasn't how Irina remembered it at all. Candy had this snug 'so there, I win!' expression on her face and Irina wondered what it would take to get rid of it. 'I'm in the country a week,' she suddenly said, though she didn't know why she felt the need to explain herself to Candy. 'I leave one flat because the girls call me a peasant and I go to another flat and there you scream at me before you even say hello. And I get shoved into this stupid world and nobody ever say what they mean and they all fake and my look is too editorial and I have to translate everything into Russian and then back into English and is exhausting.' It was the longest speech she'd ever made in her life and it didn't make Irina feel remotely better for getting it off her chest, especially as Candy was visibly unmoved. She even had the nerve to feign a yawn.

'Yeah, yeah,' she drawled. 'Remind me to cry into my beer for you tonight. You get this amazing opportunity to have a life do-over, go to amazing places, and all you have to do in return is stand in front of a camera with a po-faced expression. Big whoop.'

If Candy wanted to pull out the bitch card *again*, then Irina couldn't be held responsible for anything she might do or say. 'Hadley and Reed see each other for months,' she blurted out, and Candy's mouth and eyes turning into three perfectly round Os of horror was all the reward she needed. 'Behind your back, because you're the selfish, possessive witch and they not want to tell you.'

'Bullshit! You're just making it up to get me mad.'

Now it was Irina's turn to do the nonchalant thing, with added head toss for good measure. 'I see them suck face five different times, and when you're not around, they in her room for hours.' Candy didn't look convinced. 'Once she came out with two lovebites on her neck.'

Candy jammed her fingers in her ears so she wouldn't have to hear any more. 'But they have nothing in common. What would Reed see in someone like *her*?'

Although they were currently estranged, Irina couldn't let Hadley go undefended. 'She has the good heart, she's funny, generous and she's smart.' And before she could start feeling guilty because Hadley *was* all those things and she'd still screwed her over, she turned the knife in the other direction. 'No wonder Reed's in love with her.'

It turned out that when Candy was crying before, it had just been the warm-up to the main event. Now the noise that came out of her mouth sounded like a faulty power drill. She hunched in on herself, buried her head in her hands and cried so hard that her body shook.

Irina couldn't help but feel just a little bit guilty for reducing Candy to agonized whimpers. She crouched down and tapped Candy's shoulder in what might pass for a sympathetic manner. 'There, there,' she said. 'Is no big deal. She probably get with Reed so she can be in his film. Hadley knows is all about making as much money as possible. And people respecting you. Is all that matters.'

That just made Candy cry even harder, though Irina hadn't thought that was possible. With a deep sigh, she tore off another piece of toilet paper and handed it to Candy. 'Go the fuck away!' was all the thanks Candy was prepared to give.

Irina didn't need to be told twice. 'OK, feel better soon,' she called over her shoulder, as she nipped out of the cubicle ready to face the long line of narrow-eyed girls all jiggling from foot to foot as they waited for the other cubicle that didn't have a sobbing drama queen in it.

Irina shrugged at the crowd. 'She had bad curry. She'll be out soon.'

Javier was nowhere to be found, not that Irina was looking for him. But Dean was still alive and intact, so she went to hang out with him, until Sandrine arrived in figure-hugging red satin.

Dean had been talking about England and how he missed sausages in batter, but when his not-quite-girlfriend turned up the conversation quickly degenerated into a round of:

'Fuck you!'

'No, fuck you!'

'*No*, fuck *you*!'

Candy had emerged from her enforced exile and was sitting in a booth with her mother, looking pale and forlorn, as Bette chattered animatedly at her. So, officially she wasn't Irina's problem any more.

When another weaselly guy in an expensive suit approached and asked if she was a model, Irina decided it was time to leave. She had a big shoot tomorrow and no way was she turning up with puffy eyes and a truckload of grouch because she hadn't had a decent night's sleep.

Outside the club, Irina peered down the street to scout for a cab with its light on, when Javier jumped over the velvet rope and planted himself firmly in her path.

The best evening she'd had in months had become something that she'd only wish on her worst enemies. 'Javier,' Irina grunted. 'What do you want?'

Javier was looking all hurt and wounded, which made Irina feel hurt and wounded too. Why did he still have that power over her? 'Didn't take you long,' he rasped. 'That guy will screw anything that moves. And a rock star, Irina? You're really living the cliché, aren't you?'

Part of her, a very large part of her, wanted to deny it. But she refused to listen to that tiresome part of her brain. 'Is none of your business. Go, leave me alone.'

'It took you five minutes to find someone else.' Javier shivered inside his hoodie and folded his arms. 'Did you cheat on me when we were together?'

'I never knew we were together!' she half screamed in frustration. 'You never straight with me. You never call. You never want to see me unless I beg. Then you dump me before I even know we're dating, so don't give me the sulky face.' God, she had her rant on tonight. 'And every time I turn around, you flirt with another beautiful girl.'

'They're just friends, Irina . . .'

'Like I was a friend, huh?'

'You were never a friend. You wouldn't even hold my hand when we were walking down the street,' Javier gritted. 'And that night we went out with your roomates in London, you didn't even introduce me to them.'

That had been the night they'd taken Laura out so she'd forget that her boyfriend had cheated on her and she was on the verge of being sacked from Fierce because she was fat and moody. How Irina wished that they'd left Laura in her room that evening to eat herself to death. Hadley had got so drunk that she'd collapsed on the floor of the limo, Laura had slept with some boy that she didn't know, and Candy . . . had just been Candy. Why the hell would she have introduced Javier to them, when they were embarrassing to be seen with?

'If I know that you were my "boyfriend" ' – Irina air-quoted so furiously that she almost poked Javier's eye out – 'maybe I would have.'

Javier snorted in derision as Irina waved frantically at a vacant cab.

'You're so high maintenance, Irina,' he muttered. 'Why does everything have to be spelt out with flashcards for you? It's obvious that you didn't even understand half of what I was feeling.'

Irina shoved him out of the way so she could get into the cab. 'Because you never tell me!'

She barked her hotel address at the driver, who didn't seem in any hurry to drive off, and next thing she knew,

Javier was jumping into the cab just as they pulled away from the kerb in a squeal of tyres.

'Get out!' she spat, scooching across the seat to get away from Javier, who'd picked a really weird time to grow a pair.

'We're going to talk this out,' he announced calmly, which made Irina want to smack him. 'So you didn't realize we were dating? Never thought you'd be so slow getting a clue.'

'You not date models,' Irina reminded him stonily. 'You make that clear.'

'When did I say that?' Javier frowned, like it was all too confusing for words.

'When you drunk out of your skull in Tokyo.' Irina peered ahead to see if they were anywhere near her hotel, then nearly jumped out of her skin when Javier took her hand in a grip so strong that she couldn't shake free. Really, she didn't want to, but that was beside the point. 'Get your hand off me!'

But Javier was moving closer so he could take her chin and turn Irina's face towards him. 'Look, let's go back to your hotel,' he murmured. 'Get this sorted out. Maybe I should have been more forthcoming about stuff too.'

There was nothing to sort out. Irina was done with being Javier's hook-up, fed up with making do with the few small crumbs that he felt like throwing her way. God damn it, she was getting paid £5000 a day! That meant she deserved better than . . .

But then Javier kissed her gently like he always did with the first kiss. And just like always, it made Irina feel like a princess, like some delicate slip of a girl who was used to being treated as if she was precious.

The second kiss was a little less gentle. More tender. And way more passionate, so Irina was kissing him back, putting everything she had into it because she was useless at putting it into words.

And the third kiss had the cab-driver braking sharply so he could exclaim, 'Hey, get a room!'

It was just the reality check that Irina needed. She jerked away from Javier so she could lean over and wrestle with the door handle . . .

'Baby, what are you doing?' Javier asked, even though it was obvious, because she had both hands on his back so she could push him out of the cab, where he landed in an ungainly heap on the pavement.

'No. No!' she repeated sharply, wagging her finger at him. 'You no get the milk any more, not without buying the freaking cow!'

'What the hell are you talking about?' He was glaring at her as he got to his feet and dusted off his jeans, but Irina was already slamming the door and telling the driver that he wouldn't get a tip if he didn't put his foot down.

Chapter Twenty-Four

Even as she turned her key in the lock, Irina could hear the sounds of an argument.

By the time she reached the first-floor landing, the argument turned out to be Candy swearing, Hadley screaming, Laura crying – and Irina had a good mind to turn herself around and book into a hotel.

Sighing, she opened the front door to be met by the sight of the three of them facing off in the lounge, with clenched fists and lots of hair tossing.

If she just tiptoed down the hall, they probably wouldn't even know that she was there. Irina gingerly hauled her suitcase over the threshold . . .

'About time you put in an appearance.' Candy rounded on Irina furiously. 'Tell Hadley what you told me about her and my *brother*.'

'Half-brother,' Hadley corrected with a full-on body flounce. 'And it's none of your business, and thank you for totally betraying me, Irina, after I got you a movie role. The only place you're going to be is on the cutting-room floor once I tell Reed.'

'Don't even say his name!' Candy growled. 'He's only with you for the publicity. I mean, why the hell else would

211

he be able to stand spending time with you?'

There was a high-pitched yelping sound from Hadley before she launched herself at Candy. It was a really lame excuse for a cat-fight. Irina would have just punched Candy repeatedly in the face until she shut up, but Hadley was a hair-puller and Candy was a nail-digger, so they just crashed around the lounge in a blur of dyed hair and flailing limbs.

It was left to Laura to come in like some avenging army because she always had to stick her stupid retroussé nose where it wasn't wanted. 'You're absolutely toxic,' she spat at Irina. 'Even when you're not actually in the country, you manage to wreak destruction.'

Irina had watched six episodes of *The Catherine Tate Show* on the plane. 'Do I look bothered?' she asked in her most bored voice, which was more bored than most people could muster up in a whole lifetime.

'Toxic!' Laura clarified before her attention was distracted by a half-full coffee mug toppling over and sending a shooting arc of brown liquid over the carpet, as Hadley and Candy crashed into the table.

'Fake plastic bimbo!'

'Evil troll!'

'Well, don't just stand there,' Laura barked at Irina, eyeing the writhing bundle of girl before them. 'Help me separate them.'

And without a care for her so-called model looks, Laura

waded in, grabbed an arm, and kept yanking until Candy emerged red-faced and panting from the scrum.

Without Candy's hands wrapped around her throat, Hadley sank to the floor and surveyed the little half-moon marks that were embedded in her hand. 'You've maimed me!' she gasped, because you could always rely on Hadley to add a little more drama to any situation. If she'd been on the *Titanic* when it went down, she'd have been screaming about water damage to her Louis Vuitton luggage rather than heading for the nearest lifeboat. 'I need to get a tetanus shot.'

'You should have got a booster injection when you bought your revolting little rat-dog,' Candy hissed, rubbing her head. 'Oh my God, I think she's left a bald spot.'

Laura patted her on the back. 'Just calm down, Candy . . .'

'You leave Mr C-C out of this,' Hadley squealed. 'If these marks leave a scar then I'm sueing you and you're going to have to pay for the skin grafts.'

'Maybe I can arrange for the surgeon to sew your mouth up at the same time.'

Irina sank down on the sofa and watched as the hissy fit gathered steam. Once they got going, they could be hurling insults for hours, so she groped for the remote control to see if the Sky+ box had recorded *Skins*.

'What the hell do you think you're doing?' Candy suddenly enquired as Irina scrolled through the programme log. 'Irina! I'm talking to you!'

'Actually you shout,' Irina pointed out. 'Go away, I not be able to hear the TV over your annoying voice.'

There were three gasps of disbelief as they all turned to look at her.

'This is all her fault!'

Irina wasn't sure who'd spoken, but it didn't really matter. From the accusing looks, they'd all finally found something they agreed on.

'Is my fault that Hadley's shagging Candy's brother?'

'I am not! I'm saving myself for my wedding night. And you were sworn to secrecy anyway.' Hadley didn't know who to look at. Her gaze skidded from Irina to Candy and back to Irina again. 'I thought you were my friend, but actually you're just a vindictive, hostile person who's not capable of being friends with anyone. And if I didn't hate you so much, then I'd feel sorry for you.' And with that, she scrambled to her feet and stood there with her hands on her hips.

Irina sighed because she really hadn't meant to drop Hadley in it. They *were* friends. Kind of . . . 'Hadley . . .'

'No! Don't even say my name!' Hadley cried, holding her hand up in protest. 'In fact, don't ever speak to me again!' She whirled out of the room with as much dignity as someone could when they had the word 'juicy' emblazoned across their arse.

That left Irina alone in the company of the two-headed

Laura and Candy beast, except now they were bickering.

'I really don't see what the big deal is if Hadley and Reed are dating,' Laura was saying as she tried to see if Candy's scalp was bleeding or if she was just a big, fat faker.

Candy flinched away. 'That's because you've never had a sibling. You're the classic example of an only child.'

'And what the hell is that meant to mean?'

'You're kind of spoilt, Laura. You want everything to go your way so you can float through life without getting your hands dirty. Well, I'm sorry if my pain and hurt is an inconvenience.'

Irina was torn. It was great to see Laura getting knocked off her pretty-girl perch but, on the other hand, Laura could totally take Candy in a fight. One blow from her meaty fists and Candy would be out cold.

'I'm going to give you the benefit of the doubt because you're all upset and acting like a certifiable crazy lady, but just because I'd like to live in a peaceful, harmonious atmosphere without people screaming every five minutes does not make me spoilt,' Laura finished haughtily.

'I do not ever scream!' shrieked Candy, doing a good impersonation of a girl with some serious vocal chords. 'And you must have known they were seeing each other. You had to! I know that you hang out with *her* when I'm not around, even though you're meant to be my friend.'

Laura shoved her hands into her hair and gave a genuine scream of irritation. 'I *am* your friend, but I'm Hadley's friend as well. I've told you a million times that I won't take sides. You've had it in for Hadley from day one . . .'

'I've had it in for her ever since she started perving on Reed!'

'Do you have the incest thing going on?' Irina heard herself ask before she could engage her brain cells. Obviously the jet-lag was starting to kick in. 'This possessive thing of yours – very weird.'

It had been the wrong thing to say. Irina knew that as soon as the words left her mouth. Mostly because it reminded Candy and Laura that she was responsible for all the ills in their happy home. Maybe even beyond that. Like, it was her fault there was global warming and weapons of mass destruction.

'Oh, just shut the fuck up!' Candy yelled so loudly that she had to have done irreparable damage to her throat, Irina thought hopefully. It took a superhuman effort, but she raised one eyebrow, like all the drama was just getting too tiresome for words.

It was left to Laura to deal the killing blow. 'No wonder you haven't got any real friends,' she snapped. 'You are the most obnoxious person I have ever, ever met.'

The worst of it was that Irina wanted to agree with her. She wasn't a friend to anyone, except herself. Which was fine. Irina had her own shit to take care of and worrying about other people just got in the way.

'Yeah,' Candy sniffed, coming off the bench. 'Heard from

Javier lately or did he get tired of spending time with such a colossal beeyatch?'

Irina looked down at her chest, surprised that there wasn't a gaping, bleeding wound where they'd just stuck the knife in. Never before had she been so pleased to have a stony face as her default setting. And when she picked up the remote control again, her hand was pleasingly steady. 'Shift your fat arses,' she ordered brusquely. 'I not see the TV if you two are in the way.'

She stared fixedly at the screen until they got the message. Not that Laura and Candy had managed to bond over their mutual loathing of Irina. A moment later, she heard two separate doors slam and she could settle down to watch the TV in peace. After five minutes, she stopped pretending to be engrossed in MTV and hurried to her room so she could hurl some small electrical appliances from the window.

This last fight wasn't like their other fights. Of which there'd been many – usually when Laura took it upon herself to call a house meeting, which never ended well. Then there'd be a lot of hot air and bluster, but by evening, they'd be camped out in the living room watching *Project Runway* and bitching about the models. Irina almost felt a warm glow as she remembered happier times.

Now it was nothing short of total war. The battle lines had been drawn, the troops had been assembled and there was no hope of a ceasefire. Candy had got a man to come round and put a padlock on her kitchen cupboard, which was a damn shame as she always had the good stuff in there like Oreo cookies and these little marshmallows that Irina liked to dump by the handful into her hot chocolate.

Hadley refused to stay in the flat while Candy was in residence and she and Mr C-C had decamped down the road to Reed's house. She only returned if Candy was flying to Mumbai for a nightclub opening or going back to New York to make her poor mother's life living hell.

Irina never thought it would go down like this, but she actually preferred the times that Candy was around. And not just because it gave her a feeling of immense satisfaction to see the three former pals snapping and snarling at each other. What was far worse was seeing Hadley and Laura embarking on new-best-friend-dom. They'd sit on the sofa watching stupid chick flicks, and as much as Irina strained her ears, she couldn't hear what they were saying. Though she had a feeling that her name came up a hell of a lot. And even she didn't have the stones to wedge herself between them and demand that they change the channel.

It was a secret that she'd take to her grave, but actually she did feel lousy about what happened with Hadley. Hadley had had a tough life. OK, she'd had a tough life in a Malibu mansion, but she'd still been through lots of shit and come out the other end as much of a survivor as Irina was. Irina respected that. Telling Candy about her and Reed had been a genuine mistake that Irina couldn't undo, nor was she going to waste time beating herself up over it. But Irina hated that she'd hurt Hadley's feelings. Hadley got this tight, pinched look on her face whenever Irina was in the same room, and she'd do anything to rub it away.

Irina had taken to leaving little gifts on Hadley's bed. A gift basket from the Japanese cosmetics company, who were ecstatic about the response the ads were getting. The Christian Louboutin shoes she'd snagged from a stylist. She'd even paid full price for a Gucci dog collar and lead.

One night when she'd just got in from a gruelling outdoor shoot, modelling evening gowns in what felt like a force-twenty gale, Hadley appeared at her door with her arms laden. 'I don't want this stuff,' she said baldly, dropping all Irina's peace offerings on the floor. 'I haven't said anything to Reed, so as far as I know you're still in the movie.'

Irina roused herself from her near-catatonic state. 'That's not why I give them to you.'

Hadley folded her arms. 'If you were sorry, you could just, like, say that you were.'

'Is not my fault that Candy is the evil bitch,' Irina protested, because blaming Candy was way easier than saying sorry. Only losers said sorry.

'Oh, what*ever*!' Hadley said, sounding scarily like Candy. 'I only came in to tell you that Laura's speaking to Fierce and trying to find us a two-bedroom flat. Though we just might end up renting somewhere together.'

Irina didn't have time to mask her shocked expression. She didn't want new flatmates. Or to leave Camden. Or have to share with Russian girls. Or not live with Hadley. This was why she didn't do friends – they were far more trouble than they were worth.

'Fine, I hope you be very happy together, if you find a flat big enough for her gigantic arse,' Irina said, flopping back down on the bed. 'Close the door behind you.'

Chapter Twenty-Five

After New York, Paris was possibly Irina's favourite city. She liked the fact that the Parisians were famously rude but fawned over anyone who made the effort to speak their language. And she liked that she could take the train rather than having her legs squidged beyond all recognition in a narrow aeroplane seat. And she particularly loved pain au chocolat and almond croissants and *steak-frites*. Yeah, Paris was cool with her.

It was cool right up to the moment that she walked into the photo studio booked for her *Vogue* shoot and saw Javier. She'd been dreading this moment ever since she'd pushed him out of the cab in New York.

He didn't see her at first. Or maybe he was pretending that he didn't see her. Irina drank him in because it sucked that she thought she hated him, but when she got to be in the same room, there was no one that she'd rather talk to. No one she'd rather look at. Conflicted, table for one.

'Irina. Get yourself a coffee,' drawled a voice in her ear and she turned round to see Aaron looming behind her. From the disapproving look on his craggy face, he hadn't forgotten or forgiven her for the crap she'd pulled in Japan. Though that was months ago. And he obviously hadn't heard about her great strides in self-control.

Irina had finally gone to see the anger management specialist, only because she'd smashed so many mobiles that the staff in Carphone Warehouse were starting to give her funny looks each time she came in to get a new phone.

It had been a waste of time. The guy was a total charlatan in a designer suit, who'd told her to imagine her rage as a red cloud that she had the power to blow away with her positive energy. 'Just tell me how not to break stuff when I get angry,' Irina had snapped at last because the visualizing was giving her a headache.

She'd been expecting a cosmic box that would reassign the electricity in her body, but he'd just reached into a drawer and pulled out a bag of elastic bands. 'Put one of them round your wrist and each time you feel like shouting or breaking something give it a good snap. The pain will centre you,' he'd said. 'And stop glaring at me – you have a very grey aura around you, Irina.'

So now she gave the elastic band a quick tug. Strangely, it did seem to be helping with the rage, though she had a permanent bruise on her wrist from the continual pinging. 'Hi, Aaron,' she said brightly, though to her ears it sounded as fake as a pair of plastic boobs.

He ignored her. 'We're going to be ages setting up the lights for these hair shots. Find a quiet spot and try not to annoy anyone until you really can't help yourself.'

At this rate, Irina would completely cut off her blood

circulation from over-enthusiastic pinging. 'Fine,' she said thinly, walking over to the obligatory large squashy sofa. As she passed Javier, he acknowledged her presence with a cold look, which didn't sit well on his sensual face. He'd obviously been giving Aaron regular updates on how she'd done him wrong. Which was a case of gross misrepresentation, but Irina doubted she'd be given the chance to defend herself.

She curled up with the bag of pastries she'd bought on the way. They were still warm, but she was damned if she was sharing them with Aaron and Javier, especially as she could have had an extra hour in bed while they were climbing on ladders and fussing with different coloured filters. Not even the stylists or the make-up artists had turned up yet.

Irina contented herself with a frantic text back and forth with Dean, who was in Paris to play a one-off show for some important people from his French record company. He didn't seem wildly thrilled about the prospect. Sometimes Irina wondered if their friendship was nothing more than a simple case of 'misery loves company'. But it was good to have someone to moan at through the medium of one hundred and sixty characters.

'You're to take these,' said a gruff voice.

Irina looked up to see Javier holding out a bottle of aspirin.

'Why?'

'We're shooting six different looks and your hair is going to be tugged and tangled and combed out.' Javier trotted out the explanation like he was talking to a three-year-old. 'Your scalp's going to get sore.'

Irina's stupid heart leapt in her chest and did a couple of backflips. Javier still cared about her. He even cared about her hair follicles.

'Aaron doesn't want your complaining to slow things down,' Javier continued in a flat drawl. He seemed like a distant relative of the boy who'd whispered secrets to her in the dark.

The thought of what her head was going to feel like after five individual comb-outs was nothing compared to the pain of Javier refusing to look her in the eye. 'Fine,' Irina said again. She had a suspicion that she'd be using that word an awful lot today, even though things were pretty much as un-fine as they could get.

'Fine,' Javier snapped back at her, and he could just suck it up and stop acting like he was the injured party.

She snatched the pill bottle and waved a dismissive hand. 'Run along, pretty-boy. Do your fetching and carrying.'

Irina was still texting Dean about Javier's failings as a human being an hour later as she sat in the make-up chair and resisted the urge to scream. Her hair was positively soaked with serum so it would look shiny and sleek under the lights.

She'd never thought much about her hair. People praised

its thickness and strength and its versatility, because it wasn't straight and it wasn't curly but somewhere in between. They even liked the colour. Irina called it brown. But brown in the fashion world meant tawny or sable or chocolate or russet. Right now, Irina would happily have shaved off every last inch if it meant people would stop touching it, yanking it or discussing it.

'On set now,' someone instructed. 'Slowly, don't make any jerky movements.'

Irina was escorted the few steps on to her mark with all the attention usually given to a reigning monarch. The two hair stylists actually squeaked in alarm when she stumbled, and brandished their spritzers in anticipation.

Aaron tapped his foot impatiently as Irina was primped to their satisfaction, then shooed them away. 'OK, I'm going to do a head-and-shoulders shot, so it's all about your face,' he said, giving Irina an unfriendly look. 'Something a little softer than your usual hard-edged stare.'

Brrrrr! Seemed like someone had put the thermostat on the arctic setting. Irina closed her eyes and tried to empty her head of all the negative crap floating around so she could focus on becoming a blank canvas.

When she opened her eyes again both Javier and Aaron were staring at her with matching expressions of, well, not outright loathing. But it was clear that she was one of their least favourite people in the world.

Irina tried to do soft, she really did. She relaxed her jaw

and angled her head slightly to the side. Made her eyes a little less glarey. But nothing she did seemed to work. Aaron stopped giving her direction because he was too busy sighing theatrically. He shot three rolls, then told the stylists to dress Irina's hair for the next shot.

'Try to find your happy place while you're in make-up, if you have one,' he said out of the side of his mouth as she walked past him.

The serum had made her hair sticky, so it had to be washed out over a basin in the toilets, before someone started combing out the tangles. The aspirin really didn't help as Irina's head began to ache from the constant pulling. Her reputation being what it was, the stylists were obviously fearful that she'd use their teasing combs as stabbing devices, but it was a point of pride with Irina, by now, that she was going to suffer in silence. Apart from the odd 'ouch' which leaked out when she couldn't help it. And God help her, this was only the second look; there were still four more to go.

Three looks later and Irina's head felt as if it had been removed from her body, used as a football and then reattached. All this and she still hadn't been able to produce the required 'softer' expression that Aaron seemed to want.

Which was strange because Irina had never felt so vulnerable as she did now: perched on a hard stool with a sopping-wet towel tucked under her arms so her neck and shoulders were bare. Her make-up was a creamy blend of greys and pinks, which made Irina look younger, and her hair was a sleek curtain cascading down from a centre parting so it obscured the hard planes of her cheekbones. She looked soft, but she couldn't act soft in front of the camera, in front of anyone, especially Javier, who strode forward so he could click the light meter in Irina's face with a force that wasn't strictly necessary. God, he still couldn't bring himself to look at her. Irina stared after his departing back, remembered how it felt to press her fingers against his shoulder blades . . .

'Get out of the way, Jav,' Aaron snapped at the corners of her consciousness and Irina blinked as the flash went off, taking her by surprise.

'Don't blink,' Aaron barked. He put down the camera for one second, peered at Irina as if he was trying to move her back a few inches through the power of his mind, and then glanced at Javier. 'Stand over here, just to the side of me.'

Irina bit back a groan. It was hard enough, without Javier directly in her line of vision. She could feel her lips trembling, a scratchiness in her throat, and realized that the tears weren't too far away.

'Perfect,' Aaron announced with satisfaction. 'You've gone all dreamy and wide-eyed, Irina. I never knew you had it in you.'

In the end, the part of her that was torn with loss and longing over Javier standing just a few feet in front of her but as remote and distant as if there was an ocean between them, won out against the part that wanted to smash Aaron's face in.

It was ironic that she stopped worrying about her facial expressions for the rest of the shoot. All Irina could concentrate on was not crying. She even welcomed the pain from creating the last hairstyle because it took her mind off Javier slightly, even though she could hear his husky voice through the open door as he talked to Aaron.

The last rolls of film were shot after shot of exquisite agony. Irina could feel every inch of her body shaking as she gave up not staring at Javier as he joked with Aaron, because her pain and regret were nothing. Not important. Would just end up as different images on sheets of photographic paper.

'It's a wrap,' Aaron said, and instead of letting relief wash over her, Irina shuddered as the first sob tried to worm its way up and out. She jumped off the stool and skidded across the floor, ignoring the hair stylists who were still brandishing their spritzer bottles. 'Good work, Irina,' Aaron called after her, but she was already slamming the dressing room door behind her.

It took two minutes to pull on her jumper, grab her bag and head down the stairs. She was almost home and dry, hand reaching out to push open the street door, when Javier caught up with her. 'Irina,' he panted, catching her wrist between his fingers.

She tugged free. Her wrist was almost as painful as her

head. The elastic band had eventually snapped somewhere between the fifteenth and sixteenth roll of film. 'Fuck off,' she snarled. 'Just fuck right off.'

'Look, come back and wash all the stuff out of your head. They can put some balm on your scalp, though you'll probably have to wrap a scarf around it so—'

Irina whirled around so she could slap Javier's face. It was just as well that her wrist was sore and it lacked her usual force and precision. 'Don't! Don't act like you care! You know what Aaron was doing and you just let him!'

Javier rubbed the spot on his cheek where she'd whacked him. 'He needed to get the shots. I'm there to help him get the shots,' he said quietly. 'I don't know why you're taking it so personally.'

'You know!' Irina shouted, prodding him in the chest with her finger. 'And you let him take the advantage of me!'

'What? What do I know?'

He had to know how she felt about him. It was obvious, unless he was made of some incredibly dense material.

'What do I know, Irina?' Javier repeated softly, but she was fed up with having to spell out stuff for him. Either he knew, or he didn't. And if he did know, then he should bloody well be doing something about it.

'Stop playing games,' she said fiercely. 'I have no time for it.'

Javier raised his hand like he was going to touch her,

maybe stroke her cheek, but then decided against it. 'I've been thinking about you, about us, a lot,' he admitted, like that should be something.

But it wasn't enough. 'Stop thinking and start doing,' Irina advised harshly.

And for once, he did what he was told. He started moving forward, but then again, so did Irina. It made the kissing happen a lot quicker that way; their mouths meeting in a furious clash of teeth and tongues, fighting to push the other one up against the wall. Javier won in the end, or maybe Irina let him win because she wanted the feeling of his body pressed against hers as she wrapped her arms tight around him.

If they could just stay like this for ever then maybe things would work out. Because if they were kissing, then they didn't have to talk. When they talked, stuff always got messed up. But Javier's fingers threading through her hair, rubbing soothing circles against her aching scalp, his lips moving on hers wasn't messed up. It was perfect.

Someone called Javier's name from the top of the stairwell. They ignored it. But the voice got louder and Javier pulled away with a muffled curse so Irina could glance up and see Aaron staring down at them with a faintly disdainful smile. 'Those lights aren't going to pack themselves,' he drawled, before walking away.

Without Javier's warm body boxing her in, Irina felt cold. He was breathing hard, cheeks flushed as he ran an unsteady hand through his hair, which was dishevelled and hanging in his eyes. 'What do you want?' he asked Irina, and he sounded helpless and scared. 'What do you want from me?'

Irina stared at him in furious disbelief. 'You are the most stupid person I've ever met,' she railed. 'Is simple, you're a boy, I'm a girl. Start acting like it.' She couldn't keep doing all the work; always being the one in charge. Javier had to let her know what he felt in his heart. Irina wasn't going to say anything, unless he said it first.

She crouched down to pick up her bag and as she straightened up, Javier was reaching for her again. 'Irina.' His voice was low and urgent. 'I think about you all the time, but I just end up turning in circles. I've got to get back upstairs now but—'

'Fine,' she interrupted tersely before he could give her yet another brush-off. 'I go now too. I see Dean tonight and I don't want to be late. You remember my friend Dean, the very successful rock star, ja?'

She guessed from the thunderous look on Javier's face, before he turned on his heel and marched up the stairs, that he remembered only too well.

Chapter Twenty-Six

Dean was no help when it came to soothing either the ache in her head or the ache in her soul. 'You look like some freaky religious chick,' he laughed when Irina arrived in the hotel bar with a scarf wrapped around her head.

Irina gave Dean her most menacing scowl, which just made him laugh ever harder. She'd slathered her hair in an entire tub of intensive conditioning treatment, so it wasn't as if she had a lot of headgear options.

'Shut up before I hurt you,' she growled, looking around the bar's clientele of braying businessmen with lip-curling scorn. 'This place sucks ass, let's get out of here. I'm starving.'

They holed up in a little bistro on the Ile de la Cité, and as Irina demolished a steak so large that Dean blanched, he began to vent about the disastrous state of his love life. Though actually he didn't appear to have one.

'I just want to come clean and tell everyone that Sandrine and me aren't together,' he said bitterly. 'Then Paul mutters about our fanbase, but at the same time, they're sharing a hotel room. It makes me look like a complete tool. And she can't sing and she can barely dance, and if I'm not sleeping with her any more then why the hell should she even be in the band?'

'You should dump her,' Irina said, as she unwrapped her fifth packet of breadsticks. 'And you should dump him. Go solo or something.'

'I guess. And then he can sue me for the rest of my life, like he's done with Moll.'

Irina's ears pricked up. Dean's face had gone all pinched on the last sentence. 'Who's Moll?'

Dean became very interested in the contents of his beer bottle. 'No one,' he said shortly, before he relented. 'She started the band with another girl. Then they left, citing irreconcilable personal differences. Jane went into rehab and Molly's spent the last three years being sued by Paul. Have you ever done something so horrible to someone that you can hardly live with yourself after?'

'No.' Irina thought about her mother and Hadley and corrected herself. 'Well I did some stuff that was wrong, but I try to make up for it.'

'I'll never find another girl like Molly,' Dean sighed. 'And no, getting back with her isn't going to happen,' he added pre-empting Irina's next question. 'Some things you can't come back from.'

'*Pffft!* Find someone else. You're not so ugly to look at and you're famous. You must get the groupies?'

Dean nearly spat out a mouthful of beer. 'Don't spare my feelings, Rina. Just come right out with it.'

She flashed her teeth. 'Count on it. Maybe I find you a nice Russian girl who not put up with your rock star crap.'

'A model?' Dean sat up and started to drool. Sometimes Irina forgot that he could be a real perv. 'Couldn't hurt.'

Irina ran through a checklist of names. Famke, Katja, Nadja – they were all single, but obsessed with dating either members of the aristocracy or premier division footballers. 'How much money you make?'

Dean shook his head. 'I don't want a gold-digger. You must know a down-to-earth girl who's looking to be the muse of a quirkily attractive social commentator. That's what Spin called me.'

'Whatever. You so full of it.'

'Oh! Actually you know who I do fancy? That Laura chick, the one who does that perfume ad. She's gorgeous; looks like a Vargas girl. Why are you twitching?'

Irina could feel one of her eyelids spasming. It felt very odd. 'She's a whiny bitch. You not like her,' she said quickly.

She might just as well have not spoken. 'So you do know her?'

Knew her. Lived with her. Put up with her. And had seen her kiss Dean's picture on too many occasions to count.

'Not going to happen. Change the subject.'

'OK, what's happening with you and Javier?' Dean smirked, folding his arms and leaning back in his chair. 'Tell Uncle Dean all about it.'

Telling Dean all about it took hours. They left the

restaurant and ended up in a cavernous pool hall with blue tables in Menilmontant. Irina's game was shot to pieces as she dissected, analysed and theorized everything Javier had said to her that day and how he'd looked while he was doing it.

'You're so dumb sometimes,' Dean said finally, aiming a yellow ball into the corner pocket. 'You're acting like a girl.'

'I am a girl,' Irina snapped. 'See – tits, hips?'

'Yeah, but you're not a proper girl except when it comes to this guy,' Dean mumbled, his attention on the game. He smartly flipped another ball away and chalked the end of his cue. 'If it was anyone else, you'd march up to him, tell him how you were feeling and ask – no, *demand* that he quit all the mind games and let you know how he felt.'

Dean had a point. Several points. All good and concise but... 'I can't,' Irina admitted quietly. 'I should, but is not possible. I don't even know why.'

'Ha! I win,' Dean crowed, seeing off the last ball before he turned to her with a smug expression. 'The reason why is because you're terrified of what his answer might be.'

Irina had no choice but to sneer, while she tried to process this startling revelation. 'You talk such crap. Is a very complex situation, but you're too stupid to see that.'

'*Bock bock bock*,' Dean crowed softly, which threw Irina slightly. 'I'm making chicken noises, don't they sound like that in Russia? Come on, Rina. What are you always saying to me? Oh yeah, time to grow a pair.'

'Shut up, you idiot.'

'You just can't handle the truth, baby.' Dean grinned and kept on grinning even when she poked him in the ribs with her cue. 'C'mon let's play another game so I can beat you to a pulp a little bit more.'

He obviously liked his face the way it was because Dean stopped teasing and Irina managed to claw back the last two games. One more and it would be three all.

'You want to up the ante?' Dean asked suddenly, tapping the edge of the table with the cue. 'A little wager to make things more interesting?'

Irina didn't trust the sly look on his face. 'What?'

'I don't know. Money seems a little boring, there must be something of mine that you want.'

She thought about it for a second. 'You have a flat in London, right? I win, you let me move in and use it as a base. I pay rent if you want.'

Dean considered her proposition. 'That sounds OK, I'm hardly ever there and it's got two bedrooms – well, three, but I converted one into a home recording studio. Twenty-four track, this sweet little mixer . . .'

Irina nudged him before he could start boring on about recording equipment. 'What do you want?'

'If I win, you have to set me up on a date with your little friend, Laura.'

'She's not little, she as big as a house – and she not my friend!' He'd been playing her the whole time and she'd fallen for it like a suckery sucker. 'No way. Ask for something else.'

'So you think you're going to lose?' Dean arched his eyebrow like a pantomine villain. 'What's happened to your over-developed competitive streak?'

'I so going to kick your scrawny English arse,' Irina snarled, wielding her cue like a sword. 'I not care if you want to date that fat bitch, because you won't win.'

'We'll see about that,' Dean said, holding out his hand. 'I have a pretty over-developed competitive streak of my own. Shake on it though, I'm not having you welch on a bet once I've annihilated all these balls.'

Irina shook his hand in her most bone-crushing grip, but Dean didn't even wince. Plucking at a guitar all day must have really strengthened his fingers. 'OK, game on,' Irina said challengingly. 'Start making the plans to get my keys cut.'

Dean had totally rocked the game. One moment Irina had been chalking her cue and working out her strategy, the next there were no more balls left and Dean was doing a very undignified victory jig. 'Tell her to wear something black and slinky,' he'd leered.

She wasn't the sort of person to renege on a deal, but if Dean didn't stop texting her to ask when his 'hot date with your hot mate' was, Irina was seriously considering skipping the country without leaving a forwarding address.

But Irina hadn't had a chance to work on Laura. When she'd been in London, Laura had been in Miami. When Laura had been in London, Irina had been in Berlin. And she couldn't call Laura up because they didn't do that. They'd never even swapped phone numbers.

It wasn't as if Laura would refuse a date with someone she'd described to Candy as 'my future ex-husband because we'd get married in this passionate, romantic haze, which would burn itself out, but we'd always love each other'. God, she was so wet. But Irina didn't ever want to be in the position where she did Laura a favour. Or worse, Laura did her favour. Favours meant you were in someone's debt.

But as luck wouldn't have it, when Irina arrived back in Camden on one drizzly May evening, Laura was in situ and taking a pile of damp washing out of the machine.

'Oh, it's you,' Laura said, looking up from her pile of darks.

'And you,' Irina said, just catching her sneer in time. She propped her suitcase by the kitchen door and opened the fridge. A mound of food labelled with other people's names stared back at her. She burrowed further into the fridge and contemplated nicking one of Candy's yoghurts, when there was a cough behind her.

'My mum came down for the weekend and she brought, like, enough home-made cakes and biscuits to feed an army,' Laura said. 'I can't eat them, Hadley doesn't do sugar or carbs, and Candy's in New York.'

Jesus. Why did it take her so long to get to the point?

'I guess you could have them,' Laura continued. 'It's really wasteful to throw food away.'

Irina shut the fridge door. 'Have you spat on them?'

'No,' Laura bit out. 'I just liberally doused them with arsenic.'

'You making a joke?' Irina queried, because she was never sure with that flat accent or Laura's complete lack of a sense of humour.

'I'll give you a five-second warning if I feel a joke coming on, so you have time to prepare,' Laura replied, shoving half her washing back in the machine. 'The food's in my cupboard, do NOT eat my no-fat potato crisps, and this stuff will be dry in an hour so you can use the washing machine after.'

It was the most civil conversation they'd had in . . . well, Irina couldn't remember the last time they'd ever had one, which had to bode well. And Dean's lipstick-smattered picture was still on the wall. Now if she could just pretend that she was doing Laura a good turn out of the kindness of her heart, then Irina might even retain some small shreds of dignity.

Irina's chance came later, as she was stretched out watching *Supernatural* and methodically working her way through Mrs Laura's baked goods – though her daughter was a pain, the woman knew how to make a cake. It also hadn't gone unnoticed that there was a pile of estate agents' brochures on the table. It really did look like their not-so-happy home was about to get broken.

Laura wandered out of the bathroom, bare-faced and in her pyjamas. Just for a second, Irina's breath hitched as the other girl's beauty caught her unawares, like she was seeing her for the first time. Girls like Laura always got what they wanted, even when they didn't even know they wanted it, like dates with rock stars. While Irina had to scratch and fight and work like a dog for everything. For the millionth time, it just wasn't fair.

Irina shook her head impatiently. There was no point in seething when she had to make good on her promise to Dean. But Laura had taken one look at Irina all comfy on her nest of cushions and was backing away.

'The cake's good,' Irina said quickly, trying to keep her there a little longer. 'Thank your mother for me.'

Laura nearly went cross-eyed. 'Are you thanking me?'

'Well, your mother, but same diff,' Irina clarified. 'Her chocolate cake is almost as good as Russian chocolate cake.' Actually it was better. Much, much better.

'You're so lucky,' Laura said quietly, taking a couple of baby steps until she was almost in the room. 'You can eat whatever you like, you do no exercise and you never put on any weight.'

'Jav—' Damn! She'd declared a moratorium on that

particular name. 'Some people think I have a tapeworm,' Irina said, 'but my family are all thin.' She cast an assessing glance over Laura, who looked like she'd lost a couple of pounds, which meant that she'd upped the exercise and reined in the eating. It also meant that her mood would be edgy. Time to try a compliment. 'Anyway, the fat thing works for you. All the Russian girls hate you for bringing the curves back.'

Laura's lips trembled. 'Do you know how much it upsets me when you say the F-word?' she asked in a querulous voice.

'I didn't say fu—'

'I meant *fat*! All you ever do is ride me about the way I look and it really hurts my feelings.' Laura looked away, a sure sign that the tears would be putting in an appearance soon. 'You make me feel like this ugly lump who doesn't deserve to be here.'

Irina wriggled uncomfortably. Her months of psychological warfare had paid off, but it was starting to feel like a hollow victory. 'You got the Siren contract, ja?'

'Yeah, I did, but a season from now the athletic look will be in or the waif will be back and I'm finished.' Laura flopped down on one of the armchairs. 'I've had to work my arse off to get all of this and yeah, I've been lucky too, I know that, but not as lucky as you.'

'I'm not lucky,' Irina protested. 'I didn't get a perfume campaign worth millions. I just get on the plane, get off the plane. Model this, model that.'

'But you didn't even want to be a model and it just fell into your lap. You were booked right from the start; you've done tons of the really swank designer campaigns and just about every foreign edition of *Vogue* there is, you've done TV ads and music videos, and you get booked for way more catwalk than I do.' Laura ticked off Irina's long list of accomplishments on her fingers. 'You don't even care about how cool all that is. I've wanted to be a model for ever, but I know I have a really short shelf life. I'm like a yoghurt and you're like a carton of UHT milk.'

'I not get the reference,' Irina said crossly. 'And you talk crap. Yeah, I try to make lots of money, but tomorrow I could go out of fashion too.'

Laura snorted and started rifling through the ubiquitous pile of fashion magazines on the table. 'Ha!' she snapped, opening one and flicking through the pages before she showed Irina a spread. 'Believe me, you are going to be modelling when you're in your seventies. Look!'

Irina couldn't even remember where the pictures had been taken; all her shoots seemed to merge into one never-ending merry-go-round of studios and bright lights. The two pages were split into eight pictures of Irina. Just Irina in a plain black vest on a white background, no make-up, pulling different faces, each one more stupid than the last. She had a vague memory of a really camp photographer laughing as she pulled her ghetto face and then her haughty model face and even her Laura face, but she never imagined they'd end up in a magazine.

'No one ever says I'm beautiful!' Irina snapped. 'I get "edgy" and "striking" and "savage" and "alien" and other words that mean that I not look like the other girls.'

'But that's good! You're unique. The only unique thing about me is the size of my bum,' Laura sighed. 'I swear to God, Irina, you really need to get over yourself and start having some fun that doesn't involve eating junk food.'

Since when did Irina become the girl who nodded as she was given advice that she'd never asked for in the first place? 'I have fun,' she said sulkily. She had fun with Dean, though that usually involved swapping insults and moaning at each other. And she had fun . . . Correction, she *used* to have fun with Javier, when she hadn't been arguing with him. Mocking and fighting and throwing tantrums had been fun, but she wasn't allowed to do that any more, so right now, nothing was as much fun as a hot bag of chips laced with salt and vinegar. She was truly pathetic. But she still hadn't played her joker. 'Do you like having the fun, Laura?'

It might have been the first time that she'd ever called Laura by her name instead of 'fat arse'. Maybe that was why the other girl looked so wary, like Irina was about to stick her fingers in the plug socket. 'Sure, why?'

Irina shrugged. 'No reason.' She paused for a count of five. 'Would going on a date with that guy from The Hormones be fun?'

'No, it wouldn't be fun,' Laura said, pinking up nicely. 'Because it would mean that I was dead and in heaven. Because in heaven I go on dates with Dean Speed and I eat tons of chocolate and don't put on any weight.'

A simple yes or no would have done, Irina thought, proceeding with caution. 'I know Dean,' she said casually. 'I did that video with him, ja?'

All of a sudden she had Laura's unblinking attention. 'Ted never told me that,' she breathed. 'Oh my God, hang on.'

Irina watched in amazement as Laura jumped to her feet, did two complete circuits of the living room, then sat down again. 'OK, tell me everything and don't skip bits. How tall is he? Does he smell nice? Is he really going out with that awful Sandrine? The band were so much better before she was in it. Because Karis saw her snogging this other guy in this club in Barcelona.'

It was like mugging a crippled old lady. Too easy. 'I set you up on a date. With Dean,' Irina said as casually as if she was offering to get Laura a box of Tampax when she next went to Sainsbury's. 'If you want.'

'If I want? Get out of here!' Laura screeched.

Now it was just a matter of getting something in return from Laura – but what? They didn't wear the same size shoes and Laura was at least two dress sizes bigger. Mind you, there was always her new Marc Jacobs bag, which she didn't seem to love quite as much as she loved Dean. And then Irina realized that she was smirking triumphantly, and five minutes too soon.

'You're smirking. Why are you smirking?' Laura demanded. 'And why are you offering to set me up with Dean Speed? I bet you don't even know him.'

'I'm in his bloody video!' Irina grabbed her phone and scrolled through her pictures until she found a snap of the two of them mugging for the camera. 'See, proof!'

'But you were smirking.' Laura wasn't letting go of that fact any time soon. 'Are you setting me up just because you know it would make me happier than having a super-fast metabolism? As if! What's in it for you?'

Irina had to give the girl props. She was slightly less stupid than she'd thought. 'He beat me at pool, so I promise to get you on a date with him.'

'But you and I are not mates. You could have just said that you'd asked me and I blew him out.'

'I don't break promises,' Irina said staunchly. 'If I say I do something, then I do it.'

Now Laura was smirking as she stretched out her arms and legs and gave a luxurious little shimmy. 'I always knew this day would come, but I never expected it to be so soon or that I'd be wearing Hello Kitty pyjamas.' She was wearing one of those Pollyanna smiles that Irina particularly detested because once again, everything she wanted was just falling into her lap. But Irina wasn't even close. 'Finally, I've got power over you *and* I get to go out with the most obscenely handsome man in the world. There is no bad here.'

'But if you want to go out with him, then you have no power over me,' Irina pointed out.

'Yeah, but now that I know he fancies me I can just get Ted to call his people and make it happen!' Laura clapped her hands in glee. 'Unless you do me a favour. I was all depressed before and now I think I might keel over from sheer happiness.'

Irina hadn't thought it possible, but she preferred Laura when she was whining and weeping. 'What favour?' she asked tersely, imagining a long list of demands and counter-demands that would involve such unpleasant tasks as not eating anything with a calorie content of more than a hundred in front of Laura and doing the washing up.

It was worse than that. 'You have to say sorry to Hadley,' Laura said instantly because she didn't even need time to think about it. 'And you have to make it convincing.'

That was so typical of Laura to pick something entirely selfless, instead of aiming straight for the jugular. Irina would never be able to respect her.

'Just Hadley, not Candy?' she clarified.

A flicker of irritation appeared on Laura's face and stayed there. 'Don't even talk to me about Candy!' she hissed. 'She's worked my last nerve for the very last time.'

'So I apologize to Hadley and you go out with Dean?'

Laura nodded. 'And don't do any of that passive-aggressive shit like leaving her presents. You have to tell her that you were way out of line and that you're sorry.' She gave Irina a stern look. 'You really hurt her feelings and Candy's been making her life a living hell ever since.'

Irina stared at her feet. It didn't matter how much she earned a day or how many covers she racked up, her ability to disappoint people never changed. 'OK,' she agreed finally. 'I sort things out with Hadley.'

'Cool,' Laura said with smug satisfaction. 'And I'll give you a list of dates that I'm free for Dean.' She sighed dreamily. 'I don't know what I'm going to wear – I've been planning this since I was fifteen and I still haven't narrowed down my wardrobe choices.'

Chapter Twenty-Seven

Irina had always taken it for granted that Hadley would be around when she needed her for make-up tips or a mutual bitchfest about Candy. Her presence had always been constant during the bad old days when she'd been hungover and moping about the flat, wincing if the light was too bright or the TV was too loud.

And even when she got her shit together, she was still in London making her movie or co-hosting a lame-ass Friday night chat show or sucking face with Reed. But now according to Derek, her booker, 'She's scheduled up the wazoo. At the moment, she's taking meetings in Hollywood before she flies to Australia. Maybe you could give me a message to pass on.'

So Irina left messages because Hadley had changed her number and not bothered to inform her former sort-of-friend of this exciting development. She'd often wondered how Hadley had ever got famous when she seemed to have the killer instinct of a bunny rabbit, but now her steely reserve in not returning any of Irina's calls made perfect sense.

When Irina found out that Hadley had been back in London for three days and was still maintaining radio silence, there was only one possible course of action. She walked over to the little cul de sac in Primrose Hill where Reed was renting a house and knocked on every door until the man himself answered.

'What do you want?' he asked, rubbing a hand through his already messy hair.

'I need to talk to Hadley. Is she in?'

'No,' Reed said quickly, too quickly, with an almost imperceptible look over his shoulder.

'Fine, I wait,' Irina said decisively, brushing Reed out of the way as she pushed past him.

'You can't just barge in here,' Reed complained, but she already had and she could hear the lady of the house's voice floating down the hall.

'Mr C-C, I told you a million times that Daddy gets angry if you chew up his sneakers, even if they are really ratty. You're a very naughty doggy.'

Irina could feel Reed's eyes trying to burn a hole in her back as she strode down the hall towards a big kitchen where Hadley was perched on a stool, drinking something pale green with a few leaves floating in it. She looked startled as Irina walked in. 'What are you doing here?'

'She just pushed her way in,' Reed said behind her. 'Jesus, Hads, don't let him sit on the breakfast bar, it's really unhygienic.'

Hadley looked at Mr C-C in amazement, like she didn't

know how he'd managed to get up there. 'He's got a real head for heights,' she cooed. 'Are you my brave little boy?' Then she turned off the doting mama routine when she remembered that Irina was still there and that she was still pissed with her. 'How dare you come here?'

'I left you many messages but you never reply,' Irina said, leaning against the counter and giving Reed a glare right back with extra zest. 'You got really rude, Hadley, I never expect that from you.'

She did expect Hadley's gasp of outrage because attack was the best form of defence. Always was and always would be.

'Well, I don't think that's fair...'

'I'm sorry, OK? I'm sorry I blackmail you over the movie and I'm sorry that I tell Candy that you two were sha— *involved*, and that she's been the huge bitch ever since. I'm sorry. Now get over it.'

'It's not as simple as that,' Hadley said primly. 'It was, like, you stabbed me in the back and then spat on my bleeding body and—'

'I'm sorry for that too,' Irina replied implacably, though Hadley was stretching the metaphor way too far.

'And it's taken you *weeks* to look deep inside yourself and realize it was your deeply scarred psyche that was to blame for—'

'I'm sorry for that too,' Irina gritted. 'Whatever you and your shrink want to throw at me, fine! I'm sorry. Either accept it or not but stop psycho-babbling me.'

Irina was in the wrong; she could deal with that newsflash. But she wasn't going to let Hadley completely whip her into the bargain. 'You really need to work on your hostility issues, Irina.'

'Noted,' she said through a frozen smile, though what she really meant was 'bite me'. 'Now, you accept the apology or not?'

Hadley took a ruminative sip of the noxious green liquid. 'Accepted, I guess.' But just as Irina began to unclench, Hadley smiled a little evilly. 'That is to say, you're on probation.'

'Whatever,' Irina sighed, fishing for her phone so she could send Laura a text message: HADLEY OK, DEAN CAN DO FRIDAY. Even though she still had quite a few characters to play with, she didn't use the word 'fat', which showed what a gigantic pussy she was turning into.

Reed looked like he wasn't completely down with the peace deal that Irina had just brokered. He opened his mouth to say something, but was interrupted by a ring on the bell. 'That's my cab,' he said, picking up a leather case, before dropping a casual kiss on Hadley's forehead. 'If you borrow the car, do not go anywhere near the congestion zone, baby.'

Hadley nodded, though Irina was pretty sure that she didn't even know what the congestion zone was. 'OK, hon, don't forget to take your vitamins,' she said, absently stroking his cheek as Reed dutifully popped something in his mouth.

Irina tried not to stare, but she envied them their easy intimacy. How they could be themselves with each other and not worry about being rejected or laughed out of the room.

'I haven't forgiven you,' Reed said silkily in Irina's ear, like she could care, but then he was gone, and it was just her and Hadley, who was looking at her Sidekick. 'Message from Laura,' she noted out loud. 'Ooooh! She's going on a date with that dirty-looking boy from The Hormones.'

'I know,' Irina said, unable to resist wiggling her way further into Hadley's good books. 'Me, I set them up.'

Hadley's frequent gasps of outrage really weren't something she'd missed. 'Oh, you! Why would you do something like that?'

'Because I lose a bet, which Laura knows about but she not care less. Too interested in getting her sticky hands on Dean, innit.' 'Innit' was Irina's newest British word – though she was never completely sure where it should be in a sentence.

'But she doesn't know that Dean's your boyfriend!' Hadley looked as if she was about to fly off her stool in sheer frustration. 'And don't try to deny it. Javier told me everything!'

Irina had trained herself not even to think his name, but just hearing Hadley say it in her breathless, girly voice made all those tired feelings wash over her. Regret was an even bigger bitch than Candy. 'When did you see him?'

'I saw his book and he did some publicity shots for me.' Hadley allowed herself a tiny, triumphant smile. 'He's very reasonably priced right now and he makes me look more grown up without looking older. He's a genius!'

Oh, Irina had a few words to describe him and none of them started with a G. Well, apart from 'git'. 'And you talk about me?'

'We had far more important things to talk about than *you*,' Hadley told her sharply. 'Like what lighting worked best for me and whether a fish-eye lens would make my hips look big. Besides, you're the last thing Jav wants to talk about after you broke his heart and stomped all over it in your filthy sneakers.' Hadley looked at Irina's Vans like there were still smears of blood on them.

'I don't break his heart,' Irina burst out. Breaking someone's heart implied that they were madly in love with you, which hadn't been the case. 'He just wanted the casual hook-up, and that's what he got and then he—'

'Well, I don't know all the details because we totally didn't talk about you, but he said that you didn't have a romantic, caring bone in your body, and that you were seeing that Dean and kept reminding him about it at every opportunity. Not cool, Irina.'

'I didn't . . . I not . . . Dean's just a friend, and Javier – I hate him. He's not fit to be in the same room with me.' Irina drew herself up so she was tall and proud. 'He not know how to be a proper boyfriend even if he got instructions. With the bullet points!'

Hadley shrugged, like the conversation had gone on too long and her attention was wavering. 'Well, he did seem quite cut up, but Reed's going to set him up with a few actresses he knows. Everyone loves Javier, he's so fiery and passionate and cute. Not as cute as Reed, but semi-cute. Cute lite, as it were.'

Any time Hadley wanted to shut up about Javier and his alleged cuteness was fine with Irina. 'I go now,' she said abruptly, because only a trip to an Indian takeaway for two servings of chicken biryani and some naan bread would be able to fill the gaping hole which had suddenly opened up in her chest. 'I'm glad that we sort stuff out.'

And the funny thing was that it was true. Hadley was annoying a lot of the time. But the good, amusing annoying which made Irina feel positively well adjusted in comparison.

'Me too,' Hadley beamed. 'I'll check that Candy's out of the country and I'll move back to the apartment for a while.' Then she remembered something very important. 'But you're still on probation. There are terms, I'll let you know what they are at a later date.'

Irina couldn't wait.

★ ★ ★

There had been major motion pictures, even wars and state funerals, that had less planning than Dean and Laura's date.

Irina was actually relieved to get a sucky job in Dubai, doing catwalk for some rich oil sheikh's wives, so she wouldn't have to hear about it. But she'd forgotten about that cunning technological gadget called the mobile phone, with its stupid international roaming.

Irina had created a monster.

Laura wanted to know every single thing Dean had said about her. She wanted to check in triplicate that his relationship with Sandrine was officially over and she wanted to know how far up the waiting list Irina was for the new Mulberry clutch bag, which went perfectly with her second reserve outfit.

Dean wanted to know Laura's complete dating history. How long she'd been a fan, with particular reference to early Hormones versus late Hormones. He also wanted to know if she actually ate ('I don't want to be stuffing my face, while she's nibbling at one bloody lettuce leaf') and what the likelihood of her putting out was. 'I've changed my meds so I'm feeling pretty optimistic, if you know what I mean,' he'd told Irina before she threw her phone out of the hotel window so it landed in the infinity pool below.

And when Hadley started getting in on the act with lists of London restaurants faxed over under headings like *Best for romance, Best for hot waiters if the date isn't going too well, Best for low carb menu options*, Irina contemplated phoning Ted and asking if she never had to go back to London ever again.

But it was nothing compared to the actual day of the date itself. Laura had been in a spa for *hours*. She'd left the house before Irina had woken up and was now locked in her room with Hadley, as manic giggling and the ear-mangling sounds of The Hormones leaked under the door.

'He's not going to get on with her,' Candy muttered from the armchair, where she was sewing sequins on to something white and lacy. 'Laura's far too vanilla to keep him interested.'

Irina grunted something that was a close cousin to agreement. The balance of power had shifted once again in the flat. Laura and Hadley ruled the roost and the remote control, Irina was straddling a thin line between acceptance and merely being tolerated, and Candy was the bad seed. As an anthropological study, it was interesting to watch someone else fall from grace, rather than be the one to fall. It was also impressive that Laura and Hadley could laugh and joke not three feet away from Candy, yet pretend that she wasn't even in the same room. Candy just stuck out her chin, put on her iPod and sewed some more ridiculous garments, but Irina could tell from the pained little furrow on her forehead how much she didn't like it.

It was all kinds of odd, but Irina was starting to feel just the tiniest bit sorry for Candy. She knew what it felt like to always be the underdog and it ranked about as highly as the two weeks she'd spent working in an industrial laundry on the outskirts of Moscow.

'You know what's weird?' Candy suddenly asked, leaning forward and not waiting for Irina's reply. 'That night we were in NYC, I have this distinct memory of you locked in a clinch with Dean. I think there were tongues.'

Irina was surprised that anything had penetrated the quite spectacular hissy fit Candy had been having. 'In Russia we kiss our friends hello. Is no big deal.'

Candy didn't look like she was buying that for one itty-bitty second. 'Yeah, but—'

'Irina! Get in here!' Laura called. 'We need a wardrobe consult.'

Candy snorted derisively as Irina sprang to answer the summons. There was an unpleasant smell in her room, possibly from the unwashed crockery she'd shoved under the bed, otherwise she'd be hiding in there. Either way, anything was better than Candy's cross-examination.

'I'm having a clothing crisis!' Laura announced when Irina slouched in the doorway. Every single inch of her tiny room was covered in mounds of material. A pile of dresses. A mountain of jeans. A teetering tower of shoes. Well, at least there was a system. 'I need to know if he's into the rock-chick thing? And if you mention the F-word while you're in here, I will kill you – I'm that stressed.'

Irina tried not to breathe in the asphyxiating fumes of body lotion, Siren and the lingering odour of singed hair because Laura always turned her straighteners up too high. The whole situation made icy fingers trail a path up and down her spine. It was way too far out of her comfort zone. 'He said something about a little black dress.'

As Laura was currently wearing a pair of boy-cut panties and a camisole, that wasn't going to work as date-wear. She gave a squawk and started rummaging. 'Maybe if I put on the gutbuster knickers, I can wear the Gucci?'

'No, you have to be comfortable on a date,' said Hadley, like she was the Oracle. 'Especially if you're having dinner. I'd wear a tunic dress so you don't have to worry about unsightly bulges if you decide to have dessert.'

Laura changed direction and started rifling through another pile. 'I got a fax from Dean's assistant,' she explained, obviously mistaking Irina for someone who was even a little bit interested. 'He's taking me to that new place, Canteen, where you share tables with other people.'

'Which isn't that romantic,' Hadley piped up. 'But it shows that he wants you to be in a relaxed environment. He's obviously very caring.'

Irina gave a contemptuous sniff. 'Dean's not caring,' she scoffed. 'But cling to that illusion if it make you happy.'

'Are you sure you're not dating him?' Laura asked, eyes narrowing as she wriggled into something grey and clingy.

'Dean's a dick, innit,' Irina said, not even having to fake being offended. 'He's arrogant and selfish and he take the piss all the time. Oh yeah and he belches after food.'

'So he's like the male version of you?'

Irina glared so hard she could barely see. 'I do not belch.'

'You do after you've eaten that smelly Russian sausage,' Hadley giggled, and this was getting way off topic.

'I'm not dating Dean,' she said for what felt like the millionth time.

'Reed has this theory that she was trying to make Javier jealous,' Hadley announced, like it was all right to talk about Irina as if she wasn't actually present.

Laura was momentarily distracted from the shoe pile. 'Really? Does that ever work outside of some lame-o Shakespeare play?'

Irina wished they'd both shut up and die right there and then. Or that she had some dirt on one of them. Divide and conquer would simple things up so much and stop them ganging up on her. 'I not try to make Javier jealous because I'm over him. Please don't be judging me by your own petty, bourgeois standards,' she said haughtily, though really she wanted to scream it from the rooftops. Instead she ran her eyes over Laura, who was now wearing a skinny jeans and smock top combo. 'That make you look even more fat than you normally do,' she said, already backing out as one of Laura's shoes just missed her head and ricocheted off the doorframe.

Eventually, Laura ran out of the flat ten minutes late and Hadley, with a pointed look at the sequin-sewing lump of huff that was Candy, made her excuses and left.

As the door shut behind them, Candy gave a tiny sigh. 'You want to share a stuffed crust pizza and some garlic bread?' she asked Irina, fishing for the appropriate menu.

They shared pizza in an almost uncomfortable, almost silence until Candy finished sewing and Irina finished watching a *Behind The Music* with Notorious B.I.G. 'You know, Laura was meant to be off boys for life,' Candy remarked, apropos of absolutely bloody nothing. 'We had this whole "single girls together" thing. And she knows that I liked Dean too. I was into The Hormones way before her.'

Irina decided not to point out that Dean didn't share that like. There was no fun to be had in kicking someone who was that down. Even if it was Candy. 'They have nothing in common,' she said because it was the truth, and it made Candy perk up for a little while.

'They really don't,' she agreed, before slumping into the cushions again. 'But neither do Reed and Sadley, but they're still poncing about like love's young dream. It's beyond nauseating.'

Candy really needed to stop with the dressmaking and get out a bit more. If she had a boyfriend, then maybe she'd stop getting so pissy about other people's love lives. 'There's no boy you like?'

'No!' Candy seemed scandalized at the suggestion. 'Look, Irina, OK we had pizza together but that doesn't mean we're going to start braiding each other's hair and having deep, bondy conversations about cute boys. *Capiche?'*

Irina shuddered at the thought. 'Like, I would want to bond with you?'

'Right back at you,' Candy snapped.

'Fine.'

'Good, fine.'

Irina was saved from having to think of another four-letter word by her Blackberry ringing. As ever, her heart gave a little flutter, but it would only be Ted or Famke or one of the three other people that ever rang her.

And it was. It was Dean.

'Why are you ringing me?' Irina asked, standing up and walking out, to escape Candy's squinty line of vision. 'I tell you she's boring and wet, but you never listen.'

'This is the worst date I've ever been on,' Dean hissed. 'You have to come down here.'

'No, I don't think so.'

'Yes, you do, because I'm about to stab myself in the eye with my knife,' Dean insisted. 'She's more or less ignored me ever since she got here, apart from the tender moment when she told me that our last album sucked.'

Irina couldn't help but snicker a little. Kudos to Laura – who knew that she had such good taste? 'Tell her she has a fat arse and that you go home.'

'I can't. Come down so at least people think I scored with two models, even if one of them is blanking me.'

Anything was better than staying in with Candy. Irina was already toeing on her ballet flats. 'What's in it for me?'

'My undying gratitude and a side order of fries,' Dean said, but his voice was all throbby, which meant that he'd cave if Irina nudged him ever so slightly.

'I want your PlayStation 3 and you make me your plus one to the next MTV Music Awards,' Irina demanded. Watching VH1 earlier had strengthened her resolve to find a gangsta-rapper boyfriend.

'Done,' Dean said immediately, without even trying to come up with some loopholes to wriggle out of at a later stage. The date must be going really badly.

Irina fairly bounded down the stairs; seeing Dean getting knocked back was going to be an unexpected delight. It sure beat staying in and swapping insults with Candy, though that was fun in its own way too.

Chapter Twenty-Eight

Even as Irina marched across the restaurant, she could tell that Laura was having the time of her life. She was giggling like mad, face flushed, and when she thought no one was looking, she'd preen.

Dean, however, was sitting with his shoulders drooping. Irina could only see his back, but that was emitting so much pain and misery that Irina wanted to slap Laura. Why was she all over the average-looking guy sitting next to her when she had her crush object right there.

'Yo, wassup!' she said, whacking Dean on the shoulder as she slid on to the bench next to him. The other diners grumbled as they slid up to make room for Irina, but if they wanted to eat in a bogus canteen that completely over-charged them for self-service, then they could just get over their pretentious selves.

'I've given up on the stabbing idea,' Dean muttered sourly. 'Can you OD from eating too much salt?'

Laura looked up and gave Irina a little wave. 'Hey,' she trilled, like they were best buds. 'This is Danny. It's the weirdest coincidence, but he practically lives next door to my gran in Chester.'

Danny seemed thrilled to have Laura's grandmother as

an almost-next-door neighbour. 'Pleased to meet you,' he said shyly, holding out his hand for Irina to shake, but she simply stared at it in disdain until he retracted it.

'So, Danny, where did you go to school? I bet one of my cousins was in your year,' Laura said, and Danny turned back to her with this slightly dopefied look like Laura was the sun that he was happy to satellite around.

'We had five minutes of polite chit-chat until that tosser sat down,' Dean muttered out of the side of his mouth. 'He's a footballer or something else that doesn't require any intellect. And then he asked Laura if she used to go to some tacky provincial nightclub in Manchester and they've been yapping ever since.'

'Yeah, I like living in London,' the footballer was saying, while Laura listened attentively like he was explaining how to split the atom. 'But it's not home, is it? People are really unfriendly.'

'I know,' Laura nodded vigorously. 'You try to have a conversation with the man in the cornershop and he bites your head off.'

God, Laura had actually found someone as dull as herself. It was like watching paint dry, but more boring. 'Where are my fries?' Irina mouthed at Dean.

'You have to go up and get them yourself,' Dean snapped. 'Stupid canteen restaurant.'

Irina really didn't see what the problem was. 'Then go and get me some fries. With the ketchup.'

'I bet you get this a lot, but you're really cute.'

Laura smiled coyly. 'You're not so bad yourself. And that was an amazing goal you scored last Saturday, even though I was supporting Man U. You should be ashamed of yourself, playing for Arsenal.'

'I'll resign first thing tomorrow,' Danny grinned. 'Then I'll beg Man U to sign me up so I'm in your good books.'

They were falling in love right before her very eyes. Irina felt like she should look away – or start making with the gagging noises.

Dean thumped a plate of fries down in front of Irina so hard that they almost bounced off the table. 'Unfuckingbelievable,' he hissed, sitting down and jostling Irina with his elbows. 'Having a good time, Laura?' he asked aggressively.

Laura gave him a vague smile like she couldn't quite remember who he was or why he was sitting opposite her. 'Yes, thanks,' she murmured, before turning back to her besotted admirer.

'I told you she not worth the effort,' Irina said, picking up Dean's bottle of beer to wash down a mouthful of distinctly sub-standard fries. 'You can do better than her. I set you up with Russian girl.'

'I'm swearing off models,' Dean said morosely, and Irina had heard that from Javier so it was hard to find it amusing.

'Ah, you say that, but the men all get taken in by the pretty girls.' She pushed her plate away, because Dean's bad mood was contagious. 'Just because they have stupid, shiny hair and pouty lips. Is so predictable.'

'You're a pretty girl with stupid, shiny hair and pouty lips,' Dean pointed out, but Irina was already struggling to her feet.

'Let's go, if I have to look at those two any more, I'll puke.'

Dean didn't need to be told twice. He was already reaching into his wallet and chucking a handful of notes at Laura. 'Thanks for dinner. Let's not ever do it again.'

Laura managed to tear herself away from Danny long enough to bite her lips and flutter her hands helplessly. 'Sorry,' she said. 'I was really looking forward to this evening but . . .' There was really nothing she could say, so she looked imploringly at Irina.

'Come on, Dean,' Irina said, tugging at his wrist. 'I'm hungry.'

Dean shook her hand free and strode off, so Irina had no choice but to scurry after him, as he stalked out of the restaurant, twitching with fury.

'Seriously, next time I ask you to set me up, just bash me over the head with something heavy,' Dean said as they walked along Euston Road. A bag of chips and a couple of cans of lager had restored his good mood. 'I can't believe she dumped me within five minutes for some ball-kicker. And he was far too weedy to be any good in defence.'

'But is funny,' Irina reminded him. She'd been supportive at first, but mostly she'd laughed. In fact, she'd laughed so hard that she'd had to beg the guy in the chippy to let her use the loo. 'You should be happy she manage to find someone on her level. I not think that was possible.'

'A model and a premier division footballer,' Dean scoffed. 'How very mundane and unimaginative. And she wasn't all that in the flesh. Kind of bland actually. I like my girls more edgy.'

They crossed over into Bayham Street and Irina bumped Dean's hip with hers. If Laura and Dean had started dating, it would have been awful. She'd have lost her one proper friend. This way, everyone was happy. Well, except Dean, and he didn't seem that cut up about it. 'If you not find someone in six months, I shag you,' she offered. 'If you get it up this time.'

Dean choked on his lager. 'Joke. Say you were joking.'

'J to the K,' Irina agreed. 'But I totally get you backstage at the shows so you can see models in their knickers.'

'For real?' Dean asked eagerly.

'I promise,' said Irina, jangling her keys as Dean wrapped an arm around her shoulder.

'You're a good friend, Rina,' Dean said, kissing her sloppily on the cheek. 'You're the only person in the world who doesn't try and softsoap me.'

Irina was about to agree when Dean's bony body was suddenly wrenched away.

'Get your filthy hands off her,' said a familiar voice, and Dean was being shoved up against some railings by . . .

'Javier, what are you doing?' Irina yelled, grabbing his shirt collar. 'Have you gone mad?'

Chapter Twenty-Nine

What Javier was doing was trying to take a swing at Dean, who pulled himself free so he could leer in a way that was guaranteed to make the situation ten thousand times worse. 'What's the matter?' he enquired nastily. 'Isn't it a bit late to worry where my filthy hands have been, mate?'

'You're a lousy son of a bitch,' Javier spat, as Irina tried to wriggle in between them so she could knock their fat heads together. 'You're never going to touch her again.'

Irina ducked as the first punch was thrown and all she could do was watch in amazement at the world's most pathetic fight. It was even more pathetic than the fight Hadley and Candy had had. There wasn't so much pummelling as hair-pulling and dancing about, as they tried to get each other in a headlock.

'Not the hands,' Dean shouted. 'Or the face. I'll sue you, you wanker.'

'You can't sue me when you're in hospital having all your food through a straw,' Javier snarled back.

In Irina's humble opinion, they should concentrate less on the verbal posturing and more on the actual fighting, because neither of them was earning any macho points.

Dean was now trying to trip Javier over and Javier was clinging on to Dean's shirt, and breaking it up was as easy as pulling them apart and grabbing an earlobe apiece. 'You are complete jackasses,' Irina gritted as they yelped in pain. 'I know three ways to separate the ears from the heads with my bare hands. You want me to show you, ja?'

Turned out that they really didn't.

Irina let them go but kept a warning hand on their puffed-up chests. 'What are you doing here?' she asked Javier, who flushed dark red.

'I'm not saying in front of him,' he muttered, casting a black look in Dean's direction.

'Well, I'm not going anywhere.' Dean had recovered enough to smirk. 'So wasted trip, mate.'

'I'm *not* your mate.'

Irina could feel Javier's heart thudding away beneath her fingertips and she wanted to curl her hand over it, wanted to brush his hair back from his face and check for cuts and bruises. Ugh, she hated these tender feelings; they made her feel nauseous.

'Why are you here?' she asked again, her voice low, but Javier turned his head away.

'Get rid of him.'

Dean was gingerly prodding the corner of his mouth. 'I do have a name, you know.' He really wasn't helping the situation at all. In fact, the situation was entirely outside of Irina's remit. Two boys fighting over her? Hadley or Laura would have exploded with sheer joy, but Irina let her hands fall to her sides and shrugged.

'Thanks for walking me back,' she said to Dean. 'And if you not going to talk to me then why did you come here?' she added to Javier, who could look as downcast as he liked. Whatever. 'I'm going home.'

Going home took ten paces and she could still hear Dean and Javier behind her. Not shouting. But not sounding as if they were about to become bosom buddies.

Irina was just turning her key in the lock when Javier finally sidled up the steps. 'I was being a man.'

That warranted a sniff. 'Huh?'

'In Paris you told me to act like a man, so I came over here to be this caveman that you seem to want. Maybe throw you over my shoulder . . .'

'You throw me over your shoulder and I kill you,' Irina said, just so they were clear on that. Actually that wasn't important right now. 'You came over here to show me that you were a man? Why would you do that?'

Javier groaned. 'I wish I hadn't, because all it meant was that I got to watch him paw you and touch you and run his beady eyes over you while you enjoyed it.'

'I did not . . . Dean wasn't. He's just my friend. For real,' Irina snapped, pushing the door open. 'Stop talking in riddles and tell me why you're here.'

'Do you know something, Irina? You're the scariest, most intimidating person I've ever met, and it's hard to say

273

anything to you when you look at me like I've just crawled up from the sewers.'

'I can't help the way my stupid face looks!' She'd been thinking about inviting him in, maybe nursing his wounds, but after that he could just limp off and bleed slowly to death from the tiny scratch on his cheek. 'I don't look like those other girls that you always flirt with, I got that message loud and clear.'

Javier ruined her perfectly good flounce by grabbing her arm and hauling her up the stairs. He was taking the caveman thing way too far.

'Get the hell off me!'

'I was fighting for you back there,' Javier said furiously.

'I not need anyone to fight for me. I can stand up for myself,' Irina flung at him, marching into the flat and not caring if he was following.

She could hear his footsteps behind her as she opened the freezer door and rooted around. 'Put this on your eye,' she said, throwing a bag of chips at him on her way out.

'It's all very well you telling me to act like a man, but have you ever thought about acting like a girl?'

She slammed her bedroom door hard enough that Candy thumped an angry tattoo on the wall. Irina sat on her bed for just a second before the need to angrily pace the floor roused her to her feet.

What did he mean? Act like a girl? She *was* a girl; a silly girl who let her emotions get the better of her all the time. How could Javier not see that?

Irina stood in front of the mirror and took a long, hard look at herself to see if she could see what Javier did. She saw a tall, thin girl with a belligerent cast to her face, chin stuck out, fists clenched like she was about to go ten rounds in a boxing match. It wasn't a very user-friendly picture.

Her fingers worked at the elastic band, scraping her hair back so it fell around her cheeks in those thick waves that weren't quite straight and weren't quite curly. Then Irina dropped to her knees and started rummaging under the bed, pulling out neatly folded clothes that she'd stashed under there. Freebies that she'd sworn she'd never wear. Her hands closed around smooth, slippery satin.

Once she'd pulled it on, she scrabbled at the top of the chest of drawers, rifling through the make-up that she'd amassed until she found a tube called Sugar Kiss. Why lipsticks had such dumb names, she didn't know, but Irina pulled the top off and slicked some on, hating the greasy feel of it on her lips.

She couldn't stand to do more than glance at herself in the mirror and all she could see were pink ruffles, a hint of a ruched bodice, a foofy skirt swishing about her legs. Christ, she looked like a freaking wedding cake – but if that's what it took, then she'd even place a plastic bride and groom on top of her head. She really would.

The only clue she had that Javier was still on the

premises was that she hadn't heard him leave. And as soon as she quietly opened the door, he was there; trying to look dignified with a bag of frozen chips clutched to his head.

The dignity was quickly replaced by a look that could only be called 'slack-jawed yokel' as Irina placed her hands on her hips and posed in her nice-girl's outfit.

'What did you do?' he breathed, eyes running over every ruffle and flounce. 'You look like you had a run-in with a Barbie doll.'

Irina glowered for a second and then dialled it down to a pout. 'I *can* be a girl,' she said fiercely, gesturing downwards at the pastel-coloured frou-frou. 'See? Girl!'

Javier opened his mouth to say something, but was interrupted by Candy sticking her head out of her room. 'For God's sake, don't have arguments in the corridor when I'm trying to hand-sew!' she snarled, and Irina grabbed Javier's hand and hauled him inside her room. Which actually, wasn't very girly. She should have stood aside, with her head lowered, and let him . . .

'What you said before? You don't need to stand up to me,' Javier murmured, sitting on the edge of her bed. 'I'm on your side. But you make it really hard a lot of the time.'

'You're not on my side,' Irina reminded him, striding over so she could tower above him and glare. She really did suck at being a girl. 'First you say you don't date models and then you dump me!'

'I didn't date models, but then I met you and you were

276

rude and obnoxious and a whole bunch of other things that shouldn't have been attractive, but they were, and then I realized that you didn't even want a relationship . . .' Javier tailed off, and just as Irina was trying to work out if there was a backhanded compliment in there somewhere, he continued. 'I don't ever know what you want.'

'I want you,' Irina said quietly, her face more fiery than a thousand suns. 'Not just for the sex, but for the dating stuff too. But you never want to go on the dates with me.'

Javier leant back on his elbows and pursed his lips. God, he was so beautiful. 'What makes you say that?'

'Because you never call me,' Irina burst out, the anger rising up again. 'And after I force you to make plans, you want to stay on the beach and watch the moon rather than being seen with me.'

'It was romantic . . .'

'I get sand in my pants! What's romantic about that?' Irina demanded, hands on her hips.

'I didn't take you out on dates because I have no money,' Javier announced, his face a perfect crimson match for her own. 'Aaron pays me, but mostly I work for free and just about cover my rent. I don't have the cash for expensive restaurants and clubs and bottles of champagne. And if I don't call you, it's because it's humiliating not to pay my own way. You have your Russian thing, I have my South American male pride thing.'

Irina couldn't believe what she was hearing. 'I never ask

you to buy me champagne. It tastes like cat pee anyway. You buy me pizza and beer and that's cool.'

'Yeah, Beatriz used to say that until she started getting really successful and then she was out the door because I couldn't keep her in diamonds and designer handbags.' Javier rubbed his hands across his eyes and he looked tired. Not tired, but exhausted, as if all the life had been sucked from him. One day, Irina would meet this Beatriz and they would be having words. Oh yes. 'You remind me of her sometimes because it's always got to be about you, Irina. You're so busy being angry at the world, that there's no room in it for me.'

'I make room for you.' She was perilously close to begging now. 'I see an anger management specialist to find new ways to express my frustration.' Irina paused. 'It's not working so well.'

She expected Javier to smile, but if anything he looked even more defeated. 'We're never going to have a relationship, are we? All we do is have sex or argue, and all the big, dramatic gestures in the world aren't going to change that.'

He'd given up on her. Apart from that pathetic tussle with Dean, he wasn't even prepared to fight for them. Irina sank to the floor as a prelude to telling Javier to get out, but that wasn't what she heard coming out of her mouth. 'You say that you give me what I want, as long as it's not champagne, but what do you want from me?'

278

Javier didn't even have to think about it. 'I want you to be soft sometimes.'

He didn't want her soft; he wanted her weak. They were the same thing. And top of the list of the many things that Irina didn't do was weakness. She'd learnt her lesson young. How many times had her mother let her father come back, despite the fights and the drinking and the bruises? He'd turn up with a wilting bunch of flowers and a see-through sorry smile and she always took him back.

Being weak hadn't put thousands upon thousands of pounds in her bank account so that she was ready to buy a four-bedroom villa in the Golden Triangle for her mother.

Fighting for every single thing she'd got was the only way that Irina knew and she wasn't going to stop, even for Javier. She'd lose her edge, the jobs would dry up, and she'd be just another girl who'd given everything up for love and found that it wasn't enough. Love didn't pay the bills or put food on the table or force people to respect you. Soft was for losers.

'No,' she said, shaking her head and not looking at him because she couldn't bear to see the disappointment on his face. 'I give you anything but that. I wear pink dresses for you, I hold your hand and introduce you to the morons I live with, but I won't let you take away my hardness. It is asking me to choose you over my career so, no. I won't be soft for you.'

Javier was already stumbling to his feet. 'You break my

heart,' he muttered. 'You can't let anyone in, can you? Well, I hope you like loneliness, because that's all there is in your future.'

There should have been a snappy reply all primed and ready, but Irina had a horrible feeling that Javier was right. 'Get out,' she said flatly. 'We're done here.'

Chapter Thirty

From closely observing her flatmates in times of deep emotional distress, Irina knew that she should take to her bed with a cuddly toy, several bars of Dairy Milk and a box of tissues until she'd got over her grief.

Except she was fine, thank you very much. As she told Candy the next day.

'I heard Javier slam out of here at some ungodly hour,' Candy imparted as she mixed up some chocolate milk. 'And before that there was shouting.'

Irina waited for the inevitable explosion about waking Candy up, but it never came. Instead the other girl patted Irina gently on the arm. 'You all right?'

'I'm fine,' Irina replied stoutly. 'Is no big deal.'

'Do you want some chocolate? I've got a stash of Kinder eggs in my cupboard.'

'Not hungry,' Irina blurted out and it was a photo finish as to who was more shocked. She was *always* hungry.

'Oh, Irina,' Candy sighed with a knowing look. 'Don't pine over him. All boys are complete bastards and you're better off without him.'

Since when did Irina take relationship advice from Candy of all people? 'I'm already over him. I not need a man to complete me.' And then she shut up before she could break into a few verses of 'Independent Woman'.

Candy finished throwing chunks of chocolate into the blender. 'Damn straight! There's nothing a man can do for me that I can't do for myself,' she said fiercely, finger poised for imminent chocolate milk production. 'Friends are for ever, boys are what*ever*!'

'You may want to put the lid on first,' Irina pointed out, and she was just musing on how her snark reflex seemed to have malfunctioned when there was the sound of a key turning and Laura floated in, all pink-cheeked and dreamy-eyed.

'I'm in love,' she announced and if that wasn't bad enough, she felt moved to wrap Irina up in a Siren-scented hug. 'And it's all thanks to you.'

'Get. Off. Me!'

'Danny and I stayed up all night,' Laura beamed, letting go of Irina so she could twirl around the kitchen. She didn't even notice Candy picking up the bread knife and making stabbing motions at her back. 'Nothing happened. We just talked. It sounds sappy, but we reckon that we were lovers in a past life because we're, like, so connected and we have so much in common and—'

Going back to bed with a week's supplies was shaping up to be a very good idea. 'He's a footballer,' Irina snapped. 'He shag anything that moves and it ruin your career if you get labelled as a WAG.' She really had to learn to think before she spoke. 'On the other hand you seem happy, keep going out with him.'

Laura hadn't even heard her. 'I'm seeing him again tonight.' She sighed ecstatically. 'Isn't being in love the best thing in the world?'

At least there was work to take Irina's mind off the fact that she was completely unloveable and destined to spend the rest of her life alone until she saw out the end of her days in a New York penthouse apartment with hundreds of cats for company. She didn't even like cats that much, but she'd need someone to talk to.

Although she was sure her misery was written all over her face, her bookings were going through the roof with first, second and even third options on her for the next two months. That was fine with Irina. 'I do two bookings a day if you want,' she told Ted when he took her out for a burger. 'Especially if I'm not in London.' No way was she going to spend hours in anonymous hotel rooms to get all introspective and shit.

'Well, let's see,' Ted murmured as they went through her schedule. 'Everyone loves your new softer look.'

Irina touched her face. It was still all hard planes and angles as far as she could tell. What new softer look was Ted crapping on about?

'But there's no point in over-exposure or working yourself too hard,' Ted continued.

'I like to work too hard and make lots of money.' As far as she knew, her mother had signed the lease on a new house, after much protesting, and now Irina was working towards a New York base. At least she'd have a property portfolio to keep her warm at night.

'You've lost weight,' Ted hedged, peering at her face critically. 'And you haven't touched your fries.'

Irina pushed away her plate. 'I not have any appetite.' It was true. Eating seemed like far too much effort at the moment. She'd tried everything from sauerkraut to stinky sausages to family-sized bags of donuts, but nothing seemed to fill up the space inside her.

'I don't want to have to book you out because the papers have started bitching about you being anorexic,' Ted griped, then realized he sounded majorly unsympathetic. 'Is there something I should know? I bumped into Aaron Murray at an exhibition last week and he said that Javier . . .'

Irina was wide-eyed and suddenly hanging on to Ted's every word because he was about to launch into a big speech about how Javier couldn't live without her, couldn't eat or sleep or get through the day because everything reminded him of Irina, and that he'd made a big mistake, and actually it was really cool to date a girl who was in control and in charge and . . .

'. . . did his first big fashion shoot for *Interview*,' Ted finished, with a mischievous glint in his eyes. 'He's really going places, Aaron was like a proud papa.'

'Whatever,' Irina said heavily. 'About time he get some paid work. Now what's the big job you want to talk to me about?'

Ted shrugged like it wasn't his fault that all his efforts had been in vain. 'I know you don't like working with other models, and Lord knows they don't like working with you, but this is going to be the shoot of the year, maybe even the decade. It's a twenty-page story in *Look Book* with a gatefold front cover featuring ten on-the-verge-of-becoming-super models and Caroline Knight.' He paused and shuffled back in his chair as if he was waiting for Irina to hurl her glass of Coke at him in fury.

'Cool, when is it?'

'Irina, are you OK? I said you'll be shooting with nine other models, including Laura and Caroline Knight, who's really not your biggest fan, and you might not even be on the cover but on the inner gatefold.'

'And I say already that I do it.' It was work, and working meant standing in front of the camera and pretending to be whoever the photographer wanted her to be. Which was never the real Irina – and that suited her just fine.

'I think you must be sickening for something,' Ted pronounced. 'Or someone?'

Irina thought about getting rustic on Ted's arse, but settled for snapping her elastic band. 'As long as Aaron is not the photographer then I do it,' she decided firmly.

'It's probably going to be Annie Leibowitz and they'll be

shooting in New York,' Ted muttered, gathering up his papers. 'I have to get back for a conference call, but look after yourself, sweetie.' He hesitated. 'I think you'll learn a lot from working with Caroline.'

'Javier say that everything she does, I should do exactly the opposite,' Irina sniffed, ignoring the gigantic burning pain in her gut at the mention of his name. Possibly her burger had been undercooked.

'All I'm saying is that I think she'll be an inspiration,' Ted said loftily. 'And be nice to the other girls. You know how sucky you were when you were trying out for the Siren campaign? Be like that.'

Irina could tell that Ted was trying to goad her out of her slump, but either the anger management bullshit really was working or she was too heartsick to care. Either way, something was seriously wrong in the state of Irina.

Chapter Thirty-One

Irina ignored her pounding pulse points as she was buzzed into the Industria complex. She never got nervous before shoots, but shooting with ten other girls who all hated her guts, with no guarantee of a front cover unless Irina could well and truly bring it, was slightly terrifying. And her gameface wasn't as effective as it used to be.

Irina lingered on the stairs, took a few deep breaths and then shouldered open the big metal door. 'Hi,' she trilled, channelling her inner Hadley, as she walked into the studio. 'I bring cupcakes for everyone.' Irina held up a Magnolia Bakery box for all to see.

She'd made a point of getting here an hour ahead of call time, before the other models arrived, so she could suss out the set-up. And possibly suck up to some of the fashion grunts who were always employed in vast numbers on these shoots. As it was, the cupcakes were a big hit, especially as Caroline's people had phoned ahead to say that the studio was to be a no-carb zone.

Nothing was too much trouble for Irina; she even bent down to pick some cake crumbs off the floor before they could be spotted. Then she glanced up to see if a halo had suddenly materialized above her head.

'You're Irina Kerchenko?' one of the make-up artists queried. 'You are not what I imagined at all.'

Irina laughed gaily. 'When I first arrive, my English not so good. The language barrier was no friend to me.' She touched his arm playfully. 'I'm so excited about working with you. Your last shoot is exquisite.'

If Irina had learnt one thing about fashion folk, it was that they loved compliments almost as much as they loved being fast-tracked up the wait list for a new It bag.

The make-up artist was no exception. He was currently ducking his head and beaming. 'Everyone's going to try and out-diva each other by turning up late, so why don't I start working on your base and give it time to settle? And then I can really go to town on your eyes. But don't tell anyone you're getting preferential treatment.'

'I not dream of it,' Irina promised as she sat on a stool.

It was all going very well. Irina even heard two of the stylists gesture at her and whisper, 'She's really sweet. Just goes to show that you shouldn't listen to gossip.'

Irina was in the middle of a long anecdote about shooting underwear in the middle of a funfair when Aaron, closely followed by Javier, closely followed by two other boys with dark jeans and floppy hair walked into the studio, which was being used as a dressing room for the day.

'You're not Annie Leibowitz,' she said faltering as Aaron smiled thinly.

'Nope, guess I'm not, so you'll just have to make the best of a bad job.'

'I not mean it like that!' Irina protested. 'Ted said—'

Aaron held up his hand. 'I think it's best all round if you say as little as possible today, Irina. Stay out of my way, speak only when you're spoken to, and if you start anything with the other girls or anyone else for that matter, I'll finish it. And then I'll finish you. We clear?'

God, it was so fucking unfair! And Javier was staring at his feet while his two photographer assistant buddies were giving her the evil eye. So much for a sunny attitude and twenty-four frosted cupcakes.

Irina slumped on the stool and nodded. She'd get through this day somehow and then she'd kill Ted for setting her up. And she meant it this time. They all stalked out and the make-up artist patted her on the shoulder, though Irina wanted to bite his hand off. She didn't need petting, she needed a sawn-off shotgun and no witnesses. 'There, there,' he soothed. 'They've been here all night setting up the studio next door. Everyone's cranky.'

Everyone except Laura, who sailed in five minutes later with the sickly smile that she'd had on her face ever since she'd met Danny. 'I love shooting with Aaron,' she enthused, plonking herself down on the next stool. 'He's so funny. Have you seen Javier? Everything cool with you two?'

'Yeah, everything is just wonderful,' Irina said and she

was being deeply ironic, but Laura was already pulling out her phone.

'I went up to Manchester to meet Danny's parents last weekend,' she chirped. 'Let me show you the photos.'

Irina would rather have been stabbed in both eyes with the hot tongs. Laura seemed to think that her current state of bliss was all Irina's doing and was determined to share each new development, like Irina gave a toss. Laura yapped for fifteen minutes without pausing and slowly the other models arrived. The French girl who'd had her legs insured for £2,000,000, the Danish model who had also been up for the Dior campaign, some Mexican chick who was on the cover of the current issue of *Vogue Espana* – they all trooped in. And they all looked a little wary, because each one of them was used to being the centre of attention. Of being told that she was the most beautiful girl in the room at any one time. Well, not today.

There was a lot of air-kissing and hugs and 'I saw your last *Vogue* shoot, it was fantastic!' but Irina wasn't fooled for one second. Every single one of them was in it for themselves. And when the last girl trailed in, with booker in tow, seven sets of eyes shot daggers at her, apart from Irina who was having false lashes glued on and Laura who still thought that being nice was acceptable behaviour. 'Hey,' she called out with a little wave. 'I'm Laura.'

'She doesn't speak English,' her booker said, as the girl, a pale slip of a thing with mousey-brown hair and thin lips, picked up one of the cupcakes and started licking off the frosting. 'This is Greti, she's fourteen and from Slovenia.'

A gigantic bomb had gone off, but Laura was still smiling and completely unaware that the future had arrived. And that she was history. Curves were out and bland was the new black.

The last eyelash was glued in place and Irina was done. She slid off her stool and gestured at Greti to sit down, who slunk past Irina like she wasn't fit to be in the same room as her. Three months from now, Irina knew that Greti would shrug off the shyness like last year's coat, and if she gave Irina any trouble she'd squash her like a bug.

Irina curled up on the couch on the other side of the studio and pulled out her copy of *Anna Karenina*. She'd started reading it years ago at the Academy and found it deadly dull, but now she could totally understand the whole deal with Anna and Vronsky.

As the other girls finished in hair and make-up, they wandered out in their fluffy white robes and sat down to read magazines, knit or gossip. Anything to pass the time while they all waited for Caroline to arrive.

Caroline still hadn't shown up three hours later, when Aaron strode in and beckoned at Irina with his finger. 'We need to do some test shots,' he barked. 'Move it.'

Anything was better than sitting here with the other girls and their inane twittering. Irina followed Aaron into the other studio and then came to an abrupt halt. Not just because Javier was perched precariously on a ladder to adjust some lights, with his T-shirt showing several inches of tanned stomach. He was beautiful, but not as beautiful as the studio, which had been transformed into a luxurious penthouse apartment, with gold leaf and brocade as far as the eye could see. It was *exactly* how Irina had always imagined her New York penthouse apartment to look before she'd had it drummed into her that pale Scandinavian wood, stark white walls and minimalist furniture was what she should be aiming for.

'Hopefully it won't look so cheesy when we start shooting,' Aaron muttered and snapped his fingers in the direction of a baroque sofa and chairs grouped around a red velvet backdrop. 'We're having trouble lighting the couch. Sit on it.'

Maybe she'd lived in England too long, but Irina couldn't help but think that a 'please' would have been polite as she obediently sat on the sofa and tried not to gawp at Javier, whose tongue was poking out of the corner of his mouth as he adjusted something with a screwdriver.

When Aaron started taking pictures it was a relief. He obviously didn't think Irina was worthy of direction so she shucked off her dressing gown to reveal a black velvet gown underneath and draped herself decoratively on the couch. And then she simply stared at the camera like it was the only thing in the world that knew her secrets and never judged her for them.

'OK, we're done,' Aaron called out some time later and Irina blinked, slowly coming back to her present surroundings, which was Aaron gazing at her thoughtfully. 'That new softer look of yours is quite good. We were all starting to think you were a one-trick pony.'

Apart from a slight flaring of her nostrils, Irina remained calm. Much as she wanted to smash every single piece of expensive photographic equipment on set, she was going to rise above it. She could put up with a hell of a lot for a twenty-page shoot in *Look Book* and . . .

'I'm going to have a word with him,' Javier said softly, crouching in front of Irina so he could push a spool of cable under the couch. 'He shouldn't be riding you like that.'

'Is OK,' Irina insisted, staring at her hands. 'Is like the water off the duck's back and I can look after myself.'

'Of course you can,' Javier said, his voice hardening, and Irina risked looking up only to see that he looked as rotten as she felt, though she was wearing layers upon layers of make-up to disguise it. Javier on the other hand had dark shadows like bruises under his eyes, his hair was hanging lankly like it didn't have the energy to flop as beguilingly as usual and he'd lost enough weight that his once snug T-shirt was baggy. Which was why Irina felt the need to force feed him pizza until he got that sleek look back.

'Look, we can still be friends,' she said equably.

Javier's eyebrows shot up. 'Oh yeah, like you and Dean were "friends"?'

293

'I never shag him. I just try to make you jealous and it was a dumbass idea . . .'

'We can't be friends, Irina,' Javier cut right across her. 'It's hard enough being in the same city as you. We'll be civil if we're working together, but that's as far as it goes.'

He was infuriating! Irina started to rise from her seat to show Javier that she didn't do civil when there was a commotion in the hallway.

'Caroline Knight's here,' someone shouted. 'She's getting out of the car. E.T.A: two minutes!'

Chapter Thirty-Two

Caroline swept in with her entourage an impressive six hours late. Irina perched on one of the sofas and watched with interest as six foot of supermodel paraded up and down the studio, quacking on her phone to someone called 'Darling', just so that everyone knew that she was there, even if they'd yet to be granted an audience.

One of the senior magazine people managed to attract Caroline's attention between calls, but it was an hour before she was in make-up. And another hour before the make-up was done to her satisfaction. The other models had been ushered over one by one, but when it was Irina's turn Caroline didn't deign to look up from her Blackberry. 'What's your name again?' she asked in a bored drawl, before turning to one of her kowtowing assistants. 'Tell them to get me some champagne. There's no way I'm doing this sober. You, Russian girl, stop hovering and get as far away from me as possible.'

When Ted had had the wonderful idea that Caroline would be Irina's modelling big sister and guide her through the wacky world of fashion, he'd probably imagined that they'd go for mani/pedis together. Or that maybe Caroline would gift her protégée with discarded designer freebies.

Maybe she'd even give Irina a few posing pointers. What Irina actually did was go back to the sofa and decide that from now on she was going to do the exact opposite of everything that Caroline did. Just like Javier had said.

Yeah, the matching assistants were cool, but it was degrading to make one of them hold your ashtray. Especially as Caroline seemed to flick the ash at her assistant rather than in the receptacle provided.

And she was rude to everyone. Not just the little junior stylists and assistants that Irina was usually rude to. She was rude to Aaron, ignored all his assistants and the magazine people. She was even rude to her best friend, who turned up halfway through the third make-up attempt to drop off a package. The only person she wasn't rude to was the editor of *Look Book*, who phoned up to make sure the shoot was running smoothly.

'Sweetie, you're so kind to think of me,' Caroline cooed as she swatted the make-up artist away. 'You know how much I love working with you. No . . . No . . . Of course, I don't mind shooting with the other girls. It's really important to nurture new talent, innit?'

Yeah, Irina had been a holy terror on shoots herself because it was what models did. But now she could watch it unfolding around her, like she was a little kid with its nose pressed up against the window, and she was getting an entirely different view. She'd made the little fashion girls cry and not felt a pang of guilt. But now she could see one of the stylists shaking so hard that she couldn't hang up a dress, after Caroline had reamed her out for getting the colour of her latte wrong. Even the senior fashion editor was hissing at Aaron: 'I've just missed my daughter's third birthday party because that overpaid diva was meant to be here at ten this morning. Now it's six and we haven't taken a single shot.'

Aaron held up his hands in a futile gesture. 'What can I say, honey? I hope you didn't make dinner plans.'

But they couldn't start until Caroline took it upon herself to supervise which model would be wearing which couture gown. The black velvet was taken away from Irina and given to the shortest girl there, who had to teeter on six-inch heels so she didn't trip over the hem. At least she wasn't Laura, who was carefully eased into figure hugging, flesh-coloured satin, which made her look like the circus fat lady. Greti was swamped by a billowing grey dress which made her disappear, and Irina still had nothing to wear. 'For Christ's sake, bitches,' Caroline snapped, clapping her hands. 'Get in front of the camera. I don't want to be here all night.'

Finally they were arranged on and around the sofa and chairs, but only after Caroline had objected to the first three outfits that Irina had put on and she'd finally been given a pink slip left over from another shoot. 'No one will be looking at her anyway,' Caroline insisted. 'No point putting her in a $3000 couture gown.'

Irina didn't earn $15,000 a day, or have two assistants, but she knew that she could take a better picture than Caroline or any of the other girls who were bitching and fussing with frocks that did them no favours. Which was tough shit, because a good model, a true model, could work a potato sack if she had to. It didn't even matter that Caroline had ordered her to the back of the shot, because Irina could feel all the energy in her body rushing up to her head, then pouring out of her eyes as she stared at the camera. Like she and the lens were having their own private dialogue. It was very freaky but also kinda cool.

Aaron also thought so because as Caroline's attention was focused on the strap of her Jimmy Choo and the hapless assistant who was on her knees adjusting it so the leather didn't chafe against her delicate ankle, he winked at Irina. Like he knew exactly what she was up to and for once he totally approved.

Each time Aaron tried to change the set-up of the shot, Caroline had only one instruction. 'Move back, you keep crowding me. Jesus!' she kept shouting at Irina who was five feet behind Caroline at all times. 'Your skin is really grey in this light, maybe we shouldn't have put you in a pink dress. Oh, well.'

It was a lame attempt to psyche Irina out. But like the first time they'd ever met, Irina couldn't help but feel flattered that a bona fide supermodel was taking a lot of time and energy to try and screw things up for her. It was a damn good result for a girl from a Moscow housing project. Especially when there were nine other models she could have savaged instead. But Caroline had singled Irina out; identified her as the major threat. No wonder Irina was having a severe attack of the warm fuzzies. Her serene smile just drove Caroline to an even nastier, darker place. And as the camera clicked away, Irina sincerely hoped that it was capturing all of Caroline's insecurities and her own supreme ease.

'Stop!' Caroline suddenly shouted, snapping her fingers at Aaron. 'Show me Polaroids.'

'Come on, baby, we've got a lot to get through,' he cajoled. It was a mark of just how powerful Caroline Knight was that Aaron simply shot Javier an exasperated look and clutched his camera tighter. 'You look beautiful, Caro.'

'I don't give a toss. Polaroids now, or I walk.'

Javier gingerly came forward, clutching the Polaroids like a sacrificial offering. Caroline didn't say a word as she went through them, throwing each discarded picture on the floor at her feet. 'I'm not doing this,' she said finally. 'Not with *her*! I'm not shooting with this Russian freak. Send her home.'

There was a moment's strained silence before the fashion director from the magazine delicately picked her way on set. 'Caroline, I don't see what the problem is,' she said firmly. 'You look beautiful. You always look beautiful.'

'Get rid of her,' Caroline bit out, pointing at Irina who assumed an innocent air. 'She's sucking all the life from the shoot.'

'But we were very clear that you'd be shooting with new models and we've signed contracts with all of them,' the woman said carefully. 'Your agency did approve this.'

Caroline waved a dismissive hand. 'I'm the star. You'll sell issues because of my name, not because of some dirty-looking tramp from a Russian slum.'

It was hard for Irina to maintain a dignified composure when she wanted to knock Caroline off her heels. Then she could really kick off about strap chafing. But the worst of it was that she couldn't do anything; certainly not open her mouth and let fly with a torrent of abuse that she'd picked up in her Russian slum. Even Laura felt moved on her behalf to surreptitiously squeeze Irina's hand in a comforting gesture.

'Jeez, what a *cow*,' she hissed out of the side of her mouth. 'She's always been really sweet to me when I've met her before.'

'We will do some solo pictures,' the woman placated, her hands outstretched in a pleading gesture. 'But we need to nail the group shot. This is going to be a memorable story. The reigning queen of fashion and her princesses. It's multicultural, elegant and edgy, old and new…'

Irina's mouth fell open, along with every other mouth in the room. It was the wrongest thing to say since Britney

Spears hit the hairdressers and told them to shave it all off.

'Old? Did you just call me *old*?' Caroline went from menacing growl to piercing shriek in two seconds. 'You did not just call me *old*?'

The woman was holding her hands out in front of her, which was a good idea as Caroline looked like she was about to throw a punch. 'No, no, of course I didn't. I meant that you're a fashion legend, an icon, and Irina and the other girls are just newbies . . .'

'Phone!' Caroline screamed, snapping her fingers so rapidly that they were just a blur. 'I am going to have your arse fired!'

One of Caroline's assistants was already running on set with her Blackberry held aloft like the Holy Grail of telecommunication devices. 'Not that one. My other phone!' She pointed a finger at Javier who stared back at her with a truculent expression. Not even he could remain chilled when Caroline had him in her sights. 'You! Get me the other phone.'

Irina shifted her weight from foot to foot. Despite the fact that she was the one responsible for all this tantruming, she seemed to have been forgotten. Actually, that was probably a good thing.

Javier loped back to Caroline, clutching four phones to his chest. 'Wasn't sure which one was yours,' he murmured in an off-hand manner, which was pretty brave in the circumstances. Irina felt a burst of pride at him for not being a pussy when greater men would have caved under this kind of pressure.

Caroline was looking less and less like a glorious, golden goddess and more like a demented drag queen. 'Give!' She rifled through the phones with scant regard for their original owners and gave a squawk of disbelief. 'None of these are mine,' she yelled at Javier, who wisely took two steps back to get out of range.

It was too late. Four phones flew through the air, two of them catching him on the cheek, and ouch, *in* the eye. Irina winced in sympathy as Caroline strode from the set.

'That's it,' she announced. 'I'm going out to my car and I'm not coming back until you, you and you are fired.' She stabbed her finger at Irina, the fashion director and Javier, who had one hand pressed tightly against his eye socket, his face scrunched up in pain.

Chapter Thirty-Three

No one moved as Caroline sailed out, then everyone dived for their phones at the same time. Not Irina, as her phone was currently in pieces on the floor. She crouched down and tried to push the fascia back in place and reinserted the battery, which had skidded several feet.

The fashion director was already on the phone to the company lawyer about her cast-iron employment contract, Javier was being led back to the dressing room by a gaggle of shrieking assistants and models, and Irina was left standing on set without a clue what to do.

Should she phone Ted? Had Caroline got there first and was regaling him with all sorts of heinous accusations about her, which Ted would believe because Caroline was his good, old chum from way back and Irina already had a rep for being difficult. For the first time in her life, she could really identify with the boy who cried wolf.

And, more to the point, how dare that bitch do that to Javier? Yell at him, treat him like shit and then attack him so his pretty face might be permanently scarred. OK, they weren't anything to each other, but Irina still had a prior claim on Javier. And no way was anyone going to hurt him and think that Irina would be cool with it. She clenched her fists as she felt the familiar red mist surround her. It was going to take much more than a sodding elastic band to tamp down her rage.

'Why don't you change out of the dress while we try to get this sorted out?' Aaron suggested, as he inserted rolls of film into their canisters. 'And a word of advice, kid, never work with children, animals or supermodels.'

'Javier . . .' Irina growled. 'She hurt Javier.'

'Who's big enough and old enough to know that there are some battles that aren't worth fighting,' Aaron said calmly. 'Not if he wants to take another picture in this town again.'

'Bullshit,' Irina snapped, hitching up her dress so she could stride off the set.

The atmosphere in the dressing room was frostier than Moscow in a blizzard. Javier was surrounded by hordes of girls all stroking him and *touching* him as they proffered ice cubes and advice.

'It just stings a little,' he muttered, face red, though whether that was where he'd been struck or because he was embarrassed, Irina couldn't tell.

'You should totally sue her for aggravated assault.'

'And if she tries to have you fired, you can sell the story to *US Weekly*. Shall we get Kit to take photos of your face?'

'And you have to go to the ER and file an accident report.'

As Irina walked into the room, they all turned and gave her evils. Like, she'd made Javier miserable long before Caroline, so she was also the enemy. Her cupcakes didn't count for anything now.

'You OK?' she asked softly, as she tried to wriggle down the concealed zip of her dress because absolutely no one was rushing to help her.

'Well I don't think I'm going to be scarred for life!' Javier said with a careless shrug. 'But it's probably a good thing that I gave up modelling.'

'That bitch!' one of the models hissed. 'She was just looking for an excuse to leave so she could go out to the car. And we all know why.'

Irina didn't. 'What she do in the car?'

They all shot each other conspiratorial looks. 'That package her friend dropped off? A little pick-me-up so she'd start resembling something a bit more human.'

'Huh? What are you talking about?' Irina asked, as one of the girls held a finger to her nostril and sniffed dramatically.

'She's a total coke-whore,' someone drawled. 'C'mon, everyone knows that. You're a model, Irina, you know the score.'

Apart from a little weed, Irina didn't know anyone who took drugs. Not the new girls certainly. She'd heard whispers, but thought that the whole drugs thing was totally over, like metallic leggings.

'She do coke in the limo outside?' she clarified. 'Like, now?'

'Duh! She's even got a solid-gold tube to snort it with,' one of the make-up artists said. 'Got it from her last boyfriend, who ended up in rehab after three months trying to keep up with her. Why are you grinning like that?'

Irina held up her battered phone triumphantly. 'I take that bitch down and if any of you say a word about it, I have you killed. I know Russian mafia.'

She didn't, but that threat always worked on Laura, Hadley and Candy, and the girls in the dressing room all looked suitably scared.

'Get out,' she suggested, grabbing the first hand she could reach and tugging it towards the door. 'You all get out now.'

'Oh Irina, don't do anything stupid,' Laura tweeted, helping to shoo out the other girls. 'It's not worth ruining your career over. Javier's fine, aren't you?'

Javier leant against the make-up counter and tried to roll his eyes. Then he winced. 'It really doesn't hurt that much. And I can stand up for myself, Irina,' he bit out. 'Isn't that what you always tell me?'

'No!' Irina insisted. 'No! She not do that to you and think I just let it go.'

Her accent was so thick that Irina knew she was two syllables away from spitting out a stream of X-rated Russian, but Javier just shrugged again. It was infuriating.

'Like Laura says, this is not worth ruining your precious career over. Hey, it might even lower your day rate.'

If he weren't already injured, Irina would have smacked some sense into him. 'I not give a stuff about that right now,' she yelled. 'That whore is going to suffer.' She turned to the girls clustered in the doorway, who were all staring at her like she'd suddenly sprouted extra heads. 'Why are you still here? Get out!'

No one so much as budged, and Laura planted herself firmly in Irina's path with her hands on her hips, which were straining the seams of her dress. 'I'm not going to let you do this, Irina,' she said firmly.

'Whatever, you can stay,' Irina decided magnanimously, throwing her hands up in frustration because time was ticking on and hopefully none of them had the stones to grass her up. 'Now, watch and learn, little girls. You'll get the best view from the window.'

'Aren't you going to do anything?' Laura cried at Javier, as they were almost mown down in the stampede.

'The only thing that would stop Irina in a mood like this is a nuclear bomb,' he sighed. Then he gave Irina the oddest stare, like he was trying to look right at her heart pumping away underneath the satin and skin and muscle. A half-smile played on his lips but Irina was already calling 911 as everyone crowded around the window to stare at the long black town car idling away at the kerb in flagrant disregard for the 'no waiting' signs.

The elocution lessons she'd had for the Siren campaign had been worth every penny as Irina informed the operator in a flawless accent that she'd just seen someone doing coke in the back of a car parked outside 'the address that I'm about to give you, ma'am'. She even left a fake name, Candy Harlow, as she finished the call with a breathless, 'I think you should get here soon, she's in full view of small children'. OK, it was ten at night but she wasn't going to get bogged down in those kinds of details.

There were a few muted giggles as they waited. Five minutes stretched into ten and Irina gave a sigh of regret. She'd given it her best shot but . . .

'Hang on! Was that a siren?'

'That was *so* a siren!'

There was a lot of shoving and jostling for position as three patrol cars roared up, a couple of motorbikes bringing up the rear.

The limo was quickly surrounded as they all craned their necks to see the window slowly being wound down. It was hard to work out what was going on, but then Caroline was stepping out of the car, still in her dress with all the Swarvovksi crystals hand-sewn on it, and being pressed up against the car as she was cuffed.

'You should have phoned E!News and got them to send a camera crew down,' someone yelped as they all tried to angle their camera-phones to take pictures.

Irina shrank back from the window as Caroline glanced

up, not that she'd be able to see her, she hoped. This was either her biggest triumph or the worst mistake Irina had ever made. It was hard to tell.

Someone had already rushed into the studio and was screaming jubilantly, 'Oh. My. God! Caroline's just been arrested. They're taking her away in a cop car.'

The other girls were looking at Irina like she was their god and they were all about to drop down on their knees and give thanks to her divine munificence. It was very unsettling.

'Is nothing,' she said modestly, which was an entirely new look for her. 'I say the bitch was going down. She went down.'

'I can't wait to see her mugshot because that base I gave her is not going to look good under harsh lighting,' one of the make-up artists said gleefully. 'And can I just say that I love you?'

Irina suddenly found herself in the middle of a twelve-way hugathon, which was the most freakish experience of a singularly freakish shoot.

'Listen up, everyone!' Laura shouted over the deafening squawks. 'We are going to have a pact that what happened in this dressing room, stays in this dressing room. OK?'

There was a rousing chorus of agreement as Irina struggled to free herself from the group hug, which was making her sweaty. When she finally managed to wrest herself from the throng, she looked around for Javier, but he was nowhere to be seen. Which was fine, really it was. Though a thank you would have been nice.

'I've just spoken to the editor and he wants to continue the shoot without Caroline,' said the fashion director who was standing at the doorway. 'I expect everyone on set in half an hour.'

It was all very democratic. Everyone decided to swap dresses so they could face the camera in clothes that actually suited them. And considering they were all uppity models who should have been killing each other for prime position, it was also decided that they'd all have a chance at centre stage. Irina was happy to go with the consensus because she knew deep in her bones that she'd make it on to the cover and not end up on one of the gatefold flaps. She wasn't the most beautiful girl here, but she could out-model every single one of them. As she was zipped back into the black velvet dress, Irina wondered if her most successful relationship would always be with the camera.

Although Laura got told off for continually yapping and Greti had to be coaxed to crack a smile, the rest of the shoot went off without any more interruptions. It took hours though, as each model still had to have individual shots taken. It was exhausting, and when it looked as if the coffee had finally run out, there was a moment's panic until one of the assistants managed to find a twenty-four-hour deli that would deliver.

Irina was almost asleep and swaying on her stool as her make-up was removed. One of the stylists had to help her back into her jeans and put her shoes on because when she'd tried to do it, she'd fallen over. Laura already had her coat on and was yawning.

'Can I crash in your room tonight? My hotel's all the way uptown and I've got a nine a.m. call time.' She sounded close to tears because it was nearly three in the morning and she needed more beauty sleep than the average model.

Irina was too tired to tell her to piss off. 'Sure,' she slurred, leaning against the stylist because gravity just wasn't doing it for her. 'Whatever.'

'Well, OK, then,' Laura said in surprise. 'There should be a car waiting outside.'

Irina trailed out after her, eyes barely able to focus on the thing that was blocking her exit. The tall, lean thing with what looked like a tribal armband (or possibly random ink blots) entwined round one tanned bicep.

'I'll see Irina gets back safely,' Javier said and Irina groaned in protest.

Laura frowned. 'Are you sure? She's very . . . well, *more* cranky when she's sleep-deprived.'

'I know, but I'll take my chances.'

'I'm standing right here,' Irina bit out, but actually she was walking because Javier had one hand in the small of her back and was pushing her outside and into a car, while

Laura was left on the sidewalk bleating about having to trek all the way uptown.

She slept for what felt like five seconds until the car jerked to a halt and she was sleep-fuddled enough that Javier could tug her up far too many flights of stairs into a tiny apartment, about the size of her room back in Camden. She'd always wanted to see where Javier lived, but all she could do now was flop on an unmade bed and try to look angry. 'Why? Why do you bring me here?'

Javier sat down and propped Irina's feet on his lap so he could start doing something with his knuckles and her instep that felt absolutely amazing. 'You know that crap you said about how being soft would hurt your career? It was bullshit.'

Irina tried to summon up the strength to tell Javier just how completely wrong he was, but now he was kneading her toes, which had been squeezed into a very uncomfortable pair of shoes for hours. 'Just 'cause I let you rub my feet does not mean I go soft.'

'No, but you were prepared to ruin your career just to pay Caroline back for committing aggravated assault with a cellphone, and that made me realize two things.'

'Two things you tell me about some other time?' Irina suggested. 'Like, when I actually give a damn.'

'Going to do it right now, so shut up and listen,' snapped Javier and, while Irina was gaping in shock at his harsh command, he continued. 'Soft doesn't suit you, Irina. I get that. You need to stay hard to keep on your game and so maybe I should be the one who stops being soft and tells you how it's going to be from now on.'

Irina attempted to tug her foot free, but Javier had a death grip around her ankle. 'We're done. You make that clear before.' She couldn't hit him, not when he was injured, so she settled for a look of seething fury instead.

'Do you want to be my girlfriend?' Javier asked softly. 'Do you want to have a relationship with me?'

Irina did hit him then. And it wasn't that hard, so there was no reason for him to shriek like a girl because of the weedy blow she'd given his upper arm. 'Because I want to be your boyfriend, but only if you promise never to do that again,' he pouted, rubbing his bicep. 'And you can be as rude as you like to everyone else, but you have to start being nice to me.'

'Why would you even think that I want to date you again?' Irina snapped, shaking off the last vestiges of tiredness. 'Not that I realize we were dating before.'

'Which was my fault because I was having commitment issues, which I'm completely over,' Javier assured her and he was gazing at her fixedly, so even the bruising couldn't detract from the sincerity shining out of those deep brown eyes. 'And you want to date me again because you're a little bit in love with me.'

Javier was just full of surprises. Irina nibbled at a nail while she considered her option. She *wasn't* a little bit in love with him, she was a lot in love with him, but if she told him that and he didn't feel the same way, then she'd end up looking like a twat. 'Why do you think I'm in love with you?'

'God, will you stop answering questions with other questions?' Javier was stroking her feet again and staring down at her as she shifted to get more comfortable. 'Because you didn't give a stuff about your career earlier today. You chose *me* instead, Irina. And you have your famous, new, soft look, like you've been getting in touch with all those emotions that you used to lock away, and you've lost weight.'

'So have you!' Irina hissed and it shouldn't be so hard to stop throwing up these big barriers of hostility and just tell Javier what was in her heart. But it was. 'You totally skinny and you look like shit.'

'It's because I've been pining. It sucks, doesn't it? Especially when the person you're pining for refuses to let you in.'

She couldn't be bothered to argue any more, which had to be a first. So, Irina shut her eyes, took a deep breath and jumped. 'OK, you can be my boyfriend and sometimes you can hold my hand if you want,' she said very quietly as Javier leant forward to catch her words. 'Even when there are people around.'

Javier frowned. 'Was that a joke? 'Cause I still can't tell. Maybe we need a signal.'

314

Irina scrambled up so she could curl against him and rest her head on his shoulder. Because she could. That was the deal, so why was he tensing up like his bones were about to shatter? 'Give me a fucking hug, you idiot.'

A hand patted her gingerly on the shoulder, like Javier wasn't sure whether she was a rabid dog and wanted to check that she wasn't frothing at the mouth. Irina tried to wait patiently, though it took a lot of teeth-grinding.

And then his arms were wrapping around her tight, like he knew she could take it because she wasn't one of those fragile, delicate girls who'd shatter into tiny pieces from rough handling or an unkind word. She was tougher than that.

'You're not ever to see that Dean again,' Javier suddenly hissed. 'I forbid it.'

Irina ran her fingers through his hair, feeling the strands cling to her before she tugged his head back so he could get the full weight of her glare.

'Then you never to even look at another model or talk to one or flirt with one . . .'

'But that's my job! And anyway, lots of my friends are models. I can't just dump all my friends.'

'Dean is my good friend,' Irina said hotly. 'So if you make me lose him, then you have to lose them.'

Javier was obviously trying to come up with a get-out clause and he looked so flustered and cute, like a kitten with wet fur, that Irina had to kiss him. At least when they were kissing, they weren't arguing. And kissing led to other things, which then led to other things which were far more preferable than arguing about other people.

Later – much, much later – when Irina was tracing patterns on Javier's skin, spelling out poems and sonnets, she came up with a solution. 'You talk to your "friends" if there's another boy present,' she decided generously. 'And I not see Dean on my own, unless you give me permission.'

'That sounds suspiciously like a compromise,' Javier murmured lazily, tucking a loose lock of hair behind her ear. 'And while we're doing deals, you have to promise to never wear anything pink and frilly ever again or I'm calling it off.'

He could be so smug and annoying sometimes. Irina had really missed that.

'*Ya tebya lyublyu,*' she whispered, and Javier demanded to know what she'd just said, but Irina just wriggled to get more room, which involved elbowing him in the ribs, and told him to shut up and go to sleep. OK, she'd said 'I love you', but she'd said it in Russian and if Javier couldn't understand it, then he couldn't hold it against her at a later date.

Epilogue

'It's cold, Irina. You never said it was this cold,' Javier shouted over the biting wind. 'I think I have frostbite.'

It was hard to tell if Javier was joking. The only part of his face not obscured with a big woolly scarf and dark glasses to avoid snow glare, was his nose. Which was bright red.

Irina tapped it playfully. 'This is not cold,' she told him. 'Stop being such a pussy. You want cold, then you should come to Moscow in February, not December.'

She tucked her arm in his and, heads down, they shuffled along the gritted pavement of Kitai-gorod (because God forbid someone rich should slip on the ice and break a bone).

'Is pretty though, innit?' she asked Javier because the trees were strung with fairylights and there was a huge Christmas tree in the centre of Theatre Square. Irina never thought she'd be back in Moscow, staying in the Metropol Hotel with her boyfriend, though her mother thought they had separate rooms.

Not that her mother had had much time to pass comment on Irina's lack of morals. When the prodigal daughter had returned for Christmas with a good Catholic boy in tow, just in time to help her mother move into her new house, there were other matters to worry about.

It had been all paint swatches and fabric samples until Irina never wanted to see another floral curtain as long as she lived. And then there had been the relatives descending with furniture loaded on to trucks and the roofs of their cars.

'But I thought we'd go to Ikea,' Irina had protested only the day before, as her Uncle Vasily had hefted in a hideous sideboard, but her mother wouldn't hear of it.

'If you keep frittering away your money, you'll be destitute by this time next year,' she complained. 'And don't put your feet on the sofa. I don't care what you get up to in London, remember that you have some manners.'

There had been a party, a house-warming, which was just a flimsy excuse to have a good gawp at Irina to see if she'd actually got beautiful in the last year. 'Irina's always been striking,' her mother had declared as her two grandmothers (thankfully still alive) had tutted over the swimwear shots in her portfolio. 'Elisaveta is pretty, but her looks will fade once she gets older. Irina has good bones – she takes after my side of the family.'

'Why can't you just say I'm beautiful?' Irina had demanded, and her mother had turned to the guests and shrugged expansively as if to say, 'You see what I have to put up with?'

So the party had mostly been her and her mother

rowing, while Javier had glass after glass of vodka foisted on him by various aunts, cousins and Mrs Karminsky from the language school.

'How's your head?' she asked, as they crossed the street and headed for the slick storefronts of Tretyakov Drive.

'Between the hangover and the headache after listening to you and your mother screaming, it's just about broken,' Javier said, quickening his pace so he could pull her into the first store, where they were greeted with a welcoming gust of warm air.

'*Pfft!* I forgot how much she yells,' Irina grumbled, picking up a shoe and pulling a face.

'She loves you,' Javier remarked matter-of-factly. 'I got a big talk about how she didn't care if I was a big hotshot fashion photographer, I'd better be treating you right.'

'She liked the pictures that you did of me for *Vogue Nippon*, said I looked almost pretty,' Irina snorted. 'And then she said if I moved out of the Fierce flat and got somewhere on my own, people would think I was a prostitute.'

But she *was* going to move out of the Camden flat, even though the rent was super cheap and it was only two minute's walk from McDonald's. The whole fashion world still worked her nerves, but where else could an unqualified Russian girl with a gap between her teeth become a multi-millionaire in the space of a year? So it was dumb to pay a landlord rent when she could buy her own place. She just couldn't decide if it was going to be in London or New York. Javier and Irina had sat down and talked about it, because apparently that was what people in committed relationships did. But they still weren't sure if they could live together without killing each other.

And the others were getting itchy feet too. Laura was planning to live with one of her dull little friends from Manchester who was moving to London to go to university. Though mostly she was making googly eyes with the weedy footballer every chance she got. And Hadley was spending most of her time between LA and Reed's apartment. Irina still couldn't work out if they were doing it, or if Hadley was intent on saving her virginity as a wedding-night gift with purchase. Only Candy was still in the flat and showing no signs of leaving. Although she was emitting such bad energy that all the plants had died.

'Irina, no! It's much cheaper to buy them in New York,' Javier protested as she approached the dresses and rifled through the rail until she dug out the most expensive one. She still didn't know her bias cut from her A-line, but she had an unerring knack for picking out designer stuff with the heftiest price tags.

Irina held it against her and twirled until she attracted the attention of the security guard who blocked the door and eyed her with suspicion. Possibly they had her photo and fingerprints on file.

'I want to buy it in Moscow,' she said, putting it back

on the rail and snapping her fingers at one of the shop assistants who'd been sneering at her. 'Get me this in a size eight.'

The girl slowly uncoiled herself from behind the counter so she could give Irina a swift up and down, taking in her jeans and big, puffy anorak. 'Maybe you find something more in your price range in one of the markets.'

Javier didn't understand the quick-fire Russian, but he'd already expressed horror at how rude most Russians were after he'd tried to buy a woolly hat in a department store and had all his polite requests to pay ignored. 'I always thought you were just using it as an excuse to be obnoxious,' he'd sighed after Irina had come to his rescue and shouted at someone. 'But everyone's really abrupt here. I thought that woman was going to shoot me for not having the right change.'

Now he just leant against the counter and pretended that he was somewhere else.

Irina pulled out her Marc Jacobs purse and saw the sales assistant's eyes widen in recognition. Then she rummaged for her platinum Amex card and tapped it meaningfully. 'You either get me the size I want or you get me your manager,' Irina barked as the girl sulkily nodded. It was so good to be back home and stop with the pleases and thank yours. 'Miuccia Prada is a close personal friend of mine.'

There was the tiniest snort from the cheap seats. But in fashion, if you did catwalk for someone, then you were their friend. Well, until your look went out of style.

The sales assistant had flounced off, but she returned with another girl in tow who was staring at Irina and whispering frantically. Javier gave a long, low whistle. 'Irina, you know the story that did the rounds about how you were shoplifting from Prada when you were discovered? Was that true?'

'Ja,' Irina smiled beatifically. 'From this very store. Is ironic, innit?'

'I think we're so about to get kicked out, or beaten with clubs, I'm not sure which.'

The second sales assistant was rummaging under the counter. Irina expected an alarm to go off and the shutters to suddenly come down, which was stupid. She hadn't so much as sneaked a pair of sunglasses into her bag. Even so, Irina felt that familiar metallic tang of fear in the back of her throat and she'd almost forgotten how unpleasant it was to break out in a cold sweat. She really had gone soft.

'We might have to make a run for it,' she whispered to Javier, who looked horrified at the suggestion.

'I don't want to go to prison in this country and—'

'You? This is you?' The haughtiest of the sales assistants was brandishing something at Irina, possibly a 'Wanted' poster.

She looked again. It was the latest issue of *Vogue Russia* with her face adorned with a slash of red lipstick on the cover. 'Of course it's me.'

'You should have said. I can give you a thirty per cent discount,' the girl said, still not cracking a smile as she wrapped the dress in soft sheets of tissue paper. 'This dress is far too big for you. You're too skinny.'

Javier was getting restless and wandered off to check out the menswear while Irina signed the credit card slip with a flourish. 'It's for my mother,' she said, even though it was none of her damn business. 'She only wears Prada.'

In fact, her mother would shriek with horror when she unwrapped her Christmas present, and insist that it was too expensive and needed to be returned. But Irina knew that even if it got hung in the back of her closet never to be worn, her mother would rub the whisper-soft satin across her cheek at least every day.

She gave the sales assistant a brisk smile as she handed over the stiff white bag and nodded her head at Javier. 'Come on, pretty-boy, time to button up. I want to hit Chanel and Versace next.'

'I'm going to take you to Sao Paolo in the middle of a heatwave,' Javier huffed, holding the door open for her, even though Irina had told him a million times that she was perfectly capable of doing it for herself. 'See how you like it.'

They walked out into the winter sunshine and had a brief slapping match over who was going to hold whose mittened hand, before heading down the street. Irina's face stared snootily down from a billboard, advertising the newest scent from Chanel. She'd landed the campaign after they sacked Caroline. Or Cocaine Caroline as the papers now called her, after she'd narrowly avoided a prison sentence and had to hightail it to rehab instead. But it was too cold to stop and gloat; she only did that in private because Ted was still suspicious about the rumours that Irina had played a major role in Caroline's downfall. But she did look fucking hot in the pictures, Irina thought to herself with satisfaction, and she'd got paid more than Laura had for the Siren campaign.

'Stop looking so pleased with yourself,' Javier teased, looking up at the other Irina glaring down at them. 'And walk faster, I'm about to freeze over.'

'Pussy', Irina muttered under her breath, but snuggled into Javier's shoulder as they started walking at a quick pace. In her coat pocket, Irina could feel the comforting, solid weight of the platinum key fob she'd palmed as she was paying for the dress.

Russian Glossary

What's With All the Russian Stuff in This Book?

Blintz (also known as blini)
Russian crepe-like pancakes, which can be filled with anything from sour cream, ground meat, caviar or even jam and honey. Blintzes are most popular when filled with cheese, folded over and then fried. Yum!

Bolshoi
Moscow's premiere theatre, best known for its world-famous ballet company, which the Russians are super-proud of.

Budem zdorovy
A Russian drinking toast, it literally means, 'Let's stay healthy!'

Ja
Russian for 'yes'.

Kitai-gorod

A swanky and very old district of Moscow, near the Kremlin (the Russian Parliament) and the Bolshoi Theatre.

Moscow

The capital city of Russia.

Niet

Russian for 'no'.

Oligarch (oligarchy)

The small band of people who made huge pots of money after the fall of Communism in Russia, sometimes by getting up to all sorts of dodgy things.

Rouble

The currency of Russia. There are roughly fifty roubles to one pound.

Sauerkraut

Actually German for pickled cabbage, which is a staple of the Russian diet, especially in soup.

Slav (Slavic)

Any person from Eastern Europe, including Russians, Poles and Croatians, who speaks one of the Slavonic languages.

Technically Russians are Eastern Slavs, but let's not concern ourselves with that!

Spasibo
Russian for 'thank you'.

Soviet Union
Before Communism collapsed in 1991, Russia was part of the Soviet Union, which consisted of fifteen Soviet Socialist Republics. For more details ask your history teacher!

Tretyakov Drive
In the Kitai-gorod district of Moscow, Tretyakov Drive is one of the poshest shopping drags in the world. Gucci, Versace, Prada, Dolce and Gabbana, and Tiffany's (among others) all have boutiques on this little street.

Ya tebya lyublyu
Russian for 'I love you'.

(For a full modelling glossary, please see Fashionistas: Laura)